I0563815

MISSING MEN

.

Seated around the table in ghost-like fashion were men who had,
as it were, come back from the dead.

THE INTERNATIONAL ADVENTURE LIBRARY

THREE OWLS EDITION

MISSING MEN

The Return of Cheri-Bibi

BY

GASTON LEROUX

AUTHOR OF

"WOLVES OF THE SEA," "THE MYSTERY OF THE
YELLOW ROOM," "THE SECRET OF THE NIGHT,"

W. R. CALDWELL & CO.
NEW YORK

PUBLISHED IN ENGLAND UNDER THE
TITLE OF "CHÉRI-BIBI AND CECILY"

COPYRIGHT, 1923,
BY THE MACAULAY COMPANY

PRINTED IN THE UNITED STATES OF AMERICA

CONTENTS

MISSING MEN

MISSING MEN

CHAPTER I

COD IN THE SPANISH WAY

The Dodger landed at Palmerston, the small, rising
capital of the Northern territory of Southern Australia, with six million francs in his trunk. A fine harbor, a few huts, a few wooden churches and chapels
and a few brick houses—such was Palmerston. But
the Dodger did not stop to admire the beauties of the
landscape. It seemed to him that he could discern in
the distance, in the roadstead, a large vessel lying at
anchor which bore a look about her of the "Estrella."
Nevertheless he did not recognize her under her latest
flag. Since he left her, the transport had probably
changed her appearance, her flag, her name. What adventures had she passed through? What news was in
store for the poor Dodger?

After depositing his luggage in the hotel, he hastened
to the post office, and came out with a letter addressed
to him as he had reason to expect. At that moment
he stumbled against a short fat man who fell sprawling
against his legs.

"Little Buddha!"

"The Dodger!"

"Well, old man. . . . Here we are again. . . . I say, what's the news of Chéri-Bibi?"*

"Give me your news first. Have you succeeded in the job?"

"Yes, I've pulled it off. But how's Chéri-Bibi?"

"It'll be a great consolation to all of us that you've succeeded."

"How's Chéri-Bibi?"

"Chéri-Bibi is dead, old man."

The Dodger collapsed in his arms. It was a knock-down blow. Little Buddha carefully attended to him, and when he opened his eyes:

"Where's your luggage?" he asked.

"At the hotel."

"And the millions?"

"Also at the hotel."

"Well, old man, you do take risks. . . . I say, look here, you are a chicken-hearted chap. . . . You don't seem to have much red blood in your veins."

He carried rather than led him to his hotel which was the only one in Palmerston at which a traveler with millions in his trunk could stay. Little Buddha lost no time in giving the order for a handcart. Nor did he remove his eyes from the trunk. The luggage was taken, at his request, to a ship's boat which had been waiting for him, and in which the Dodger let himself slide more dead than alive.

"Push off," Little Buddha ordered the sailors. The boat left the harbor and headed for the outer roadstead.

"You did well to hurry up. You'll just be in time for his burial!" said Little Buddha.

* See "Wolves of the Sea," by Gaston Leroux.

The Dodger raised his eyes to heaven and silently wept.

"His burial is a figure of speech," explained Little Buddha, "considering that we're going to put out to sea and drop him quietly overboard lest the authorities should interfere with us. Do you follow me? We are always up against the authorities you know. In that respect nothing has changed. But answer me. Haven't you finished blubbing?"

"What a bit of bad luck," sighed the Dodger. "If I hadn't missed the earlier boat at Batavia I might have arrived in time to close his eyes."

"No; make your mind easy. We didn't anchor here till this morning and he was already gone."

"But how did he die? . . . Tell me about it."

COD IN THE SPANISH WAY

"He died of the same complaint as the Marquis, it appears. Only the Marquis is quite well."

"It's always like that," sobbed the Dodger. "The good are taken and the bad left."

"Well, you know, we shan't be half pleased to see you back with the money. We were beginning to be bored stiff on the ship."

"Did you see him before he died?"

"Yes, now and then . . . but he had lost the power of speech. . . . We could see that it was all over with him. Everyone was very much upset . . . but since there was nothing to be done, we gradually got used to the idea. We had to. . . . The Kanaka did his utmost to save him."

"Yes, the Kanaka killed him with his dodges. . . ."

Oh, what a pity. . . . Chéri-Bibi. . . . Chéri-Bibi.
. . . It won't be long before I follow him, you may be
sure."

"You'll make a mistake seeing that we're rich now."

"Oh you, Little Buddha, you've got no heart. When
I hear you talk like that I feel that I could do you in."

"You don't say so! . . . You must have been very
fond of him."

"Fonder than I am of my own life. . . . If you knew
what a friend he was to me. And then I tell you he
was a decent fellow, a good sort. Men made him go
wrong. . . . Men and worse . . . bad times . . . and
worse . . . fate. *Fatalitas* as he used always to be
saying. Ah, what bad luck, I shall never see him
threaten the Heavens with his clenched fist and say
Fatalitas again. . . . Where have they put him?"

"On his bed in the Captain's cabin. His sister is
watching by his bedside."

"Sister St. Mary of the Angels. How is she? . . .
There's a good girl if you like."

"She's all right. . . . Everyone's all right."

"Yes, only Chéri-Bibi is dead. To think that I
should have traveled all that distance only to hear such
news."

The boat was alongside. It was a dull, rainy, gusty
day, and everything seemed gloomy and even dismal to
the sorrowing mind of the poor Dodger. His return
was so utterly unlike that which he had expected after
so many vicissitudes.

In his mind's eye he had pictured, confidently waiting
for him at the accommodation ladder, the terrible visage
of Chéri-Bibi whose expression would contrive to soften
for him. And now his eyes encountered the inscrutable

though fine and regular features of the Kanaka whom he had always detested. What business had he to be among them? Why should he bring them wealth now that he was assured that it would not make Chéri-Bibi rich? He would have liked to disappear beneath the waves dragging the millions with him.

He loathed the miscreants. They had committed a thousand horrors. True, he acknowledged that he himself had been guilty of a few peccadilloes, but they were the result of hard luck just as they were in Chéri-Bibi's case. He had killed, in justifiable circumstances, a couple of warders. But after all warders and police spies were of no account. It was their delight to treat the miseries of the convict world with kicks and blows from fist and revolver. Thus at least thought the Dodger who was already examining his conscience, for he felt that it would not be long before he joined his "dead pal" wherever he was; probably in the lower regions.

He heard the Kanaka greet him as in a dream. He shook hands here and there, and caught the voices of the Countess, Little Buddha and others speaking to him but gave no heed to them.

And he allowed himself to be taken to Chéri-Bibi.

The Captain's cabin was transformed into a mortuary chamber. A large black cloth bearing a white cross was over the convict whose head lay all white on the pillow and it seemed as if he were sleeping. One hand hung down. The Dodger seized it as he fell on his knees. It was the hand of a friend if there ever was one. He had often held it in his own. He recognized its rough, gnarled, hard skin and its scars; and tears coursed down his cheek upon it.

Then he raised his head to take a last look at him. Chéri-Bibi lay there as he had known him in moments of comparative calm when he was not being too keenly pursued, and when he could "breathe freely" between two evil deeds forced upon him by his inveterate enemy, Fate. But he reflected that Chéri-Bibi would never "breathe freely" again. . . . Then he saw near him a woman who was praying, and he recognized Sister St. Mary of the Angels.

"You loved him dearly, Sister," he said. "You loved him in spite of his crimes. So do I. I cannot too often say that. He was not as bad as people made out, I assure you. It was all the fault of *Fatalitas*."

And he staggered out of the cabin.

He began his eulogy of Chéri-Bibi with Little Buddha, he continued it with Sister St. Mary of the Angels, and he went through the entire crew with it. From cabin to cabin, from deck to deck, from quarter deck to forecastle, he sang the dead man's praises.

It was obvious that he was in a painful state, and they did not attempt to talk business with him that day. Moreover, Little Buddha had reassured them. Nevertheless they kept a strict watch over his trunk.

In the evening he made his way to the Kanaka's cabin, and after closing the door, partly undressed and took from his inside pockets a million francs in bank notes which had been sewn into them.

"May the will of Chéri-Bibi be done," he said. "Here is your million francs, Kanaka. No one will ever know a word about it. The other millions are in the yellow trunk. Take them and distribute them. I don't want to see anything, know anything, have anything. . . . I only want to be left in peace. . . . I don't want any one to speak to me." And he walked away and seated himself on the poop under the flag.

Next day the ship sailed on her piratical course to the Malay Archipelago, and Chéri-Bibi's body was cast into the sea. Was it a civil or a religious ceremony? God alone who heard the prayers of Sister St. Mary of the Angels could say.

At all events if Chéri-Bibi were not received into Heaven he was deeply mourned on board ship. The Kanaka delivered a splendid oration to which the convicts listened in solemn silence and with great emotion. The Dodger continued to give voice to his grief. And while his comrades went back to their duties, he began his pilgrimage to Chéri-Bibi's cage, and cell, and cabin; to the storeroom in which he had defended himself with such vigor; to the boiler in which he had hidden himself at the risk of being boiled with the soup; and in short, wherever Chéri-Bibi was wont to bend his steps.

When he returned on deck he came up against a big fellow whom he at once recognized as the Marquis du Touchais. It was obvious that this distinguished nobleman had greatly changed. But although his cheeks were less rounded, less full than before, his features with their Bourbon lines denoting ancestry were still well-shaped. The Marquis was, in particular, less stout, but he still retained the stature and the powerful shoulders which had been conspicuous in the sporting world. Now, however, he walked with a stoop.

Moreover, he continued on the sick list and under the Kanaka's care in the special part of the sick bay which he had shared for so many months with Chéri-Bibi. His friends were told not to tire him, and he lived a somewhat secluded life, speaking as little as possible, much cast down, it would appear, by his evil fortune, and longing with impatience for the moment of his deliverance to come.

The Dodger stared and passed him with clenched fists. Oh, it was this man who deserved to be at the bottom of the sea. . . .

At that moment their eyes met and the Dodger gave a start, clutching the rail of a ladder to prevent himself from falling.

When the Marquis had disappeared he murmured:

"What's wrong with me? I can't set eyes on a Marquis without feeling as if I were going to faint. True the look of him makes me feel ill. Perhaps it is because he has blue eyes like Chéri-Bibi. And, curse me, everything that reminds me of Chéri-Bibi makes my head go round. . . . All the same, they were not like Chéri-Bibi's little round eyes which smiled so funnily when we were having a joke together. . . . But what's wrong with me! . . . What's wrong with me?"

He could not help it. A strange force which he was powerless to resist impelled him to seek out those eyes once more. . . .

He waited for a couple of hours until the Marquis du Touchais, who was shut up with the Kanaka and the principal officers, came out from the ward room. But he was disappointed for the Marquis was wearing dark spectacles.

The officers had formed certain resolutions with a view to secure the safety of the crew. The Marquis was to be landed in a small fishing village on the coast of Borneo from which it would be impossible for him to obtain help by messenger under some three weeks.

From there he would be able to reach the China line
of steamers, and return to France as he pleased. Moreover, the Marquis had undertaken not to divulge his
adventure until two months had elapsed under pain of
severe reprisals. Thus he was receiving quick and
favorable treatment because he was the owner of the
millions which were to be paid for his liberation. When'
once the program was executed in its entirety the
Marquis would have nothing to fear from the convicts
who, on the contrary, would regard him as one of their
benefactors.

The shipwrecked friends of du Touchais, the old officers, Captain Barrachon, Lieutenant de Vilène and the
rest, and the old crew and military overseers and their
families, would be landed, with two months' provisions,
on a small desert island in the Pacific which was shel-
tered from storms and wind by coral reefs. The little
island was remote from the trade routes. The Kanaka
would take measures to inform the Australian Government of the existence of this new colony so that these
persons might be rescued in due course, within two
months at most.

The convict staff, of course, were not such simpletons
as to expect all on board to keep the secret, and it was
for this reason that they deemed it desirable to take
every precaution of time and circumstance.

All parties, for that matter, declared themselves satisfied with the arrangements since it was no use going
back on them, and the crew in the very natural delight
with which their newly-found wealth had filled them,
were bent on celebrating the happy day; but the
Kanaka called to mind that they had that very morning attended Chéri-Bibi's funeral, and they must honor

his memory by postponing public rejoicings until the
time came when they could "enjoy themselves among
themselves."

They passed a vote of thanks and suggested a com-
plimentary reception to the Dodger who declined to
accept "anything." They ended by respecting his
grief.

The "Estrella" was shaping her course for Borneo.
During the short voyage the Dodger continued to live
with the shade of Chéri-Bibi. He was like a man under
a delusion and his shipmates began to look upon him
and to treat him almost as a madman. Sometimes he
talked to himself, or at least the men thought that he
was talking to himself, but he himself imagined that
Chéri-Bibi was with him and understood him. He was
sailing not with the memory of him but with him.

"He's still on board. I feel it, and I'm certain of
it."

And when in his overexcited imagination he fancied
that Chéri-Bibi was not with him he looked about for
him.

He looked for him everywhere as if Chéri-Bibi were
having a game with him and hiding himself. He hardly
ate anything, and his meager form fell away still more.
It seemed as if the least breeze would sweep him from
the deck and fling him to the waves or the clouds. A
mere shadow so to speak.

One evening the Dodger dropped in an increasingly
lugubrious state of mind on to a bench on the upper
deck. He felt worn out, ready to give up the ghost.
Suddenly a white object on the bench attracted his
attention. It was a handkerchief which had been left
behind; a rather fine handkerchief which he was me-

chanically passing through his fingers, when he was stopped by a knot, a large and curiously formed knot tied in the handkerchief. The Dodger scrambled to his feet, distraught, trembling in every limb. The knot was a very special one which Chéri-Bibi used to tie in his handkerchiefs when he wanted to remember anything. . . . What did it mean? . . . Who was daring to tie Chéri-Bibi's knots . . . unless it were Chéri-Bibi himself?

"I tell you he's not dead. I tell you he's not dead," some invisible being cried to him in tones that deafened him.

Moreover, it was not the first time that he had come across living traces of Chéri-Bibi since his body had been flung to the sea. As he wandered anew over Chéri-Bibi's accustomed walks, he found the black ashes of pipe-tobacco still warm in the very places in which Chéri-Bibi liked to sit and smoke and dream; in those places which no one ever frequented, such as the prow, beyond the skylight, at the very ship's head, where he used to ensconce himself, dangling his legs over the sea. . '. . What did it all mean? . . . It was certain that he was not dreaming. . . . And the handkerchief? Whose handkerchief had been tied with Chéri-Bibi's knot? . . . Some one had left it there and some one perhaps would return for it. . . . And he drew back and leant against the davits of the ship's launch and waited. . . . waited.

Meanwhile his thoughts turned to a slight incident which occurred the evening before and to which he was wrong not to attach importance. It was a trifling thing in itself. Some one in the main alleyway had coughed, and the Dodger felt as if he had received a shock. He could have sworn that it was Chéri-Bibi's cough. He made one bound as quietly as he could to the alleyway, and his eyes fell upon the Marquis walking imperturbably away with his hands in his pockets.

The Dodger could have cried out in his disappointment and yet he had heard Chéri-Bibi cough. He would have recognized that cough in a thousand, and here was the confounded Marquis coughing like a convict! . . .

Therefore the Dodger hid behind the davits. The signalman struck the bell for the ten o'clock watch, and a big shadow, bearing slightly on one side, appeared. The Dodger put his arms round the davit to prevent himself from collapsing. . . . Nevertheless he slipped and fell over on his knees with chattering teeth. . . . That shadow was the very image of Chéri-Bibi's shadow.

The sky was slightly overcast and the moon lay behind the clouds. Had the Dodger found himself face to face with the phantom Flying Dutchman he could not have been more affrighted. It was Chéri-Bibi come back from the kingdom of the dead, and walking as he used to walk when he was alive, with the same peculiar carriage, the same waddling gait, the same dragging of the feet, and the same rolling of the shoulders. . . . There was no possibility of doubt. It was not a dream this time. After seeing, with his own eyes, Chéri-Bibi dead, and placed in a sack and thrown to the sea with a good-sized cannon ball at his feet, he now saw him alive, walking placidly on the deck as if he were still in command of the ship.

"Mother!" cried the Dodger.

The other who was almost touching him stopped in

front of him without the least agitation; and in the rays of the moon which had now wiped the clouds from its face, the Dodger saw with wide open eyes the Marquis once more.

The Marquis betrayed no surprise at seeing the Dodger on his knees, his teeth chattering with fright. A fellow of such small importance would obviously not be worthy of his attention. He turned his back on him and continued his silent way, and the Dodger no longer saw Chéri-Bibi and his peculiar carriage, his shuffling feet and rolling shoulders. It was indeed the Marquis from behind as well as in front!

In the Dodger's brain thoughts were whirling in pitiable confusion. He crept along on deck like a wounded man who has lost the use of his legs; he leant against "the wall" for support. The Marquis came and went as if he were not there.

"A funny bird, say what you like," thought the Dodger. . . . "The Marquis has turned out to be a funny bird since his illness. We never see him with his friends. He never visits any one, or speaks to any one, and he waits until night-time to take a walk on deck and commune with the stars!"

At this moment the Marquis, who was apparently fatigued, sat down on the bench on which the Dodger had left the handkerchief. He caught sight of the white linen, picked it up, looked at it and used it. The Dodger felt that his hair, which had not been cut during his travels, would stand on end. He had heard Chéri-Bibi blow his nose!

It was too much for one night and he fell into a dead faint.

The coolness of the early morning revived him. He

looked around him. The Marquis was gone. That part of the deck was deserted. He collected his thoughts. Obviously the Marquis had recognized his handkerchief since he had used it; therefore it was he who had tied the knot. The Marquis when he was not wearing spectacles had a certain look in his eyes of Chéri-Bibi; the Marquis at night-time when he thought that he was unobserved walked like Chéri-Bibi. It was as though he found relief from the restraints of day-time. But, indeed, in spite of all, the Marquis was the Marquis and Chéri-Bibi was Chéri-Bibi. No; if he were Chéri-Bibi what had become of his ears and his squat nose and a number of other peculiarities which disfigured him in the eyes of every one but the Dodger? They were buried in the sea with Chéri-Bibi himself.

Suddenly the Dodger gave a start as if he had received an electric shock. His thoughts went back to the Kanaka and the Countess covered with blood coming from the cabin in which the Marquis and Chéri-Bibi were held prisoners by the strange illness which they treated with the surgeon's knife. . . . He recalled the cries and groans and the sudden silences such as occur when patients have been given an anesthetic prior to an operation. He remembered, too, what had been said about the Kanaka and the Countess's trial, and the strips of human flesh that they were said to have cut from their patients. . . . Well, was he on the right track! Was it possible? . . . Was it possible that x . . . If they were not cannibals what had they done with those strips of flesh? . . . They had always refused to say what they had done with them. It may have been that their tricks were not invariably successful. And the proof of it was that on the "Estrella" one of the sick persons had died from them. . . . Oh, but . . . Oh, but . . . it would not be safe to change the flesh of people, particularly if it were done against the will of one of them. . . . Oh, but . . . Oh, but . . . Was such a thing really possible?

It was claimed that such things were possible. The Dodger remembered how amused he was one evening, after supper, when the boatswain read an article from the "Matin" * in which it was stated that surgeons were

* Here is the article in question:

At a meeting of doctors, surgeons, physiologists and scientists held at the Academy of Medicine in Paris, Professor Pozzi read a paper of the highest importance dealing with the very successful experiments in grafting on animals which had been made by M. Alexis Carrel, a French surgeon established in New York. M. Carrel is one of the governors of the Rockefeller Institute.

During a recent journey to the United States undertaken in scientific interests Professor Pozzi verified for himself the surprising results obtained by M. Carrel. He returned to France profoundly impressed by them.

The first experiments made by the French scientist consisted of the patching up of undeveloped parts. In January, 1917, M. Carrel cut from a bitch of medium size a part of the abdominal aorta covering an extent of two centimeters. He patched up the duct with a piece of peritoneum previously taken from the same animal and preserved for some days in vaseline. The dog was none the worse for the experiment. Twenty-two months later, on the 22nd November, 1918, he made a laparotomy; the abdominal cavity of the animal was opened, and it was found that no trace remained of the first operation.

"I saw the animal," said Professor Pozzi, "at the end of the séance, last month, and she was in perfect health."

But that was not all.

M. Carrel, emboldened by his first success, experimented in the substitution of entire portions of veins or arteries by other veins previously taken from other animals.

On the 7th June, 1917, he grafted a segment of a jugular vein on the carotid of a dog. On the 28th October of the same year the circulation was entirely normal. On the 1st February, 1919, the dog was killed in a fight with other dogs. It was found that the vein had "arterialized" and that the line of suture was almost invisible.

"This series of experiments is particularly interesting," said Professor Pozzi. "They admit of being surgically applied to now able to graft on a living animal any organ or limb taken from another living animal. Well, what surgeons had done so far with animals only the Kanaka had done with men. Nevertheless it must have cost the men dear.

human beings and they suggest the possibility of treating aneurism by the removal of the tumor, and the substitution for the carotid of a segment of the femoral vein taken from the subject himself."

Grafting various organs from animal to animal was likewise successfully attempted by M. Carrel.

"I saw two dogs from which he had temporarily removed and then replaced the spleen. They were quite healthy, but the result of the experiment cannot be decided until the dogs have been killed for dissecting purposes.

"The left kidney of a bitch was removed on the 6th February, 1918. A few minutes later, after washing it and plunging it in Locke's solution, the kidney was replaced in the abdominal cavity. The same operation was made with the right kidney a fortnight later. On the 5th May last the dog was frisking round me. A few days before she had had in quite normal circumstances eleven pups.

"Experiments of a still more daring character were then undertaken. In 1918 M. Carrel succeeded for the first time in grafting the leg of a fox terrier, which had been recently killed, on to a dog whose leg he had just amputated. The muscles, nerves and ducts were joined one to the other. The circulation was established in the dead limb. The dog died twenty days later from broncho-pneumonia.

"During my visit I saw a black dog on which three days before a leg belonging to a white dog had been grafted. The dog's condition was quite satisfactory."

One question of importance had to be solved, namely, how to have at command for the surgery of the future the necessary ducts and limbs in order that they might be utilized as occasion requires.

M. Carrel had discovered means of preserving the vitality of the tissues, which are to be transplanted, by immersing them in a special chemical solution, and in placing them in a refrigerator the temperature of which is maintained between zero and one degree centigrade below zero.

M. Carrel does not hesitate to affirm that the grafting of limbs will be attempted, in the near future, on man with limbs obtained by amputation or from the bodies of persons who have died violent deaths.

"All the same," added Professor Pozzi, "M. Carrel declares that it behooves us to be extremely careful, and not to draw inferences too hastily from these experiments on animals and apply

'And that was why he preferred to put up with his ten years' hard labor and to keep silent.

Such strenuous cogitation caused heavy drops of perspiration to break out on the imaginative Dodger's temples. . . . Good Heavens, it was possible for people's faces to be altered in that way. . . . Not forgetting that if it were possible, it would not have been very difficult since Chéri-Bibi and the Marquis's heads in length and breadth and shape were pretty well of the same dimensions. . . . But how had the Kanaka managed with the nose . . . to place the Marquis's Bourbon nose on Chéri-Bibi's face? He must have removed Chéri-Bibi's nose and grafted that of the Marquis on his face. What a piece of work! What a piece of work! . . .

"In any case, he's got some pluck, has the Kanaka," thought the Dodger admiringly. "They say that surgeons nowadays shrink from nothing. . . . And his hands. He must have done the same thing with his hands. . . . And I took the dead man's hand and wept over it. . . . Without a doubt it was Chéri-Bibi's hand . . . and it didn't belong to him any longer. . . . To

them to man. Thus he has resisted up to now the requests of two of his patients who, with the daring characteristic of Americans, entreated him, one to replace an arm that had been amputated, and the other to substitute a healthy kidney for his own, which suffered from Bright's disease, by obtaining the limb or the viscera from the body of an executed criminal.

"In the present state of his investigations I would not allow," said the Professor with a smile, "an unhealthy kidney of mine to be replaced by a healthy one; but I unhesitatingly say that I would allow an artery to be replaced by a piece of fresh vein if I were threatened with aneurism.

"However that may be, M. Carrel's brilliant experiments hold out splendid hopes to the science of healing, and they pave the way to a new era in surgery."

change the hands must have been more painful than anything else. . . ."

His thoughts sped back to Chéri-Bibi's terrible moans: "Not his hands. . . . Not his hands."

"Oh, well, if anybody had told me about it . . . I shouldn't have got in such a state, of course. . . . Damn it, Chéri-Bibi get out! He's the only man who'd have played us such a trick. It's up against old Bertillon and the finger print dodge now that a man can change his hands as he changes his gloves. . . . And what about the tatoo marks on his skin? Did Chéri-Bibi change his skin from head to foot? . . . I'm sorry they dressed the corpse. I should have liked to see for the last time the flowery designs that Chéri-Bibi had had tatooed on his skin over his heart. . . . What a queer business. . . . His big ears and his thin nose . . . and so on and so forth. It's all up with the measurements of prisoners now. . . . No, hang it all, it's too good . . . it's too good to be true. It's out of the question . . . I'm talking nonsense."

He began to laugh like a madman, not knowing what to make of the many grotesque thoughts which were "buzzing in his head." That Chéri-Bibi's death had sent him "dotty" was self-evident. He crawled to his cabin and threw himself on his bunk, where he lay awake and dreamed until about six o'clock in the morning, when he fell into a heavy slumber.

He slept until the evening. Men came in to inquire after him. They were rather uneasy about him, but he declared when he woke up that he had never felt better, and was famishing. They asked him what he would like to eat. He thought for a moment and said:

"That's my business. I'm going to cook myself something nice."

He dressed and made his way to the galley in which he had once been the cook's mate. Here he set himself seriously to work. He prepared some codfish. It was a Spanish dish of which he had the recipe, and in the old days Chéri-Bibi was inordinately fond of it.

"Poor chap," some one said. "He still fancies he's cooking something for Chéri-Bibi. How devoted he was to him!"

As a matter of fact the Dodger had never shown so much care and attention in the whole course of his culinary career. He prepared the dish in such abundance that it looked as if Chéri-Bibi, whose appetite was equal to that of six men, was really in the land of the living.

The dish consisted of:

1¼ lbs. of cod

1¼ lbs. of potatoes

1 lb. of tomatoes

3½ oz. of red powdered pimento in lieu of fresh red Spanish pimento, of which he would have used 14 oz.

1¾ oz. of onions

1-3 oz. of garlic

1-3 oz. of flour

A little pepper freshly ground

Salt

A small bunch of bay leaves in lieu of thyme and parsley

Stale bread crumbs.

His comrades left him to himself, for they were fully

aware that they must not interrupt the Dodger when he was concocting this particular dish of cod.

He cut the cod into pieces, boiled it, drained it when it was cooked, took the bones out, and kept back half a pint of the water in which it was boiled as dressing. He sighed with regret as he thought that if he had fresh pimento he would have peeled them, and cut them into long thin slices, and sprinkled them with a little pepper, but as he had rot got them he had to do without them. He peeled and chopped and half cooked the onions in oil, with the tomatoes cut in slices, the garlic, the bay leaf and the rest of the pepper; he added the dressing and let it all boil for ten minutes; and then he used the flour to thicken the sauce, and continued the cooking for a few minutes longer, took out the bay leaf, and tasted his handiwork, smacked his lips with satisfaction, but added a little salt to the seasoning since the cod had been soaking too long, and strained the sauce and the dressing.

Meanwhile the potatoes had been cooked in steam. He peeled and cut them into slices. Then he took a fire-proof dish and spread a layer of potato slices on it, then a layer of cod slices, and above that a quarter of his powdered Spanish pimento in lieu of slices of pimento, added a little sauce, and repeated the operation in every particular four times. He sprinkled bread crumbs over it, put it in an oven for about half an hour, until the dish had acquired an oily consistency the appearance of which alone was enough to send an epicure into raptures. When he opened the oven a splendid odor, an appetizing fragrance as from the Arabian Nights, permeated the galley.* The Dodger

* Try it and you will see how excellent it is. G. L.

closed his eyes. "Oh, Chéri-Bibi, if you were here!" he cried. He opened his eyes, placed the dish on a napkin, took two spoons, and walking quickly through the alleyways, which were deserted at this hour, reached that part of the deck where the Marquis was in the habit of taking his walks when the crew, except the night watch, were asleep. And he placed his steaming and odorous dish not on the bench where the Marquis usually sat, but some twenty paces away on a large pulley. Having done so he concealed himself as on the previous night.

It was not long before the Marquis appeared. It was so obviously the Marquis this time that the hapless and trembling Dodger felt his heart sink within him and he was almost suffocating.

The Marquis sat down in his customary seat, but suddenly he raised his head and sniffed. He seemed to be inhaling with a certain uneasy enjoyment an unexpected odor. He rose to his feet with quivering nostrils. He took his bearings, and after some hesitation walked to the place from which, on this fine starlit night, the agreeable flavors were being wafted. Oh, the poor Dodger's beating heart! . . . Now the Marquis is but two steps from the odoriferous pulley. He stoops over the dish, over the cod cooked in the Spanish way.

He casts a rapid glance on either side to see that he is unobserved.

And he flings himself greedily on the dish crying: "*Fatalitas.*"

"*Fatalitas*" repeats the Dodger in a delirious voice. "Oh, Chéri-Bibi . . . Chéri-Bibi."

They rush forward, shake hands and hug one another.

"Hush, not too much row. . . . Besides the cod will get cold, Dodger."

And they fall to. And both of them eat from the dish.

"Well, I say, you're a Marquis now?"

"Hold your tongue, so that the Kanaka may never suspect that you know."

"What's it got to do with him? I shan't leave you again. . . . That's understood, eh?"

"Yes, that's understood. . . . Oh, this splendid cod, my dear old Dodger. . . . You'll come and cook some for me now and then at my own place at home."

"Of course, it all belongs to you. . . . You're Cecily's husband now."

Chéri-Bibi dropped his spoon. He had eaten enough cod.

"Oh, don't speak of it," he said. "The mere idea of it sends me crazy."

CHAPTER II

THE car stopped on the summit of the hill at Dieppe, a little outside Le Pollet.

"Must I wait for you, Monsieur le Marquis?" asked the chauffeur.

"No, Carolle, you must return to Treport, and stay there until you receive my orders."

The Marquis and his secretary alighted from the car.

"Well, my good Hilaire, here we are at the end of our trials."

"You must be greatly excited, Monsieur le Marquis," said Hilaire, looking at his master, a fine figure of a man, tall and extremely stout, while the secretary was a puny mortal wearing a traveling suit which seemed too big for his narrow frame and lank slender limbs.

"Yes, Hilaire, I am excited, as you may well believe, so excited that I'm not sorry to arrive at nightfall in a place where every paving-stone, you understand, every pebble brings some memory back to me.

"What long years have passed since those fatal happenings which forced me from the place and with which you are familiar. It was here that I lived as a happy boy and young man. Oh, blessed soil, land of my fathers! Now I come back to it after so many hopes shattered, so many struggles and vicissitudes. Is it true that the dearest of my wishes is to be granted?

31

Oh, my dear Hilaire, I never expected that I should die one day an honest man in this Caux country where I was born, and have a grave, one day, in this dear spot.

"Hail, O my country. I see once more your humble dwellings, the smoke ascending from the housetops in the quiet evening, little children chasing one another with happy cries, and the white caps of the good wives of Le Pollet who sit on their doorsteps the better to watch the passer-by.

"Here we can see the lights gleaming through the windows. How my heart beats at the sight of this porch from which I used to step into the noisy diligence which bore me to Birelle or Criel and through the great open country. Heavens, Hilaire, let us stop here. You see that road whose ascent branches off towards the cliff? That's the way to Le Puys, where I knew my earliest joys and greatest sufferings. It was here that my little sister and I used to fly like the wind to get to the great hawthorn bushes entwined with honeysuckle and dog roses which shaded Cecily's house. . . . Cecily! . . . Cecily! . . . How is it that on this day which ought to be the happiest day of my life, an uncontrollable sadness creeps over me and fills me with secret misgivings, as if I were hastening to a fatal catastrophe, a disaster which nothing can avert?"

"Let's go on a little, Monsieur le Marquis. . . . People are beginning to stare at us."

"You're right, old fellow, we mustn't attract attention. I am not anxious for the Marquis du Touchais to be recognized, nor that people should welcome my happy return before I have fully savored the joy of seeing alone many faces and places which hold me by such tender memories. Ah, there it is . . . there . . .

the shop front. , . . Nothing has changed, Hilaire.
. . . Nothing has been changed. That is the iron shop
front belonging to the butcher with whom I served my
apprenticeship."

"I confess," said Hilaire, "that I'm not much struck
with those particular iron bars, for they recall to my
mind the most unpleasant time of your life!" And he
endeavored to drag the Marquis off by respectfully
taking his arm.

But the Marquis shook himself free:

"Look at that fine calf, Hilaire, it is splendid," he
said. "And the heart, liver and lungs are magnificent.
They always had the best pluck here, because they
never bought spotted meat, that is to say diseased
meat. I need only point out to you, in proof of what I
say, those lungs which are quite 'fat' as they say in
the business, in other words, first rate. It's like that ox
still hanging on the gambrel: it is a pleasure to see it, I
assure you."

"I beg of you, Monsieur le Marquis, to notice that
people are flocking round us."

"Yes, yes, Hilaire. I'm coming. , . . You are quite
right . . . but you must forgive me, you know. It
was here that I first learned how to use the knife!"

They crossed the bridge and once more the Marquis
encompassed in one glance the harbor and the quays
where he had played in the heyday of his youth.

He pointed to the dark outline of a steamer and said
to his secretary:

"There, that's the Newhaven boat. We'll come and
see her off to-morrow. Remember this evening to look
up for me the time of high tide. And now I'll show you
Duquesne's statue."

They were held up by a great block of carriages on the way to the races, such as may be seen in the height of the season, and he said:

"I'm glad to notice that we still have a certain amount of traffic."

When they reached the Square which contained the statue of the great French sailor, the Marquis placed Hilaire in a favorable spot from which, though the evening shadows had fallen, he was able to admire the noble attitude of the hero of Dieppe in his top-boots.

"When my sister and I were young," said the Marquis, "we never passed this statue without my saying: 'You see, Jacqueline, it's not bronze, it's . . . Duquesne." *

The Marquis recalled this schoolboy playfulness with emotion and it seemed to him that he was a boy again.

"Where shall we dine?" asked Hilaire, who was feeling hungry.

"Look here, Hilaire, if you've no objection we'll leave the swagger hotels alone this evening, and I'll take you to a modest eating-house, in the harbor where, in my apprentice days, my friends and I used to regale ourselves when we were on holiday. It will cost us two and a half francs each, including wine, but not including extras of course, and we shall have a good dish of fried fish."

"I notice, Monsieur le Marquis," said Hilaire, who was not very keen on the eating-house, "that you've become rather economical lately."

"I never liked squandering money, and upon my soul,

* In the Northern patois "chêne" is "quêne"; the ch very often becomes qu; so that the pun is: "Ce n'est pas du bronze, c'est du quêne (chêne)." "It's not bronze, but oak."—*Translator's note.*

without being a miser, one can remember that a sou's a sou."

"You were not so calculating when you were poor."

"There's no merit in not calculating when you have no money."

"That's true," admitted Hilaire.

"But what are you complaining of? Are we denying ourselves anything, and aren't we living up to our position? You see, Hilaire, the one thing I don't like is waste. It doesn't benefit any one. Besides, we've got to make up the loss of six million francs, don't forget."

"Hush!" Hilaire broke in, gripping his master's arm.

"I'm not saying a word that the whole world mayn't listen to," went on the Marquis as he rubbed his arm. "I repeat, six millions . . . that's money. What a number of honest men we could make with six millions!"

He pushed open the glazed door of a restaurant opposite the Fish Market in the arcade to which they had returned.

About a dozen sailors and clerks were dining some-what noisily. The proprietor of the establishment—Oscar by name—darted towards them, gratified to see such well dressed customers coming into the place. But the Marquis knew his way about, and had no need of his services, for he went direct to a sort of special room cut off from the ordinary dining room by glass parti-tions from which depended short dingy-looking cur-tains.

"It smells of burnt fat," said Hilaire with a look of disgust.

"It smells of the fried fish of Dieppe," returned the Marquis. "Monsieur Oscar, please give us four por-

tions of fried fish, some crab and prawns, and four portions of calf's head cooked in oil, and two jugs of cider,
to begin with."

"Do you expect friends, sir?" asked M. Oscar,
obsequiously.

"No, but I know something about the size of the
portions here, and I want to make quite sure."

"Do you know me, if it's a fair question?"

"Not at all, but I saw your name on the door. In my
time the proprietor was called Lavallée."

"He's dead," said Oscar, "and I took over the business."

"Is business still good?"

"Business is bad, but such as it is I'm trying to sell
the place. The big restaurants do me a lot of harm.
Customers are very particular, and I have to get my
fish from Paris."

"How's that?"

"Because the big hotels buy up all the fresh fish in
Dieppe."

"You see yourself that we should have done better to
go to a big hotel," said Hilaire dolefully.

"You'll be quite satisfied, sir," Oscar declared. "I'll
run to the kitchen myself."

The Marquis sighed:

"It's hard that one can't get a bit of fish in a seaport
town," but he at once added: "Look here, Hilaire, I
don't care one way or the other. It's the setting of the
place that I've come to see."

"It's a pretty sight!" said Hilaire.

But he put a bridle on his ill-humor when a dainty
little serving girl made her appearance. She was
young and smart, and wore a white cap over her ears,

and her bright looks, sly smile, sprightliness and activity and the graceful manner in which she laid the table sent him into raptures.

"What is your name?" he asked, reddening.

"Virginie, sir, if you please."

Hilaire at once engraved her name upon his heart.

Thus, as befits the awakening of love, Hilaire remained silent during the whole of the disagreeable meal, and hardly touched the "horrible scraps," as he called them. The Marquis talked enough for two, bringing to mind twenty anecdotes of his youth, and striving, apparently, to escape from himself. Hilaire, who knew him well, was not deceived, and he felt that all his chatter carefully dissimulated the one thought which preoccupied him but which he did not express.

Meantime a newsboy came into the restaurant shouting the name of an evening paper, and selling it to sailors in the adjoining room.

"Hullo!" said one of them almost immediately, "it seems that it's all up with the famous 'Bayard.' "

At these words the Marquis and Hilaire gripped each other and listened with strange anxiety.

"Yes, look here, it's in the paper. At the finish they caught her after chasing her for a year, and they've sunk her."

"Read it! . . . Read it!" cried several voices.

The man read out:

"The 'Times' has received a telegram from its Singapore correspondent stating that an end had been made at last of the notorious 'Bayard' and her convict crew. The French cruiser 'La Gloire,' which was on her track during the whole of last year, and from which she succeeded in escaping in the many groups of islands of the Malay

Archipelago, came up with her in the Molucca Sea, near the Sula Islands. 'La Gloire' at once opened fire. A quick engagement ensued, and the 'Bayard' was blown up. Three fourths of the crew were drowned. The remainder, who had taken to the boats and were attempting to escape, preferred to be shot rather than to surrender. 'La Gloire' picked up over a hundred dead bodies among which they were able to identify the Kanaka, the leader of the gang, and his terrible wife, the Countess. It is known that the Kanaka took over the position of Captain of these abominable pirates after Chéri-Bibi's death. Thus ends the amazing organization which had occupied the attention of the whole world for such long months and which terrorized the entire China Seas."

The reading had finished.

The two men in the private room, who had turned whiter than the tablecloth, breathed a deep sigh of relief and muttered: "That's a good thing!"

The sailors in the other room indulged in various comments on the Marquis du Touchais and his luck in escaping from such bandits.

"All the same, it cost him five million francs," said a sailor, for most people were acquainted with the facts and knew that the Marquis, Captain Barrachon and many others had barely escaped with their lives; and the Marquis himself on his journey through Paris had freely allowed himself to be interviewed by representatives of the great newspapers.

"I've heard that the Marquis is coming back to Dieppe soon," said another. "The 'Belle of Dieppe' will be pleased. She'll begin to ride the high horse again, while the Marchioness, who is good, will be crying her eyes out. . . . Say what you like, certain things are not right. . . ."

"It seems this evening that she's going to open the Ball in Aid of Poor Seamen in the great hall at the Casino."

"Yes, the dear lady is to be accompanied by the Deputy Prefect. It's the first time that she's taken part in any public charity since the death of her brother in Australia."

"Her brother was a nice object. He died from dissipation and, they say, was an opium smoker. She can't be over-sorry at the loss of him."

"If her husband had gone under like her brother, she would have been well rid of him, poor thing. But knowing that the Marquis is coming back to her one of these fine days, she can't be jumping for joy. Not to mention that she got on very well without him. If I'd been in the Marchioness's shoes, I wouldn't have provided those ruffians with five millions so as to send me back a bird like him."

"The Marquis made a heap of money out of the St. Julien property in Rouen. His solicitor had no need to ask any one's permission to get him out of the mess, you may be sure."

"Anyway I pity her."

"Did you see the 'Belle of Dieppe' coming back from the races to-day? She had a dress on that hit you in the eye."

"All the same the Baroness Proskof is a beautiful woman, but only the Marquis knows what she's cost him."

When the diners reached this point in the conversation they were obliged to move their chairs to allow the two customers from the private room to pass out.

"Hullo," said one of the sailors when the two men

were in the arcade outside, "that man and the Marquis are as like as two peas."

"It isn't the Marquis. You don't suppose he'd come here to dine. . . . You've gone cross-eyed."

The Marquis when he was outside looked at his watch in increasing agitation.

"It's only half-past eight," he said.

"It doesn't begin until ten o'clock," said Hilaire.

"The program says that the ball will be opened at nine o'clock. . . . When I think that in half an hour . . . I'm frightened, Hilaire, I'm trembling like a child. . . . I can tell you now. . . . The thought of seeing Cecily again appalls me. . . . Yes, at first I was immensely elated. . . . And it was that which made me suffer and endure everything . . . it was that which enabled me to bear torture. The thought that I should be her husband, her master . . . that she would belong to me . . . that this woman whom I idolized, and who was so far, so far above me, was to be mine . . . mine . . . that I should live in the same house with her, see her every day, breathe the atmosphere that she breathed, and hold my arms out to her. . . . Was not this the most perfect happiness, a heaven upon earth? Well, Hilaire, for more than a year I have put off opening the door of that paradise."

"You did well, Monsieur le Marquis," returned the secretary, "if only because you've waited until the day on which we've learnt of the death of the two persons who alone knew your secret. Now we may feel safe. Besides this last year has benefited you and benefited me too. You have traveled and seen people and the world. You have learnt a good many things. You have mixed in 'society.' You know how to hold your

own, how to succeed in society. You have conferred
with your solicitor. You have examined your accounts.
You know the extent of your fortune. Wealth does
not astonish you any more. You know how to talk to
women. You are a real nobleman. Your manners have
become polished, your language more refined. I listened
to you just now saluting your native country in the
choice language that one reads in books. No vulgar
word escapes you any more, and though the opportunity has often presented itself, you have never once
allowed yourself to utter the *Fatalitas* which in the old
days so often embellished your speech. For my part, I
have followed you in this prudent course. I have
benefited from the lessons that we have taken together,
and I no longer recognize myself."

"You still have the same old kind expression on your
pale face, my dear Dodger."

"Don't mention that name, Monsieur le Marquis. It
is buried with all our troubles."

"You have the stuff of an upstart in you, my dear
Dodger. I am not at all offended when you forget
yourself and call me Chéri-Bibi as you did in the old
days—provided we're alone of course."

"Don't go for me," said the Dodger in hurt tones.
"I may look like an upstart, but I often find you now
rather bombastic. It's certain that something more
than your features have been changed."

"What does it matter if my heart is the same."

"I must admit that in that respect you haven't
altered. You are still in love with Madame Cecily.
. . . You think of nothing but her. . . . See, here's
the Casino already illuminated. What do you propose
to do?""

"Come Dodger, my dear Dodger, let's have a turn on the pier. . . . There's plenty of time."

"How you're trembling. . . . I feel very sorry for you. Lean on my arm. . . ."

"You see, Hilaire, I'm very unhappy. Understand me. . . . This woman . . . this woman is my very life. . . . And I have every right to her. . . . That is the terrible part of it. Suppose I make her suffer. . . . She doesn't care for me. She is happy without me. If I were a decent man, and had a heart as you say I have, I should slink away this evening without seeing her. Can you imagine the torment through which I am passing, and why we stayed for three days in idleness at Treport, when everything called me here? I don't know where to turn my steps. . . . I waver. . . . I'm like a man groping in the dark. At one time I had an idea of living in America . . . of settling down there. But I couldn't. . . . No. . . . No. . . . The thought of her attracts me as iron attracts the magnet."

"As the magnet attracts iron, you mean," Hilaire thought it well to interject.

"As you please. . . . So I sailed for Europe. And then we reached Paris . . . and afterwards came still nearer her. Now we are quite close, and I must see her. At first I shall try to see her from a distance. . . . This ball has decided me. When I learned that she would be present I said to myself: 'Here is an opportunity. I will go to the Casino—after paying for a ticket, of course. I will stay outside the ballroom.' But we can see the dancing through the great glass windows . . . we can watch the scene. I shall see Cecily again. I am longing to know if she still retains the beauty of long ago which I have carried in my heart. Let us sit down here, my dear Hilaire, my dear old Dodger and only friend. I am very glad that when you came to collect the millions you did not see Cecily."

"Yes; as you know, Monsieur le Marquis, the business was settled through the solicitor. And I personally am glad that the solicitor died; because being dead he won't recognize me!"

"Maitre Régime, who succeeded him, is a very excellent man, Dodger. . . . But I was saying that I was glad you didn't see Cecily, and I'll tell you why. Tastes differ, and perhaps you would not have considered Cecily as beautiful as I could have wished, and I should have been greatly grieved, and would never have forgiven you, you see, Dodger. I can't understand any one not admiring Cecily."

"Now I know what to expect," thought the devoted secretary.

They were on the pier and the breeze from the offing wafted them alike the scent of the sea and the opening sounds of revelry.

"Here goes," cried Chéri-Bibi. "The die is cast."

He rose and hurried the Dodger off to the Casino. A crowd was already assembled at the great gates, and carriages and motor cars were bringing a constant succession of well-dressed people. Our two men passed through the reserved courtyard, and quickly made their way to one of the large windows overlooking the ballroom, and posted themselves in a secluded corner which was screened from indiscreet observation. They could see without being seen. Chéri-Bibi sat down to allay his excitement, his eyes fixed on the ballroom in which groups of dancers were already beginning their evolutions. On a platform near the orchestra a number of valuable prizes were laid out which were to be drawn for in the lottery at the end of the evening. Sprightly young girls and charming young women came backwards and forwards to examine the prizes, passing them from hand to hand, and smilingly commenting on them. Young men with flowers in their button-holes were moving from chair to chair to greet their friends or to "put themselves down" for dances. Some of them were showing off, strutting about and assuming ridiculous airs. A man of about forty came in, extravagantly well-dressed, holding his handsome but frivolous head, high. His appearance gave no pleasure to those who do not care for dandies. Chéri-Bibi, who as it happened did not like them, rose and swore under his breath. He recognized the man:

"M. de Pont-Marie," he said. "Now there's a man I've always disliked."

M. de Pont-Marie offered his arm to an elderly, white-haired lady whose distinguished features could be seen under her lace wrap.

"See, the Dowager Marchioness du Touchais," said Chéri-Bibi to the Dodger.

"Do you know her, Monsieur le Marquis?" asked the Dodger.

"I should think I do—it's my mother!"

He had not descried Cecily. His eyes dived into the different groups, roaming among the young women, because Cecily was still a young woman to him, though she must be thirty-five now, and "in the full flush of her beauty," as the Dodger expressed it consolingly. Apparently she had not yet arrived. She was not behind time, for the Deputy Prefect had not yet put in an appearance.

For a moment it occurred to Chéri-Bibi that she was present; and that perhaps she was under his very eyes but that he failed to recognize her. . . . The mere thought caused great drops of perspiration to break over his forehead which he wiped with feverish and agitated gestures, no longer able to keep still.

But it was impossible. His heart was thumping in his chest with heavy, dull blows that resounded like the beating of a drum; and he knew that even if his eyes had failed to recognize Cecily his heart would have stopped and said "There she is!" for his heart would have stopped beyond a doubt. And indeed, he might have died from that very fact. He leaned for support upon the Dodger, who felt that he was trembling.

At one moment there was a sort of commotion in the ballroom. The dancers turned round. People who were seated rose to their feet. Every face wore an expression of curiosity and young men flocked to the door as if some one had arrived and was creating a sensation.

"It's Cecily or the Deputy Prefect," thought Chéri-Bibi, half-dead with emotion, for he could not conceive why there should be any excitement unless it were on account of Cecily or the gold-laced representative of the Government. But it was neither the Deputy Prefect nor Cecily. A brilliant couple had arrived.

The lady wore a conspicuous head-dress of plumes. The Dodger, who had devoted some time to the study of literature since he became Chéri-Bibi's secretary, considered that she was of "proud beauty." Tall, of an ideal grace of form, and expressing in her entire person, her bearing, her manner of looking and smiling, a most voluptuous charm, she advanced like one accustomed to carry everything before her, a veritable belle of the ball. She wore a daring princess dress of straw-colored Indian silk, clinging closely to the figure, while an enormous sash of crimson crêpe de chine was slung over her shoulders.

Chéri-Bibi in his wrath was about to ask: "Who is this minx?" when he perceived her "partner." Her partner was the Baron Proskof, who had returned to France and to his wife as soon as he could. By a miracle she had escaped from the wreck of the "Belle of Dieppe" in a boat which was picked up by the vessel which had crashed into them.

If Chéri-Bibi had retained any doubt as to whether this superb creature was the Baroness, he would have been quickly informed by the remarks which were passed at the windows near him. The spectators whispered "the Belle of Dieppe" and perhaps he would not have resisted the longing to express somewhat openly his own thoughts about such a person, but there was no time. At that moment Cecily arrived.

Chéri-Bibi had mounted a chair and he collapsed. The Dodger caught him in his arms, pulled him together and spoke a few encouraging words, to which he replied with a vague shake of the head promising to be sensible, and then returned to the window, against which he flattened his face, as pale as death.

The Deputy Prefect advanced to meet the lady President of the "Aid for Poor Seamen," led her to her seat, offering his arm and talking to her with every mark of attention. Chéri-Bibi at once felt a loathing for the Deputy Prefect.

She possessed a wonderful charm, did the young Marchioness du Touchais, a charm rendered all the more affecting by her natural air of melancholy. Even as her rival shed a radiance in her path, so Cecily appealed by reason of her quiet beauty and her grace and good form. For she was as graceful as the Baroness, if not more so, if it be true that grace is that quality, innate in some women, which consists in perfect refinement of manners, ease of movement, unfailing taste in dress, and simplicity in the midst of opulence. The Marchioness wore a white silk dress trimmed with black Chantilly lace.

"Heavens!" said Chéri-Bibi in his innermost conscience where his love for Cecily found utterance in a lyrical outburst which went beyond the language of ordinary mortals: "Heavens! behold the sweet light of my life; she who holds the four corners of my heart; the dear object of my fears; of hopes so fraught with grief. How comely she is! Her unhappiness has but made her more beautiful in my eyes. As a woman she surpasses the promise of her girlhood. See how she moves and tell me if fairies stealing across the flowered meadows have lighter feet. See how she smiles and tell me if sorrow that laughs, and is akin to pity that weeps, is not the fearer of the two. . . . O young fools who "like the fickle multitude" revolve round this buzzing queen who is her rival, how can you see her pass without being enslaved forever."

Thereupon he sighed; and after feeling astonished at the lack of cordiality which the Baroness's friends showed when they bowed to his idol, a wave of his customary fury shook him from head to foot when he saw the Deputy Prefect dance with Cecily.

The Deputy Prefect had a way of smiling at Cecily which Chéri-Bibi intensely disliked. Besides he found

that this high official made too free with the Marchioness's figure. He held her too closely; it was not good
manners; and he had a conceited look about him as he
whirled her round which deserved chastisement. Of
course the explanation was very simple. Chéri-Bibi did
not understand why any one should dare touch his idol,
and he cursed the customs of society which under the
guise of charity permitted tricks the impropriety of
which revolted him.

In the end he removed his eyes from the Deputy
Prefect because "it hurt him" and interested himself
only in Cecily. She danced without effort, with an
absent look, her mind elsewhere. Chéri-Bibi saw her
pass quite close to him, and he received a shock which
made him lean, gasping, against the wall. The window
had been partly opened. As she went by it seemed to
him that her presence lingered with him. Those ver-
milion lips, those adorable eyes, that yielding form,
that dress which was raised and held in her hand showing her exquisite ankles, her little feet in their fine silk
stockings and satin shoes. . . . Oh, it was all Cecily,
his Cecily. . . . And she belonged to him . . . him.
He had only to set his mind to it. The thought of it
. . . the thought of it was, in truth enough, as he told
the Dodger a few minutes before, to send him crazy.
. . . To-morrow, the day after to-morrow; in short,
whenever he dared . . . that very evening if he had the
courage, he had but to come forward and say: "Here I
am!" The mayor, the rector, Providence, the law if
necessary, all society in heaven above and in the earth
beneath would be at one in bringing Cecily to him and
saying: "Take her. She belongs to you." He pressed
his clenched fingers to his heated brow. . . . Oh, yes,

he would dare, he would dare. To begin with, now that he had seen her nothing else was possible; that is to say, nothing that implied flight, self-denial, parting forever, renunciation of so much beauty and youth. He could no longer do without her. Whatever happened she should be his. . . .

The dance was over and the Deputy Prefect took Cecily back to her place with the Dowager Marchioness. Chéri-Bibi quieted down somewhat. Thenceforth he was sure of himself, and of his intentions.

He made up his mind once for all. He would be the Marquis du Touchais to the death.

Suppose that some one had told the little boy living in Le Pollet that it would be so—the youngster who scarcely ventured to lift his eyes to the young lady at the Bourreliers'. . . . At that moment Chéri-Bibi no longer regretted the past, nor any of the amazing events in his career of crime, the years spent in prison, in a convict settlement, his destitution, his innocence ignored by the blindness of his judges, his frightful revolts, nor his moments of terrible hatred against an implacable destiny; and for the first time in his life he thanked the *fatalitas* which had led him through paths of perfidy and bloodshed to the arms of Cecily . . . the arms of Cecily. . . . He saw them for the first time. Oh, those beautiful arms . . . the arms of Cecily . . . his wife!

The orchestra was striking up the first bars of the next waltz. Chéri-Bibi saw M. de Pont-Marie, with his monocle in his eye, bow with—to his mind—an idiot smile to Cecily. She smiled in return, and rising, seemed to accept his arm with pleasure. Then they began to dance. The feeling that he experienced as he watched the Deputy Prefect and Cecily dance was nothing compared with the storm which in a flash overwhelmed him. The Dodger, whose arm he held as in a vice, repressed a desire to cry out, and thought it as well, after shaking himself free, to witness Chéri-Bibi's outbursts of love and hatred from a safer distance.

M. de Pont-Marie was a blackguard. He danced with his eyes fixed on Cecily's, and though indeed he did not smile, as he danced, like the Deputy Prefect, nevertheless his detestable character as a coxcomb, as a connoisseur of women, was reflected in the ardor with which he expressed his secret feelings. At moments his lips whispered words that Chéri-Bibi could not, of course, hear though he could imagine the sense. They were from all appearance "burning words." How Chéri-Bibi suffered. Cecily blushed and turned her head.

"The monster," Chéri-Bibi thought, feeling a wild and bitter desire as the two drew nearer to fly at the little beast's throat. "He takes undue advantage of this entertainment at which the Marchioness was obliged to be present. He makes the most of the fact that during the dance which Cecily was kind enough to give him she could not publicly treat him as he deserves. And he says things for which if he had the audacity to utter them in her house, she would have him thrown out by her flunkeys."

And M. de Pont-Marie's eyes gleamed and his hand pressed Cecily's hand though she obviously resented it. How Chéri-Bibi suffered! It was enough to make him shout with impotent rage. . . . And the dance pursued its course . . . and she continued to listen to him.

The wretched Chéri-Bibi called to mind the abominable insinuations of the women on the "Bayard" when they accused his Cecily of giving ear to the amorous nonsense of this de Pont-Marie. . . . If it were really true! . . . Absurd. . . . The thought of it was too awful; it made him miserable to entertain so monstrous an idea. . . . His Cecily . . . his pure Cecily . . . to love a stupid ass of that type. . . . An idiot with a monocle. . . . The short sight which was suggested by a monocle was equivalent in his eyes to a diploma of idiocy.

But it was he, Chéri-Bibi, who was the idiot, and the proof was that in the very middle of the dance the fair Marchioness released herself, gently but firmly, from her partner and asked him in decisive tones—Chéri-Bibi had the divine joy of hearing her—to take her back to her seat.

It served de Pont-Marie right. Chéri-Bibi began to laugh as if he were out of his wits. The other pulled a face . . . such a face! Well, she had put him in his place. There was no mistake about that. Chéri-Bibi jumped for joy. He did not hear the people near him say "That poor fellow is off his head" as they watched him in bewilderment.

The Dodger had to pull him by the sleeve to bring him back to a sense of realities and good manners. . . . Oh, but Chéri-Bibi was delighted now. True, he had never doubted Cecily; but even so, if ever any one told stories—men and women alike are so disposed to be spiteful—he knew that Cecily was not in love with de Pont-Marie. He had just received the proof; more than that, this scene at the ball demonstrated that she had never allowed Pont-Marie to say a word to her that was in the least degree "unseemly."

His enthusiasm was complete when he saw the young
Marchioness du Touchais lean over and whisper to the
Dowager Marchioness, and induce her to leave the ballroom. They rose, and Chéri-Bibi, repressing a desire to
clap his hands, said to himself:

"You are quite right, my dearest. I certainly share
your opinion. Fly, my dove, back to your nest. This
ballroom in which one meets people like the Baroness
Proskof and de Pont-Marie is no place for you."

It so happened that Baroness Proskof and her husband were near the door at the moment when the two
ladies were about to pass out, after taking leave of the
Deputy Prefect and a few friends, on the plea that the
Dowager was tired. The Baroness had requested the
Baron in a loud voice to take her for a while to the
card-room, and a meeting was inevitable.

The "Belle of Dieppe," with unexampled arrogance
passed directly in front of Cecily, stopping her from
continuing her way, and even jostling her slightly. The
entire assembly perceived the incident and there was a
faint murmur of disapproval. The Dodger had the
work of the world to restrain Chéri-Bibi, who wanted
in double quick time to jump from the window and bring
the Baron to account. A lady seated on a settee said
plainly:

"It's a shame. The poor young Marchioness has
done the right thing in leaving. It's not the first time
that that woman has insulted her."

Chéri-Bibi hastened to the vestibule, dragging with
him the Dodger, who was holding on to his coat, and he
saw the two ladies pass out on their way to the iron
gate. He followed them. By an unkind fate, when
they reached the gate, they once more met the Bar-

oness, whose husband was calling for his carriage. When Cecily left the ballroom, apparently, the Baroness, realizing that there was no further opportunity of insulting her, considered that the evening was at an end and determined to turn elsewhere for amusement.

The two ladies were waiting for their motor-car.

As ill-luck would have it, rain had begun to fall, hard and fast, and a certain amount of hustle and hurry occurred in the movement of the traffic. The Marchioness's car appeared at the same time as the landau drawn by two horses belonging to the Baron.

The "Belle of Dieppe" at once raised her voice and ordered the coachman to make haste and draw up beside her by the shortest way. The coachman in carrying out her instructions obstructed the Marchioness's car, which had to come to a stand in order to avoid an accident.

The Baroness took advantage of the incident to pass in front of Cecily. She was placing her foot on the carriage step when she quickly drew back with a cry of terror. An unknown individual had seized the two horses by their heads, and under his irresistible pressure they backed, neighing and struggling in his iron grip, so that the carriage was forced to the rear with startling and unexpected rapidity.

However, the space was cleared, and the Marchioness's chauffeur was able to draw up alongside the pavement. The two ladies quickly mounted the car, while the unknown individual shouted in stentorian tones:

"Respectable women first!"

The car drove off in style while Cecily, leaning out of the window, tried in vain to catch sight of the man to whom she was indebted for this extraordinary turn of

the tables. But he was out of sight. And Baron
Proskof, who was brandishing on high his card, with a
view of challenging the unknown man and did not know
to whom to hand it, was a source of amusement to the
crowd.

"It's time we went back to our hotel," said the
Dodger to Chéri-Bibi after this lucky stroke. "But
allow me, my dear Marquis, to observe in all friendship
that we have got back again to that quarrelsome disposition which has already cost us so much trouble. And
then chauffeurs and coachmen should be left to look out
for themselves. To take horses by their bridles and
to force them to back is ostler's work, Monsieur le
Marquis."

CHAPTER III

CECILY was playing with her son. Greuze himself had never delineated with greater charm a mother at play. They were chasing each other in the shady walks of the Villa at Le Puys. Little Bernard, who was seven years of age, was already a lovable little scamp who did with his mother as he pleased. Cecily's tender weakness was rendered all the more excusable by the wretchedness of her home life.

Her son was everything to her. She felt no happiness apart from him. Although he was already more than she could manage, she regarded him as the sweetest child in the world. It was true that he in no way resembled his father.

On the morning after the Ball in Aid of Poor Seamen, she pressed the little fellow to her heart with unwonted emotion which he at once noticed.

"What's the matter, Mummy? Are you upset? Have you been crying?"

And as his mother turned her head away without replying to him, he gave a sturdy kick and smashed his mechanical horse. Whereupon Cecily was greatly touched and with the adorable infatuation of mothers said to herself: "The moment he knows that I'm worried the poor little fellow can't bear the sight of his toys."

It was she who had taught him to read and write. Bernard was very intelligent, and had proved an apt pupil, and his mother was inordinately proud of him. Her son was destined to have a high career. Heaven, which, on the one hand, had sent her great trials, had, on the other, given her the consolation of this child. She was happy only when she was with him, and she gave way to his every whim.

The child, for that matter, worshiped his mother, whom he considered beautiful, the most beautiful of all mothers, as he said, and he liked to cover with caresses her comely cheeks and splendid bare arms, lifting the sleeve of her gown like a young lover.

"Bernard, come and kiss me."

"Oh, Mummy, how nice you look."

A footman announced M. de Pont-Marie.

"Oh, it's my friend Georges. Ask him to come in at once. . . . Mummy, let's run and meet him," exclaimed the boy delightedly, for M. de Pont-Marie had known how to win his heart by loading him with toys and sweetmeats; and Bernard had a sweet tooth.

But to Bernard's astonishment his mother requested the man to take M. de Pont-Marie to the small reception room, and, holding the boy's hand, she led him to the study, where she handed him over to the governess.

"But I want to see my friend Georges."

"Some other time, my pet. You must do your lessons now." And turning to the governess, she said: "I give him into your charge. Don't leave him." She kissed him warmly, but the child was in the sulks as he let her go.

Cecily was greatly perturbed. She went to her boudoir in order to calm her agitation. M. de Pont-

Marie's audacity knew no limits. To return that morning after what had happened the night before! . . . She gave a sigh. What a set of base creatures, in truth, men were. She had known but one, one only, whom she could place above the common herd. But he had a heart of gold. He had lived but for her, and his image, encircled, alas, in a frame of sorrow, never left her. At the remembrance of him Cecily could not keep back the tears. But she quickly dried her eyes, for she called to mind that M. de Pont-Marie was waiting for her.

She rose, assumed an appearance of anger, and entered the small reception room, greatly disturbed in reality, and paler than usual.

Facing her stood the "friend of the family," who bowed with formal politeness, waiting for a signal from her to be seated like a stranger paying a visit.

Cecily pointed to a chair, sat down herself a little way off, and began:

"I am glad you called this morning, M. de Pont-Marie. You will know all the sooner what I have to say. You must not come here any more, my poor friend."

"Madame!" protested the "poor friend," at once rising from his seat:

"Yes, Monsieur de Pont-Marie, you are a gentleman. How could you have behaved as you did last night?"

"I assure you that any gentleman in my place would have done the same thing. You are very attractive. No gentleman, certainly, could have resisted the pleasure of telling you so. I told you so. I can't see that I've committed any great crime."

"But, Monsieur de Pont-Marie, what is the use of it

all? You say you love me. I don't love you and I
never shall, and my duty is to refuse to listen to you
any longer. The first time you spoke of such things, I
overlooked it. In the face of my threat to close my
door to you, you showed such sincere contrition that I
had compassion on you, and also to some extent, I must
confess to be honest, on myself. . . . I was alone,
neglected; I had no friends; my husband had deserted
me. I was sick at heart. For some months you seemed
to have changed your life completely; you surrounded
me with kindly attentions, apparently disinterested,
you pitied me greatly, and you so fully understood my
sorrow that I felt a real sympathy for you. I do not
deny it—far from it; and then suddenly I find myself
in the presence of a man, like other men, who is bent on
taking advantage of a poor woman's weakness and
loneliness. . . .

"I asure you that I have had a great deal of anxiety,
and it was pardonable in me to overlook your first
mistake. You have known how to ingratiate yourself
with my son Bernard, who is always greatly delighted
to see you, and to play, as he calls it, with his good
friend Georges. It was understood that no mention
should be made of the past, and you would honestly
make an effort not to refer to it. So gradually I gave
way to the pleasure of our meetings. I enjoyed once
more our quiet conversations, and our constant and
perfectly friendly intercourse. I see, to-day, that in so
doing it is I who am to blame. Well, Monsieur de Pont-
Marie, you must forgive me, as I forgive you the fervid
and somewhat ridiculous words that you spoke last
night; but you must understand that the experiment
has lasted long enough, that it is final and we must not

meet again. We must shake hands for the last time
and say good-by."

"But Cecily, I love you."

"Good-by."

"That's out of the question. You don't understand.
Don't you see that I love you to distraction? Yes, I
have been prudent. For two years I have not spoken a
single word of love. I have had the incredible strength
of mind to conceal from you the feeling which stirred
my heart . . . to conceal from you that there was no
more passionate lover than myself; that the fragrance
of your dear presence delighted and made me dizzy;
that even the friendly pressure of your hand gave me
unspeakable joy; a look from your eyes enraptured me.
But if I have shown such immense courage, it is simply
because I knew that you were not like other women. I
knew how to appreciate you, to give you your due
position, to see you as you really are—the most virtu-
ous and most desirable of women, worthy of every
sacrifice. I thought that, in the end, you would recognize that one cannot live in close friendship with a
woman like yourself with impunity, and realize that I
adored you; and finally that you would have compassion on my long self-denial, my respectful silence, my
unspoken love. I thought to myself that so much
restrained feeling would have its reward, and you would
be mine one day."

Cecily rose and went towards the door, but de Pont-
Marie resolutely barred her way.

"No, you will not leave me until I have said all that I
have to say, until I have shown you my innermost soul.
Cecily. . . . Why do you not allow yourself to love?
Why are we not lovers? It is your right—it is our

right. You can be mine since you no longer belong to any one. . . . Your husband! . . . At one time you believed him dead and you were glad. Oh, don't deny it. . . . I was here when news came of the loss of the 'Belle of Dieppe.' I know quite well that you almost fainted. It was I who caught you in my arms. Divine moment! . . . And don't tell me that you did not faint with joy, because you loathed the monster, who took from you all your life, all your illusions, who trampled under foot your most sacred feelings, who had but made you suffer and insulted you with the scandal of his mistresses. Yes, you believed that you were free . . . free. . . . Well, are you not in reality free, I ask you? It is more than a year since he escaped from that strange adventure on the 'Bayard,' and he has not once sent you any news of himself. He has written to you? Has he taken any notice of his son? Has he written to his solicitor? Yes, he has seen his solicitor; and he has concerned himself with his fortune, his property, his money. And he continues to travel about the world seeking distraction. . . . But if his wife does not exist for him, why should he exist for her? You are not bound to that man any longer. You owe him nothing, not even a thought. You are free, I say. You are free and I love you, Cecily . . . Cecily."

"Let me pass, Monsieur, or I shall call my servant. Please. . . . Please, Monsieur de Pont-Marie. Do you want to create a scandal? . . . Come, let me pass. But this is awful. . . . You must be mad! . . ."

The other had thrown himself on his knees, and was holding her round the knees in an iron grip. Terror-stricken and not daring to cry out, she tried in vain to shake herself free. With convulsive fingers she pushed back his head, but he imprisoned her hands, covering them with kisses.

She defended herself with desperate strength, but de Pont-Marie took her roughly by the waist and continued to overwhelm her by his wild language.

"I love you. . . . I love you, Cecily. Why do you repulse me? We might be so happy . . . Cecily."

He clasped her to him, crushing her against his breast, and she moaned as she threw back her head.

But suddenly he let her go, and leapt away, uttering a cry of pain.

Cecily had driven the pin of a brooch into his cheek. He was bleeding. He might have been seriously wounded. He snarled, wild with rage:

"You dislike me as much as that! Well, my beauty, you're not going to have it all your own way. I tell you that I want you and I mean to have you."

At that moment, certainly, M. de Pont-Marie had nothing of the polished gentleman about him. He was like a venomous and raging brute longing only to take vengeance on his prey. Cecily trembled before him like a fledgling pursued by a hawk. His attitude was so menacing that she hesitated no longer. The governess and her son were but a few steps away. With one hand she distractedly opened the window. She was about to call for help when with a terrible gesture he compelled her to pause.

She kept silent, for he went back, took a seat and said to her in a muffled voice:

"Sit down. You needn't be afraid. . . . I won't place my hand upon you again. But, shut the window. I have something to say to you. . . ."

And as she stood there without moving he rose and

closed the window. She might have slipped out by the door, and she did in fact turn towards it, but with a word he riveted her to the ground:

"It's about Bernard."

"What about Bernard?" she asked, at once on the defensive holding her breath.

"Yes; and you quite understand that what I have to say must be between ourselves. . . . Do please compose yourself. . . . Look at me. My outburst is over. I am now calm. We shall need all our self-possession. Cecily, you were wrong to behave towards me as you have done. I've no reason now to treat you with any consideration. I have tried to win you by constant friendship and devotion . . ."

"By hypocrisy you mean," she broke in.

"If you like to call it so. We have reached the point when we can waive all compliments. And since hypocrisy has not succeeded, I will speak plainly. Cecily, you are not an honest woman."

She rose as she spoke:

"You scoundrel!"

But de Pont-Marie was in no way disconcerted.

"I repeat, you are not an honest woman. You were unfaithful to the Marquis."

"Coward. . . . Coward. . . . You know very well that what you say is false. You take advantage of my being alone to insult me. . . . Go. . . . Go. . . ."

"I defy you to turn me out."

"At once, you scoundrel."

She put out her hand to the bell-pull.

"That's right, ring away, and every one shall know that your son is not the Marquis's son."

She dropped into a seat, wild-eyed, more dead than alive.

"Ah, you can't deny it," went on de Pont-Marie with a harsh chuckle.

"What do you expect me to say to such an infamous suggestion?" she stammered.

"Strong language. You are always ready to use strong language. You will do better to be sensible, I assure you, and listen to me like a good girl. Pull yourself together, Cecily. . . . Some one might come in."

He rose, walked to the glass, smoothed his rumpled hair with the back of his hand, put his collar straight, tightened the knot of his tie, and wiped, with his handkerchief, the spot of blood which lay upon his cheek.

"A little more and I should have been marked for life. That would have been a pity. I value my looks."

He turned round and saw her before him in a state of such fear and trembling that he felt, perhaps, a touch of pity for her. He sat down near her and in a voice that was once more calm and polished he went on:

"Cecily, you loved your cousin, Marcel Garavan, a Captain in the merchant service who died in New Orleans some four years ago. Don't let's have any useless denials. As for me, I'm speaking like a man who does not intend to make any more bones about it. This young man had no money, and nothing in the world would have induced your father to allow you to marry him. I need not dwell on the melancholy events which made you the Marchioness du Touchais. Eight years ago while the Marquis was finishing a tour of the Norwegian coast with his friends, of whom I was one, Marcel Garavan came to Dieppe to pay a visit to his cousin. He admired you. You loved him. The result can be imagined."

Cecily seemed to be turned to stone. Her eyes were staring at the miserable wretch before her without giving the least sign of life. . . . She was waiting. . . . She was waiting for the appalling word which was to come, which she could feel was coming. De Pont-Marie paused a moment obviously reveling in the torture that he was inflicting on her.

"Marcel Garavan's stay in Dieppe," he went on, "was extended and then ceased abruptly at the news of the Marquis's return. In due course the Marchioness du Touchais had a child, young Bernard. But she took good care to go to England for her confinement. It was thus that she was able to fake the date of the birth of the infant of whom the Marquis believed himself to be the father. His delight knew no bounds. Not that he loved Cecily; not that he loved his son. The Marquis du Touchais never loved anything but himself and his race. Now his race was saved. He had feared lest his family might become extinct. The Marchioness gave him a son. All was for the best. He learnt the news when he was in the Azores, where he had landed from the 'Belle of Dieppe' after a fresh cruise in the Antilles. As you may well believe, there were rejoicings on board. I know it. I was present. . . . Is not all this the truth, Madame? . . . You don't answer me. . . . Am I to understand that we are agreed?"

The lips of the statue opened a little.

"Agreed upon what, Monsieur?"

"Upon what I have just told you, and on the rest which you can guess. . . . The rest is the ignorance in which it is necessary to keep the poor Marquis, because

you know him. He is a man without much principle,
but he has a prejudice, if you like—a family prejudice;
and he sticks to it. Yes, he sticks to being the father of
his son, and you know that he would rather choke the
life out of you with his own hands than allow some little
thief to enter his house and steal his ancestral name.
Young Bernard du Touchais hasn't a drop of du
Touchais blood in his veins. . . . Don't forget that.
. . . I was saying that he would choke the life out of
you. That is an extreme measure to which the Marquis
would certainly not have recourse because in the circumstances it would serve no purpose. A case in the
courts, a denial of paternity and divorce, would quickly
get rid of the mother and son, and enable him, now that
he is rich, to marry again and have children, who this
time would be his lawful children. What conclusion
must we draw? Here is a secret known only to you and
me. I will give you a piece of advice. Let us remain
friends, and closer friends than ever in order to guard
that secret. . . ."

He had done speaking. He bowed and went towards
the door. But at a word from Cecily he turned to her.

"Monsieur, I see that you will shrink from nothing,"
she had the strength to say. "But your wickedness
won't avail you anything. And no one will believe this
abominable story that you have invented."

"Not even the Marquis?" asked de Pont-Marie, going
up to her.

"Neither the Marquis nor any one else. . . . Unless
you have manufactured proofs, and in that case it will
be easy to expose your imposture."

"I understand you, Cecily, and I've always said that
you were very quick-witted. You want to know if I

have the proofs. Yes, I have the proofs. I have Marcel Garavan's letters. I hope that I've told you what
you wanted to know."

"Letters!" cried the hapless Cecily, clutching him
with a wild gesture that startled him.

He threw her off.

"Yes, the letters which you think are still in your
secret drawer. Do you mean, you haven't had the
curiosity to read them during the last three days? . . .
How women forget!"

"Scoundrel!"

"Oh, nothing is to be gained by abuse. I don't see
why I should keep the principal item of my program
from you. I have taken the villa at Pourville, a quarter of a mile from here, that struck our fancy when we
went for our last walk with Bernard. I am having
certain alterations made. The place is nice and quiet.
Everything will be ready in a week from now. To-
morrow week at three o'clock in the afternoon I shall
expect to see you there."

"Never."

"You'll think it over, I'm sure."

"Never. . . . I loathe you. . . . I would rather die."

"That wouldn't save your son. You're thinking only
of yourself. You must give a little consideration to the
future Marquis du Touchais."

"But have you no pity on me?"

"I love you. That's all I need say."

"I'll kill myself and my child."

"No, you won't. And, look here, I have had enough
of this. You must promise me now that you will come.
I am tired of all this shuffling. I want you. I want to
make sure of you. Say that you'll come, or I shall at

once carry out my threat and send the letters to the Marquis."

"Scoundrel. . . . Scoundrel. . . ."

The poor woman wrung her hands and gave way to despair. She fell on her knees in her turn and implored her persecutor to have pity, if not on her, at least on her son. Her sobs and entreaties would have softened the heart of a tiger. But de Pont-Marie did not even listen to her. She was very comely in her terrible expression of grief. He told her so.

"You are more beautiful now than you were at the ball. I want your answer. Some one is coming. Get up unless you wish to be caught by your servants."

He helped her to her feet. Some one was in fact coming; and the sound of footsteps could be heard approaching the reception room. She retired to the embrasure of a window, not wishing her agitation to be seen. M. de Pont-Marie whispered:

"Well, have you made up your mind to come?"

At that moment a footman entered.

"Madame," he said, "the Marquis wishes to know if you will receive him."

"What Marquis?"

"The Marquis du Touchais, Madame."

If a thunderclap had fallen in the room the effect could not have been greater. There was a formidable silence, and then M. de Pont-Marie cheerfully exclaimed:

"The Marquis do you say? What a pleasant surprise. Ask him to come in. Is he not in his own house? I shall be delighted to see him again."

"Yes, ask him in," said the Marchioness in an almost inaudible voice.

The footman went out.

"Well, are we agreed?" asked M. de Pont-Marie eagerly. "You will come?"

"I will come. . . ."

And she flung at M. de Pont-Marie distractedly:

"Tell my husband that I've gone to fetch my son and will be back presently."

She went away wishing to be alone for a few moments to collect her thoughts and compose her distraught features.

Georges de Pont-Marie was beaming. He had triumphed. In truth it was very good of the Marquis to arrive at that decisive moment. Cecily could not possibly fight against him now. As he reached this point in his self-congratulation Chéri-Bibi came in.

He was carefully dressed. The Marquis du Touchais had never looked smarter, more dandified, more pommaded, more spick and span. Nevertheless he was a little pale. Pince-nez with slightly smoked glasses and gold rims rested on his Bourbon nose, the family nose.

He expected to be confronted by Cecily. He had a feeling of satisfaction that she was not yet there. Her absence would give him time to compose himself, but when his eyes fell upon Pont-Marie, who smilingly came towards him with outstretched hand, he could not repress a slight grimace.

"Well," cried the triumphant de Pont-Marie, "this is a surprise, and a pleasant one. Is this how you treat your friends? Not to let any of us know that you're coming. . . . Well, Maxime, what's the matter with you? Aren't you going to shake hands?"

"Yes, yes," answered Chéri-Bibi quickly. "What nonsense."

And he shook hands without effusion.

"But aren't you going to talk? Tell us about yourself," exclaimed de Pont-Marie. "I find you entirely changed."

"Where is the Marchioness?" asked Chéri-Bibi.

"What did you say?"

"I asked you where the Marchioness is."

"Oh, yes. . . . I was right, you have changed. Your voice, too, is different, you know."

"Yes, yes, I know. I've had bronchitis badly . . . throat troubles which are very dangerous for the health."

"I can quite believe you. Apart from that you look well. Still very smart. . . . Still a lady's man. You still have a good constitution. Upon my word you look stouter. You must be careful, you know. A little waist is all very well, but one mustn't overdo it. At our time of life we must keep an eye on it. I personally diet myself."

"Tell me, Monsieur de Pont-Marie . . ."

"What! Monsieur de Pont-Marie. You are very ceremonious all at once. Why not call me 'Monsieur le Viscount' like my servants. You're very funny."

"I say, Georges, will you do me a favor?"

"How deep your voice is. . . . I shall find it no easy matter to get used to that voice. And how solemn you look. You walk like a ghost at a feast. . . . A favor? Whatever you like. What is it you want?"

"I want you to clear out."

"You want me to go?"

"Yes, you follow me, it's a long time since I saw Cecily . . ."

"Well, I'm hanged. . . . Not to mention that during

the three months that you've been in France you might
have remembered your friends in Dieppe. Of course,
you were always like that. Between ourselves you were
always a little mad. . . . So you want to talk to Cecily.
. . . That's all right. I'll go. You can invite me to
lunch another day. . . . Until we meet again, my dear
Maxime."

"Good-by, Monsieur."

"What's that?"

"I'm sorry. . . . Until we meet again, Georges."

"That's something like."

M. de Pont-Marie again shook him by the hand and
left him, muttering to himself: "The Marquis is somewhat icy. Of course, people have been gossiping and
telling him the story that I've been making love to
Cecily. And then I don't know what it is, but his mind
seems to me rather affected. Mixing with convicts
hasn't been a success!"

As soon as he was alone Chéri-Bibi walked gravely to
a full-length portrait of Cecily, painted when she was a
young girl.

She was dressed in a white muslin frock and wore a
rose in her hair. His mind harked back to the Cecily
of the evening before at the ball in the Casino, and
drawing a mental comparison he said: "I like her quite
as well like that."

A door grated on its hinges. He gave a start and
turned pale. It was not she but a man-servant who
laid some newspapers on the table. Chéri-Bibi had no
courage. Not that he imagined for a moment that the
change in him would incur the smallest danger of
detection; his experience had assured him of that long
ago. If any one had loved him, a vague suspicion as to

the Marquis's identity might have been awakened in that person's mind. But the Marquis had never been loved by any one. Chéri-Bibi had nothing to fear from the intuition of the heart. No. He merely dreaded to find himself in his wife's presence.

At length she appeared.

He saw her steal towards him slowly like a shadow, her little feet dragging, in a light blue kimono flowered in gold. He likened her to a princess in a fairy tale, and stood still, without speaking, his lips closed, his throat dry. She, too, looked at him without saying a word, and they stood like two statues. It seemed as if the silence might last. He tried to speak. He had prepared a few phrases. But his mind was a perfect blank. He was unable to say "How do you do." A delicate fragrance was wafted to him from her and intoxicated him. His head "turned giddy." He thought with dread that he was going to faint. His heart ceased beating. He was afraid lest he should die; and he would have liked to rush from the room.

With the gesture of an automaton she motioned him to a seat, into which he sank slowly. Then she spoke. It was none too soon, for he felt that he was going mad. She said in an even voice:

"I went to fetch your son. I thought he was in the house, but he is on the beach with the governess and will be back in a moment."

"I shall be glad to see him," he returned. "I hope you are quite well."

She hesitated slightly at the sound of his voice, but it was long since she had heard him speak, and its new tone was not more unpleasant to her ears—far from it—than its old.

"Yes, I'm quite well. So is your son. I am glad to see that your sufferings in that unfortunate adventure have not, apparently, left any ill effects."

"They were terrible, Cecily."

He had called her Cecily . . . her! He would never have believed that the name would slip out so easily as that. He often said to himself: I shall never dare to say Cecily . . . like that . . . quite simply. It seems to me that I shan't be able to help myself. I shall call her 'Mademoiselle' as in the old days when I delivered the meat. He had called her Cecily; like a man speaking to his wife, in fact. Thenceforward, there would be no difficulty. The blood began to flow freely in his frozen veins, and he was gaining confidence in himself when his "wife," who had been silent for several moments, said:

"Cecily! It sounds strange to hear you call me Cecily in the new voice that you have brought back with you. You never used to call me Cecily when we were alone."

"Now that's a piece of bad luck," thought Chéri-Bibi. "What did these people call each other among themselves in society? Monsieur? Madame? How absurd? Yes, but they had quarreled. Come, Chéri-Bibi, now is the time to brazen it out."

With a swift movement he went nearer his wife. His eyes encountered, resting on the arms of her chair, her white trembling hand. He gazed through his smoked glasses and saw the sunken eyes, the lines of the arched eyebrows, the dark circles of sorrow and fear, and he observed that the color of her complexion was recent, made up, and false, consisting of paint and powder, and laying bare, in the deadly pallor of her lips, the artificial life which she led. His eyes were bedewed with pity. "Poor woman," he thought, and he tried to take her hand which she withdrew.

He was abashed, but his immense love lent him strength.

"It's true this is the first time I've called you by your Christian name, Cecily," he said, "and I hope you'll allow me to continue to do so. If it doesn't offend you overmuch it will give me pleasure. Many things have happened since we saw each other, dear." She did not flinch at the word "dear." "Yes, many things. . . . I said just now that I've been through terrible experiences."

"I know that from the newspapers, Monsieur, and from your solicitor."

"Oh, she called me 'Monsieur,'" thought Chéri-Bibi. "It's just as I imagined; they say 'Monsieur' and 'Madame' in private. What a husband and wife!"

"Yes, the newspapers have described them, and so has my solicitor," he went on. "By the way, I am anxious to thank you for so promptly seconding his efforts to secure my liberation. Obviously I ought and might have written to you. I did not do so for the same reason that has kept me away from here for more than a year. I should like to make myself clear. I certainly behaved badly to you. For a long time I have not deserved that you should take any interest in me. . . ."

It was a luckless phrase and Chéri-Bibi at once regretted it, for he saw a change pass over the expression of her face. The mask of icy politeness with which she had listened to him was transformed in a flash, and it was with almost an insulting dignity that she flung at him "Really, Monsieur."

"All the same," Chéri-Bibi thought, "how badly the beggar must have treated her to make her speak like that." And he bowed his head under the crushing pressure of her resentment.

Cecily, moreover, stared at him and listened without understanding, because from her experience of the Marquis, she had no cause even to suspect the greatness, the beauty, the generosity, of the sentiments which a beneficent love had implanted in the heart of this man who had returned to her after so many eccentricities. She wondered, of course, "what he was driving at," and what new ordeal lay in wait for her behind this fantastic attitude of repentance in which, of course, she could not believe.

The man whose name she bore, moreover, had accustomed her to stand in fear of him. She had never ceased to tremble under the yoke. After the frightful tyranny by which he had humbled her, he was quite welcome to say: "I certainly behaved badly to you." Clearly the wretch was deficient in moral sense. He was about, perhaps, to ask her "to forget." That would be the finishing stroke!

As it happened Chéri-Bibi did not fail to make the suggestion with a somewhat crude diplomacy which might have been pardonable in any but Cecily's case.

Emphasizing the mawkish and tearful note which, in his belief, was entirely necessitated by the actual position, and the memories of the Marquis's perfidy and wickedness, of which the house was full, he pleaded with incredible artlessness "extenuating circumstances," or

at least certain reasons which led him to hope for forgiveness in the more or less near future.

He enlarged with piteous weakness on the final disasters which had "opened his eyes." He had undergone a
long captivity among criminals. He had looked death
in the face. He was recovering from typhoid fever.
And, in short, he let himself go to such an extent on his
misfortunes that he surmised that Cecily, whose tender-
heartedness he knew, would be moved by them.

In order to make sure he ventured to lift his eyes
from the carpet whose pattern he had been meekly
studying during his melancholy speech; and by degrees
his gaze grew bold enough to meet the beloved eyes
which, a little while before, had startled him by their
flash of pride. She was weeping.

Yes, Cecily, his Cecily, wept as she listened to him.
Therefore he had found the path that led to her heart!

It was a pathetic sight when, in a transport of
delight over his victory, and no longer knowing what he
was doing, the hapless Chéri-Bibi rose and stammered:

"Cecily . . . you are crying. . . ." He could not
see her face now for she had turned away. "Why do
you turn your head? Don't be ashamed of tears which
are a proof of your goodness of heart. . . ." As he
spoke he furtively went nearer her. "Look at me
Cecily. I too am weeping. . . ." It was true that he
wept. "Cecily, let me kiss you."

He was stooping over the adored head, and carried
away by an emotional impulse his trembling lips were
touching lightly her hair, when to his cost, Cecily who
in no way suspected the enemy's approach, pushed
him away with a fierceness which was extraordinary in
so frail a being; but she saw "what was happening"

and her strength was increased tenfold. She rose from
her seat crimson, breathing heavily, superb in her
indignation at this attempt to kiss her, as though the
suggestion were a cruel outrage, and looking more
beautiful than ever in his eyes cried:

"You. . . . You want to kiss me!"

He gazed at her petrified, staggered, dismayed. Fortunately for their future relations she was unable, in
her wrath, to measure the extent of his dejection; or
else she who remembered the Marquis in his domineering
moods, would have thought that he was smitten with
idiocy, and that there was no point in concerning herself further with so pitiful a wreck.

Cecily in a temper! She angrily dried her beautiful
eyes still swollen with the tears which had inspired
Chéri-Bibi so inopportunely. And she cried out between her dry sobs which stifled her:

"Let you kiss me . . . kiss me. What can you be
thinking about? Have you gone out of your mind
all of a sudden? Have you lost your memory? How
could you suppose that I should allow myself to be
treated like a girl whom you pay to gratify your
whims. Oh yes, you saw me cry. And your outrageous
egotism led you think that I was crying on your account! . . . I was crying for myself . . . for all the
sufferings that I have endured through you . . . for
all the shame that you have heaped upon me. When
I think that you did not hesitate to turn your mother
and me out of your house . . . out of the Château du
Touchais of which you were so proud . . . to hand it
over to that woman who is your mistress, and who only
last night at the ball, dared to insult me before five
hundred people with her smiles and remarks and gross

insolence . . . when I think of it all. . . . And when
I see you try to move me to pity for some mysterious
reason or purpose of which I know nothing, I ask myself if I am dreaming. And you wanted to kiss me . . .
you! Oh Monsieur. . . . Monsieur. You must know
quite well that it is impossible. You must know that
one thing will always stand between us what ever you
do; one thing that I can never forget . . . never!
Remember the night of your departure for Norway?"

"What did I do on that night?" Chéri-Bibi wondered utterly cast down.

"Of course you are here in your own house. You
are the master. You can come or go. You can do as
you please. That's your affair, and it's not for me
to interfere. But after all you are a gentleman, or at
least you assume the manners of one."

Her last phrase made the wretched Chéri-Bibi redden
with embarrassment.

"Well. . . . Conduct yourself, I beg, in such a way
that an explanation as unnecessary as the one which we
have just had need not be repeated. That's all I ask
of you."

She was in a state of intense excitement. Once more
she repeated, "Let you kiss me . . . him!" but this time
she found relief in the sobs that choked her and sank
into a chair almost fainting.

Suddenly she rose for there was a knock at the door.
She quickly dried her eyes.

"Come in," she said.

The footman entered and stood in the doorway somewhat ill at ease as if he had a message which he did not
like to deliver.

"What is it, Jean?"

"It's the Baroness Proskof's footman, Madam."

The Marchioness turned scarlet when she heard the name, and stared with a look of violent hostility at her husband whose unabashed composure she observed. Truth to tell, the name had no power to disturb him unduly, and the foolish fellow seemed not to realize that its mention in that house was a fresh insult to his wife.

"Come, Jean, tell us. . . . What does she want?" Cecily asked in a breathless voice.

"The Baroness Proskof has heard of the Marquis's return, and she is expecting to see him about the lease."

"All right, all right. Let him tell the Baroness that I'll be with her immediately," said Chéri-Bibi with an eagerness that brought down upon him another "outburst" from the Marchioness.

"Go then, Monsieur. . . . They can't do without you there. . . ."

And she swept out of the room, holding her head high, leaving him in a state of confusion. Nevertheless as she was disappearing he made a gesture of dissent and stopped her.

"Madame, I should like to tell you that I shall be back to lunch," he said.

"That is as you please, Monsieur. I repeat: You are in your own house."

When she was gone he left the room with a short sharp movement of his hand on his hat that he put on defiantly, grumbling:

"But she's not going to have it all her own way like that. She's really too bad. And I won't be made a fool of by her."

CHAPTER IV

CHÉRI-BIBI'S DUEL

WHEN Chéri-Bibi returned to Cecily he seemed self-possessed and more satisfied with himself, and he was ravenously hungry.

From the distance he caught sight, on the front steps, of the figure and the white cornette of a nun. He recognized Sister St. Mary of the Angels. He went up one avenue while she came down another. The lawn lay between them. He bowed to her as they passed and she returned his greeting and then continued her way. Chéri-Bibi had made up his mind to avoid, as far as possible, his sister who was back in the hospital at Dieppe, and in particular not to speak to her. He was determined that she should not hear his voice. It was his wisest course. Moreover, he had not come into contact with her on board ship in the latter part of the time. He had not spoken a word to her since his "death." . . . Poor Jacqueline.

"All the same," he thought to himself, "suppose that we had been told when we were children that I should enter this house as the Marquis and she would come out of it as a sister of mercy. . . . *Fatalitas*."

His reflections were cut short by the sight of a charming group standing on the steps. It consisted of Cecily and her son.

Bernard ran forward to meet his father. From the

79

affectionate manner in which he threw his arms round his neck, Chéri-Bibi perceived that the boy did not dislike him, and that Cecily had done nothing to turn to her own advantage that part of the boy's filial love which belonged by right to his father. "Excellent woman," he said to himself. "She possesses all the virtues. Happy the man who is loved by her." He petted the boy, and since he in no way resembled his defunct father, Chéri-Bibi told himself that he was immensely fond of him.

"Have you brought me back many toys from the savages?"

"Yes, my son, a truck load of them; but I must tell you at once that those people get their supplies from the best shops in the metropolis."

Chéri-Bibi who was still disposed to be slightly pompous liked to use this word to describe Paris. He saw that Cecily who was in front of them heard it and smiled; and he was in a tumult of happiness.

"Well, she may reproach me to her heart's content. I will bow the head and say: So be it. . . . The dear woman! That light summer dress suits her to perfection. And yet in itself it is scarcely anything: a little muslin thrown over the dearest shoulders in the world. She's an angel from Heaven. I could kiss the ground she treads on."

She was walking ahead holding the boy's hand, and Chéri-Bibi followed close enough to be fully conscious of her presence. At table he sat between his wife and son. The thought entered his mind that it needed very little, in sooth, to render him the happiest of men. Lunch was served on the veranda which overlooked the sea. A few white sails could be discerned on the horizon.

There was an azure sky and a light breeze swept the flowers in the garden. The service was perfect, the napery, silver, crystal, porcelain and flowers on the table a resplendent sight, and Chéri-Bibi's heart was overflowing with love.

"So you received a visit from Sister St. Mary of the Angels," he said.

"Yes, she came with rather bad news. The Marchioness, your mother, is indisposed. Last night both of us went to the Ball in Aid of Poor Seamen, and she caught a chill while waiting in the rain at the Casino gate for our car. I'll go and see her with Bernard after lunch."

"Cecily you have always been charming in your relations with my mother, and I thank you for it, while I have behaved very badly towards the poor dear. Her door is closed to me and it serves me right. But since you're going to see her, you may give her a piece of news which cannot fail to please her, and it may help her to get well. In a week from now she will be able to return and settle down for good in the Château du Touchais."

"If what you tell me is true," returned Cecily who did not conceal her surprise, "the Marchioness will certainly weep for joy. She has often admitted to me that her greatest grief was to find herself excluded so brusquely from the place with which all the memories of her life are associated and in which she hoped to die." And she asked without looking at Chéri-Bibi. "But are they leaving the Château?"

"Yes, they are leaving it."

"Are they tired of it?"

"No, they're not tired of it. They're leaving it because I'm turning them out."

"He has had enough of the 'Belle of Dieppe.' He
has a fresh mistress somewhere," Cecily thought.

"Really!" she said, "Well I won't hide from you
that as far as I am concerned I'm not sorry. And if
the 'Belle of Dieppe's' reign is over, it is just as well
. . . Oh I speak simply because her presence so near
us is rather embarrassing."

"Of course, of course. I know a man who is much
to blame in the matter and who will always feel remorse
for it."

Cecily could scarcely believe her ears. She looked
at Chéri-Bibi who lowered his eyes and blushed like
a child. With his face in his plate he confessed his
fault, carefully choosing his language, because Bernard was present.

"When I think of all you have had to put up with,
Cecily, I feel that I don't deserve to be sitting at this
table."

Nevertheless she saw that he was eating with great
heartiness as he made his extraordinary confession, and
she could not help thinking: "In any case remorse has
not taken away his appetite."

"That woman has made me suffer," she said, "less on
my own account than on your mother's and the du
Touchais's name. But since she is to go, don't let us
speak of it: a good riddance! She didn't lay down her
arms even at the very end. Last night, at the ball,
she found an opportunity of insulting your mother and
me, or at least of defying us and showing an imper-
tinence for which in the end she paid the penalty. Since
you have just come from her she probably told you

about the incident which occurred at the Casino gate
in the presence of some two hundred people."

"No, Cecily, no. She didn't breathe a word about it."

"Obviously she can't be very proud of it. You must
know, then, that at the moment of leaving when she saw
us she ordered her carriage to take the place which belonged to our car, and she did it so rudely that the
people round us expressed their disapproval. Fortunately a stranger who observed what was happening
made a rush at the horses' heads, and with immense daring and strength backed them out of the way shouting:
'Respectable women first!' and everybody applauded.
The Marchioness was delighted, and I myself would
have given something to know who the man was who
treated her as she deserved. I should have liked to
thank him, but he had already disappeared."

"If I knew who forced that wicked woman's horses
back," said young Bernard, "I'd give him a kiss."

"Kiss me then," said Chéri-Bibi.

"Do you mean to say it was you?"

"Yes, my son, it was I."

The boy flung his arms round his father's neck and
kissed him delightedly while Cecily looked on in confusion and bewilderment.

"Now, mummy, you give him a kiss too."

Chéri-Bibi, embarrassed and quivering, put the boy
back in his seat.

"Come, Bernard, be good," said Cecily self-conscious.
"Let your father have his lunch in peace."

"But you can very well give him a kiss since it's
father."

"I've already told you that little boys should be seen
and not heard."

She no longer ventured to look at Chéri-Bibi; and to all appearance was concentrating her attention on a fresh dish that was brought in for the boy.

"Then it was you?" she said. "You were in Dieppe? . . ."

"I had just arrived. It was too late to come to the Villa without causing you inconvenience. Besides, I had not given you any notice, and I decided to stay the night at the hotel. Before I turned in, I went for a stroll round the Casino. It happened by chance that I saw and took a hand in the affair. That's all there is to it. There's nothing to thank me for."

"You might have been run over."

She said no more, suddenly becoming pensive, leaving father and son to make game and chatter and laugh between themselves.

Lunch was nearly over when a footman came in to inform the Marquis that his secretary and Maitre Régime were in the drawing room.

"Very well. Ask them to wait. I'll be with them in a moment."

"Don't let me stand in the way if you have to talk business," said Cecily. "You can join them and I'll have coffee served in the drawing room."

"That's right. You are very good. You think of everything. Excuse me, therefore. I have, in fact, a little business to do."

"It's very curious," said Cecily in an undertone after he was gone. "I find him different past all knowledge."

"You see how nice my father is and how brave. He told me that all my presents will soon be here in his car. He has a ripping car, and you know, mummy,

I want him to teach me to drive. We shall have some fun together."

At that moment the enigmatic figure of M. de Pont-Marie appeared in the wide arch of the open veranda.

"I hope that I'm not disturbing you."

He came in without ceremony as was his custom. He was never announced. When Cecily caught sight of him she staggered back in fear. Nevertheless she succeeded in controlling herself. And in the presence of the man servant who was waiting at table she apologized for her sudden start, and asked M. de Pont-Marie to join her on the veranda. Since her terrible interview with him she had had time to think things over, and she concluded that the blackmail to which she was being subjected had no other object than to force money out of her. She knew that de Pont-Marie was financially embarrassed and reduced to the lowest expedients. She had rather expected him during the last few days to have recourse frankly to her for assistance, and she would not have hesitated to open her purse to him in a friendly way. She now realized that the miserable wretch, in order to get out of his difficulties, had prepared a regular trap for her which he had dissembled under a show of love, and preceded by the theft of her most private correspondence. She would have to pay dearly; the sacrifice would doubtless be very great; but she was resolved to stop at nothing to get back the letters, to save the honor of her son, and to prevent the terrible outrage with which this mean rascal had threatened her.

Granted that it was merely a question of money, there was no need to give way to despair. She must retain her self-possession in order to make the best terms she could with the sorry creature. In her husband's absence she had taken over the management of her fortune, and, moreover, since her brother's death considerable sums had come into her possession.

De Pont-Marie expected to find Cecily with the Marquis. He bit his lip when he perceived that she was alone, and he waited with curiosity to see how she would treat him for he would be able to draw a more or less happy inference from her demeanor. In any case he assumed that she would not have the audacity to show him the door in view of the weapon that he held against her.

He at once gathered that she was conciliatory, coldly polite no doubt, but quite affable. She asked him to be seated while he waited for the Marquis, for de Pont-Marie had stated that it was the Marquis whom he wished to see.

"He is with his secretary and solicitor and won't be long."

"Did he tell you about that stupid quarrel?" asked de Pont-Marie.

"Not a word. . . . What stupid quarrel?"

"As he hasn't thought fit to tell you about it, you will forgive me if I prefer to say nothing. In these affairs," he went on with deliberate clumsiness, "the great thing is to say little and act quickly."

"You have either told me too much or too little."

And turning round to the boy she sent him away.

"Bernard, dear, go to your governess. I will come to you presently."

When they were alone she went on:

"Now, Monsieur, there is no reason why we should make mysteries of these things. Since you are here so soon after what passed between us, something of consequence must have happened. What is it?"

"As a matter of fact you are right. You are a sensible woman, and then Maxime, between ourselves, has not, up to the present, been very friendly. All the same I've come to place myself at his beck and call. He's going to fight a duel. That won't unduly upset you I fancy."

"No, as you say yourself I am a sensible woman. What is he going to fight a duel for?"

"Don't say, what for whom?"

"Well, 'for whom'?"

"For you."

"For me?"

"Exactly, I mean what I say. Maxime is astonishing us all. He is defending his wife now. It's wonderful. He is a little behind hand in my opinion. But better late than never you know. Besides what he did was done extremely well."

"But in what way am I concerned in it?"

"The thing occurred at the Proskof's and I was present. The Baroness gave utterance to a scarcely proper remark about you. She was not overpleased because the Marquis gave her notice to leave, her lease of the place having expired."

"What did she say?"

"Do you want to know?"

"I insist on knowing."

"She said, 'It's to let that Bourrelier wench live here.' "

"And then?"

"And then your husband hit the Baron a tremendous blow sending him flying among the furniture and smash-

ing priceless china. Oh it was splendidly done. Maxime had a reliable punch. Thereupon he went off
saying: 'I shall expect you to send me your seconds.'
The Baron asked me to act for him, but I declined. I
have always been a greater friend of Maxime's than of
the Baron's. Besides, Madame, I am also your own
friend, and I've come to offer the Marquis my services."

"Here he is, Monsieur," said Cecily who was much
more disturbed by this disclosure than she wished to
appear; and she went into the garden calling Bernard
but in reality to keep herself in countenance.

Chéri-Bibi came into the veranda. He observed
Cecily's hurried departure and her obvious excitement.
When his eyes encountered de Pont-Marie he gave vent
to a stifled groan: "Here he is again!" Moreover, de
Pont-Marie's presence at his house after the scene that
he had witnessed the evening before at the Casino ball,
caused him to suffer acutely. He could not understand
why Cecily did not close the door against him.

"What do you want?" he asked with scant courtesy.

"I am here to place my services at your disposal. I
have not forgotten that we used to be great friends. I
don't know why it is that we are not so to-day, but
anyhow I am still the Marchioness' friend."

"I know that . . . I know that."

"If you want a second for your duel, here I am!
The Baron is sending you his own men almost at once."

"I am much obliged to you for thinking of me. It's
very good of you. But I have already chosen my seconds. Would you mind waiting here a moment? I
want a word with my wife and I shall be with you
again immediately."

Without waiting for a reply, he hastened to join

Cecily whom he could see walking alone in the shady avenue of lime-trees where he had so often beheld her long ago lost in girlhood's day-dreams. She was in a state of agitation.

"I have just seen de Pont-Marie," he said when he caught up to her. "He's a man that I can't stand at any price. I shouldn't express my feelings if I did not believe that you shared them. I don't know what he was saying to you just now when I entered the veranda, but clearly he was worrying you, because you left him with a look of distress on your face. I've asked him to wait for me and I've come to you for your opinion. I have a strong inclination to throw him out by the scruff of his neck."

Chéri-Bibi observed, to his great astonishment, that his expression of opinion did not, by any means, produce the effect that he expected. Cecily turned pale and stammered:

"Why should you? . . . You haven't had any difference with de Pont-Marie I hope. I look upon him as a friend with whom I should like to keep on good terms."

"I . . . I am convinced that this coxcomb does not deserve your friendship and still less your forbearance. Last night at the Casino he behaved almost indecently to you, so that you were obliged to 'put him in his place' and return home. I saw the incident. I was present. And when I came to your reception room this morning and found him with you, I said to myself: 'Hullo, here's that silly ass come to apologize to her.' And when I met him again on the veranda I was obliged to think: 'She's forgiven him.' But noticing that you left him as if you were upset, I added forthwith: 'He doesn't deserve it.' If ever he shows a lack of respect for you, you must tell me."

"You forget, Monsieur, that if I had relied on you to make me respected," returned Cecily in a tone which he had not heard from her during lunch time, "I should have run the risk long ago of not being worthy of respect. You appear to have strangely misconstrued M. de Pont-Marie's attitude last night at the Casino. I have nothing to say against him. I suddenly felt indisposed, and that is why I left early with your mother who was very tired."

Chéri-Bibi suffered excruciating torture as he heard her defense. He felt confident that she was not telling the truth.

"Bad luck to me," he groaned to himself. "She's in love with him. It's no good doubting it any more."

In an access of rage he said:

"I beg your pardon, Madame"—now it was he who called her Madame—"for having made so stupid a mistake. Am I to invite him to dinner?"

"No," she replied in gentler tones, "but to lunch the day after to-morrow."

Chéri-Bibi left the avenue of lime trees as if staggering under a blow.

"The day after to-morrow," he swore to himself, "I shall be dead."

Cecily, on the other hand, though she was swayed by a thousand conflicting emotions, congratulated herself on the thought of this invitation which would afford her an opportunity of talking to M. de Pont-Marie, and perhaps of making some definite arrangement with him before the week was out. She had no wish to become acquainted with the mysterious Villa at Pourville.

In order to distract her mind which was growing obsessed by her "new husband," she called the governess and Bernard, and told them to get ready to go out with her. She intended to visit the Dowager Marchioness who would be astounded to learn of the exemplary conduct of the son whom she had banished from her good books, and sworn never to see again. They took the sunk road which led between two sloping banks, overhung with a dense arch of foliage, to the rustic dwelling to which the old lady had transferred her household goods with the assistance of the aged Rose, her companion, who had given up her life to her service. The Dowager Marchioness, who was very conscientious but very proud, preferred when she left the pretentious Château du Touchais to take this humble country cottage rather than to live in the middle-class Villa Bourrelier where, moreover, she ran the risk of encountering her reprobate son.

Cecily met Rose on the threshold of the cottage.

"I'm glad you've come," she said. "The Marchioness is not at all well."

Cecily entered the house at the moment when two gentlemen immaculately clad in frock coats and glossy silk hats were going up the road from which she had just come.

"The Baron's seconds," she thought.

They were, in fact, the Baron's seconds and Chéri-Bibi was waiting for them at the Villa Bourrelier. He had returned to the veranda where he met de Pont Marie once more, with his own seconds M. Hilaire and Maître Régime, his solicitor from Rouen, who happened to be taking a holiday in Dieppe. Maître Régime had turned as pale as his shirt-front when he discovered that his assistance was required in the wording of a document which would need no government stamp. Maître Régime was an excellent lawyer, with a paternal countenance, and his plump little hands had surely never held a sword. He endeavored, indeed, to advance this argument to his client; but M. de Pont-Marie replied, with an ironical smile, that it was not for him to concern himself with that point inasmuch as it was pretty certain that the fight would be with pistols since the Baron, who was the aggrieved party and had the choice of weapons, was a crack shot.

"But, Monsieur," exclaimed Maître Régime, "I have never in my life loaded a pistol."

"We'll have them loaded by the gunsmith!" replied M. de Pont-Marie in an absurdly tragic voice.

Irritated by quibbling which as far as M. de Pont-Marie was concerned had no object but the disparagement of Maître Régime as a second, Chéri-Bibi turned abruptly to the solicitor.

"Now, Monsieur, are you my friend or are you not?"

"Undoubtedly, Monsieur le Marquis, undoubtedly, but the nature of my profession. . . ."

"Will you be my second—yes or no?"

Maître Régime gathered from the tone in which the question was put that if he declined to be the Marquis' second, the Marquis would decline to be his client. He accepted the duty with a groan.

"Do you suppose," asked M. Hilaire who was almost as pale as the solicitor, "do you suppose, M. de Pont-Marie, that the Baron will choose pistols? Is he as good a shot as you say?"

"He won the first prize at our shooting match. He hits the bull's-eye nearly every time."

"All the better if he does," growled Chéri-Bibi, lighting a fine cigar, "it will be over sooner."

"What do you mean?" exclaimed Maître Régime, clasping his plump little hands as if he were about to offer up a prayer.

"I mean that if he kills me with his first shot there will be no necessity for him to fire another."

"Do you wish to exchange more than one shot?" enquired de Pont-Marie in a voice of simulated indifference.

"I not only desire it," returned Chéri-Bibi, glaring at de Pont-Marie so fiercely that he assumed he was suffering from the hectic fever which many men bring back from foreign parts, "I insist on it. . . . I won't have a mock duel. I want a result. Do you hear, you fellows, who are to be my seconds, I want the firing to continue until there is a definite result."

The result, he thought in his desperation, would be his death and the end of his sufferings.

"One must never say die," said de Pont-Marie. "Who knows what may happen in a duel? It's one thing to aim at a target and another to aim at a man who is shooting at you. Besides, if my memory serves me, the Marquis himself used to be a pretty good shot."

"He's a much better shot with a revolver," broke in Hilaire hardly knowing what he said. And he added, "Couldn't they fight with revol . . ."

He did not finish the sentence for he started back under a withering glance from Chéri-Bibi.

"Monsieur, my secretary is driveling."

Hilaire dropped into the background and held his peace. The conversation was beginning to flag when the footman came in bearing two visiting cards. These

were the cards of the Baron's seconds. Chéri-Bibi went
to the drawing room to receive his visitors, and to put
them in touch with Maître Régime and M. Hilaire. Afterwards he left the house, and found M. de Pont-
Marie still in the garden. He could not bear the sight
of the man. Even before Cecily's prevarication he detested him, but now he hated him with an intensity
which, in itself, was stronger even than his unhappy
love.

When de Pont-Marie caught sight of him he drew
near and Chéri-Bibi ground his teeth with every step
that he took.

"Why doesn't he clear out? Can't he see, the silly
ass, that his presence alone makes me ill?"

"Marquis, why didn't you accept me as a second?"
asked de Pont-Marie, adopting an easy bearing and,
seemingly, making up his mind to ignore anything unusual. "Those two wretched persons are shaking in
their shoes; that's evident. Believe me, I don't understand you. Come out with it, Maxime, what is the
trouble between us? . . . I have a right to know. . . .
People have been gossiping about me. They think perhaps that I come here too frequently. Such people
don't know me, Maxime, and they don't know your
wife."

"My wife. . . . I won't allow you, you understand.
. . . I won't allow you to bring my wife into this. . . ."

"There, you see, you are annoyed with me. You
have some feeling against me. . . ."

"No," Chéri-Bibi interrupted quickly. "No, no, I
have nothing against you. I apologize to you. I've
come back from abroad not quite myself." And he
added, sinking his voice, after a slight pause: "To prove

that I've nothing against you I ask you to lunch with us the day after to-morrow. Is that agreed?"

"But, old fellow, I really don't know if I can . . . anyway, tell me that we are friends as we used to be."

"Yes, yes . . . as we used to be."

"Then call me by my Christian name as before. Say: 'If you come to lunch I shall be pleased, Georges.'"

"All right: 'If you come to lunch I shall be pleased, Georges.'"

"Give me your hand on it."

"There you are."

"Look out, you're hurting me. You almost smashed my fingers. . . . Oh! I say you know. . . ."

"And now good-by for the present," said Chéri-Bibi.

"Yes, good-by for the present. By the way, does your wife know that you've invited me to lunch for the day after to-morrow? Will she be pleased?"

"Certainly she knows and, of course, she'll be pleased."

Chéri-Bibi strode quickly away for he felt that he could no longer restrain himself, and might do something rash. When he reached the veranda he flung himself into a chair exclaiming:

"Cecily! . . . Cecily!"

He sat motionless for nearly a quarter of an hour plunged in misery and then he rose in calmer mood.

"Courage," he said to himself. "Your appeal against the sentence has been rejected."

He would know how to die. The thought was uppermost in his mind now that he knew Cecily loved that coxcomb de Pont-Marie.

His seconds came to him. The discussion was over.

They had agreed among themselves that four shots
should be exchanged at twenty-five paces, at the word
of command, and the Baron's seconds gave them to understand that their man would do his utmost to bring
about a decisive result. The duel was to take place at
nine o'clock the following morning in the Du Touchais
Park.

Maître Régime, whose agitation only increased with
his responsibility, took leave of the Marquis and went
back to bed again for he could barely stand upright.
The Marquis' secretary, on the other hand, was weeping. He gathered that Chéri-Bibi had undergone such
mortifications from Cecily that he had determined to
allow himself to be shot like a rabbit. Chéri-Bibi did
his best to console him by telling him that he would not
forget him in his will, and that he might consider himself henceforward beyond the reach of want.

"You are too good," groaned the poor fellow. "You
may be certain of one thing—I shan't survive you."

Meanwhile the Marchioness and little Bernard came
in. The boy kissed his father affectionately which re-
doubled the secretary's grief. Cecily stared with astonishment at the great booby who "blubbered" as he
turned his head away. Chéri-Bibi introduced him and
asked his wife if she would be kind enough to find a
corner for him.

"There's the Lodge with the bedroom on the ground
floor. I think it would suit your secretary admirably."

"Yes, the Lodge will do. Would you mind showing
Hilaire the place? You must excuse me but I shan't
be dining with you this evening. Perhaps you'll send
me up a cup of tea at eight o'clock. I have a great

deal of work to get through and I shall be shut up in my study."

Thereupon the secretary started to weep like a fountain.

"Come, Hilaire, don't be a baby."

"All right, Monsieur le Marquis."

"Did you see my mother, Cecily? How was she?"

"She's better. She was very pleased with the news that I brought her, and Rose and I both hope that she will soon be well. Besides the doctor expressed himself as quite satisfied."

"Did you remember me to her?"

"No, she would not allow me to speak of you."

"What an extraordinary lot of women," thought Chéri-Bibi. "I should never have believed that women of the upper ten could be so resentful."

He left them and locked himself in his study which had once been the study of M. Bourrelier senior. Meanwhile the Marchioness took the unhappy Dodger to the Lodge.

"What is the gentleman crying for?" asked young Bernard.

"You heard what my son said, M. Hilaire," said Cecily after she had sent the boy off to his governess. "He is surprised to see you so upset."

"Do you know, Madame," the Dodger replied blowing his nose noisily, "that my master has made up his mind to get killed?"

"I know, M. Hilaire, that the Marquis is going to fight a duel, but I am equally aware that he is an adept in the use of arms, and will know how to defend himself."

"You are mistaken, Madame, if you will forgive me for saying so. These gentlemen are going to exchange four shots, and the Marquis told me that he should fire in the air. You see, therefore, that he wishes to be killed."

And he burst into a fresh display of grief.

Chéri-Bibi, who was not a communicative person in the important events of life, had, in fact, said nothing of the sort to his friend the Dodger.

"Are you very much attached to the Marquis, Monsieur Hilaire?"

"Oh, Madame, how could I be other than devoted to him. He is so good. . . . I know that he was not always so, and that he is greatly to blame in his treatment of you. . . ."

"Monsieur Hilaire," interrupted Cecily in a tone of voice that struck a chill into the doleful secretary's heart. "Here are your rooms. . . . Good-by, Monsieur Hilaire."

Hilaire stood, to use his own expression, flabbergasted. When he recovered his breath he exclaimed:

"How on earth does one talk to these ladies? What's the good of being tactful, one can never please them. Certainly Chéri-Bibi's Cecily takes it out of me. . . . I prefer Virginie. . . ."

After wiping his eyes he looked round the flat. He was immensely struck with it. His study, his bedroom, his bathroom! In other circumstances he would gladly have danced a jig at the sight of so much splendor. But the deadly fate which continued to dog his master's footsteps, threw him into the depths of a fresh depression. He brushed his clothes, "tried" the washstand, and after putting his tie straight, walked slowly to the door muttering at every few steps:

"It was too good to last!"

Nevertheless he retained a hope that when Chéri-Bibi saw the detestable countenance of Baron Proskof he would feel a new inclination for life, and demonstrate that he, too, knew how to handle a pistol.

He turned his steps through the row of arches to the little eating house where that morning he had lunched and gossiped with the charming Virginie. In the society of that fair-complexioned daughter of the Caux country, he forgot the great hotels and the inferior quality of the fish. But now he had the ill-luck to find the place closed, the shutters up, and a notice posted on the door: 'Opening shortly under new management.'

"As long as Virginie stays," thought the Dodger, "it's a matter of indifference to me who the proprietor is."

And thus poor man in his journey through life does not suspect that the pebble which he unconsciously brushes against with his foot, may cause him to stumble in the mysterious path of his destiny.

Until the evening he sat on a stone on the quay, leaning on his elbows, like an old pensioner with no other diversion than to gaze into the distance. He did not dine. When he returned quite late he observed a light in the study on the ground floor of the Villa. And he thought in gloomy despondency:

"The Marquis is making his will"

He was right in his conjecture. But it was some hours since Chéri-Bibi had finished his "last will and testament," dealing with the distribution of his property. It was his moral testament that he was preparing, the last memory of himself that he was about to leave to Cecily, his supreme farewell to life and love. In speaking to her from beyond the tomb, as the

Marquis du Touchais, he was careful to deal briefly
with the past in his expression of sorrow; but he hoped
by a dazzling picture of his love of the moment to excite
a feeling of remorse in the pitiless heart of her who
did not know how to forgive.

More than once Chéri-Bibi was obliged to interrupt
the flow of his impassioned confession to allow his
tears to flow. And thus it seemed that at the moment
when he believed Cecily would be his, he was to lose her
forever. A few hours had sufficed to decide irrevocably
his fate. The tragic hour was about to strike when
fatality would write the word "Finis" to his wondrous
story. At least so he believed, and with wet eyes
through which he caught the vague image of Cecily,
and with a heart bursting with impotent despair, he
rose and lifted his hands on high imploring her pardon.

Some one was pacing the room above despite the
lateness of the hour. It was Cecily's room, the forbidden temple in which the little feet of his cruel god-
dess were moving in their "perfumed sandals." It was
in carefully chosen language that Chéri-Bibi spoke of
her for the last time. His elementary education, which
was completed too late by his reading of the classic
authors, led him to adopt a somewhat antiquated style;
a style which appealed to him, after he had cast aside
slang, by reason of its dignity, its loftiness, its elabor-
ate distinction.

"My misfortunes have enlightened my mind," he
sighed. "The blood on my hands grows pale and is
being expunged. It was written that the stain should
he blotted out by this unforeseen expiation. To-day
the words of my mouth are pure, and Cecily is my
executioner."

But why had she not retired for the night? . . . Why was she not peacefully sleeping if the fate of her unhappy husband was as indifferent to her as she seemed to pretend? If she loved another, was she not on the brink of deliverance?

In the room above, the sound of her footsteps ceased to be heard, and Chéri-Bibi dropped once more into his chair before his unfinished task. Suddenly he drew himself up and his heart leapt within him. Her fragrant presence wrapped him all about. He turned round. She stood before him like a pale, compassionate ghost. He tried to take her in his arms, but she glided from his hands like a shade. He groaned. And then she said in the soft voice which he knew of old:

"What are you doing? Why aren't you getting what rest you can? To-morrow morning you have to fight this duel. Won't you need all your strength and all your self-command?"

"No, I shall not need them. When I am dead you will read what I have written, and perhaps you will discover that I was deserving of your forgiveness."

"I shall not read it," she returned in an increasingly gentle voice. "I shall not read it because you will live."

She took the sheets of writing paper that lay on the desk, put them to the light of a candle and threw them into the fireplace, and soon they were little more than ashes. But first the light was switched on in the room, and Chéri-Bibi was unnerved by the disturbing vision of Cecily in her night attire. She had thrown a thin dressing gown over her disorder which added a sense of unreality to this charming and startling apparition. She was like a delicate picture at once of sorrow and love. He fell at her feet. He had the sensation that she bent over his bowed head and—happy, unforgettable, exultant, divine moment—touched with her cool lips his tremendous forehead. He closed his eyes like a fool. When he opened them again she had vanished.

He rose with renewed strength like Hercules before the Nemean monster. He would live. He would love. He would be loved. Like a man possessed he paced the room in which a few minutes before he was prostrate with despair; and in the pale beams of the early morning the mirrors reflected his triumphant glance. He opened the window with a conquering hand. He breathed the fresh air of the dawn as though he could not inhale enough to fill his big happy heart. Cecily would be his. There was no longer any room for doubt. Heaven, earth, the waves of the distant sea, the whole world were his. The sun would rise that day but to witness his triumph. Woe betide whoever stood against him in the path of life! That little Baron Proskof, so clever with his pistol, would miss him, while Chéri-Bibi, so clever with his revolver—a much more difficult weapon—would not miss the little Baron Proskof. Because sometimes fortune showers all her blessings at one time; glorious weather, success in one's undertakings, and luck in the battle of life. Yes there are moments when it is impossible to die! Chéri-Bibi was stifling with the joy of living; he had to tear off his collar, his tie, open the front of his shirt, for he was gasping for breath. And in his glad enthusiasm, in the flush of his high spirits, he exaggerated his dishevelment, and took pleasure in contemplating himself in the great mirror hanging above the fire-place in which a few minutes before Cecily, with a simple gesture, had taught him that his love was not hopeless.

And thus he gazed at himself, proud as a demi-god who eagerly throws off his armor the sooner to achieve victory. Suddenly he turned pale and staggered back. His hand went to his heart. It was as though he were about to fall in a huddled heap stricken with death. He uttered a hollow groan. He drew himself up as wild beasts in the jungle draw themselves up after they have received the shot which, for a moment, has struck them down and which the hunter thinks will be mortal. And he leapt from the window into the garden. He ran without stopping to the Lodge where Hilaire was sleeping, and knocked at the window on the ground floor. The window was opened; and the hapless Dodger fell back at the sight of this wild-eyed, pallid, sinister face.

"What's happened?" he asked in a startled voice.

Chéri-Bibi went in to him.

"This has happened," he exclaimed showing his bare chest.

The Dodger saw tatooed on Chéri-Bibi's skin some half dozen designs representing anchors and hearts pierced with arrows, and in addition, the indelible sentence: *To Cecily for life Chéri-Bibi.* The poor man's name was engraven on his chest!

"What difference can it make to you?" asked the Dodger who failed to grasp the reason of so much excitement for so small a cause.

"Wretch! Don't you understand that I am to fight a duel this morning and it's ten to one that I shall be hit and the seconds and doctor may have to open my shirt front?"

"Oh I say, I say," exclaimed the Dodger simply, placing his hands before his face in an attitude of dismay.

Chéri-Bibi was silent. He buttoned his shirt over his secret. He was breathing hard in hoarse gasps like a wild beast that is trapped.

"Let's get out of this place," he cried suddenly. "Come. . . ."

He led or rather carried the Dodger into the garden and thence to the cliff which they reached by climbing over a low wall which Chéri-Bibi had often struggled with in the days of his youth.

They turned their steps towards the shore. It seemed to him that the air from the open sea would freshen his mind and perhaps inspire him with an idea. For after all something would have to be done. . . . Something. . . .

"Why didn't he remove your skin as well?" sighed the Dodger.

"Yes, why? . . . Why didn't he? It's too late to ask him now since he's dead. Oh, I frequently begged him to take away that particular bit of skin, but he wouldn't hear of it pretending that it was dangerous since it was so near the heart. He preferred to change my hands telling me that that was much more essential. In that respect, he was right, but he might just as well have done both. The skin over the heart is not more sensitive than the skin on the hand. He must have had some scheme at the back of his mind! I always suspected as much; and I was afraid of it. I never really felt safe until I heard that his body was picked up. Meanwhile we're in a pretty pickle!"

"Yes," admitted the Dodger, "we are in a pretty pickle. Things were going too well."

"Of course, things were going too well," said Chéri-Bibi.

"I often said to you: 'Monsieur le Marquis, don't make any more blunders. Compose yourself or there'll be trouble.' Oh damn the duel!"

"There's only one thing to be done," said Chéri-Bibi, "and that's for me to fire at once trusting to luck to kill him."

"But suppose you don't kill him? Suppose he hits you?"

"I intend to stand with my side face towards him. I shan't move my arm. I shall fire with my fore-arm pressed to my body. In this way there is a chance of being hit in the arm."

"What's the good! They'll take off your shirt just the same."

"Damn and damn again."

"Yes, it's devilish bad luck. There's only one alternative, and that is to refuse to fight."

"You must be mad. I'd rather die than be taken for a coward."

"What rot you talk. I can see you lying wounded while the seconds pull you about. Suddenly they draw back and utter exclamations. Every one flocks round you. Some one asks what's the trouble and they all read: 'To Cecily for life Chéri-Bibi!' . . ."

Chéri-Bibi turned his face to the luminous sun rising in the firmament. Had he been able to emulate Joshua's feat of arresting the sun he would not have hesitated though he unloosened a thousand catastrophes in the solar system. But since he was power-

less, he contented himself with lifting his clenched fists
and crying in infuriated tones:

"O thou sun who makest the light of day to revolve
round the world, have pity on my unjust torment."

"This is not the moment for bombast. Look in front
of you, Monsieur le Marquis."

The Dodger pointed to a form which stood above
the horizon of the pale sea on the path skirting the cliff
in which the two despairing friends had just entered.

Chéri-Bibi was not wearing his smoked spectacles
that morning and his sight was as keen as his secretary's.

He gave a start and muttered:

"The Baron!"

It was indeed the Baron who was coming towards
them, his hands in his pockets, taking the early morning
air. Apparently the eve of battle had found him rest-
less and unable to sleep, and he had determined to re-
lax the tension of his nerves by a healthy walk on the
deserted cliff.

Chéri-Bibi told the Dodger to be silent but to keep
by his side as they pursued their way.

The Baron, in his turn, caught sight of them and
recognized them. It was too late for him to go back.
It would have seemed as if he were running away. Moreover, the cliff was public property.

The path along which they were walking, the
Baron coming towards the two others, was extremely
narrow and close to the edge of the cliff. In order to
allow the Baron to pass, Chéri-Bibi or the Dodger
would have to make way. Chéri-Bibi, who was nearest
the edge, and who was also the best mannered, the most
familiar with the usages of the polite world, made the

first movement to draw aside. Baron Proskof took advantage of it, while raising his hat, to slip into the narrow passage which was open to him.

Unfortunately at that moment a series of false movements occurred between Chéri-Bibi and the Baron such as often comes about between two persons who meet face to face and desire to treat each other with courtesy. In these false movements, there was one which was falser than the others, and it sent the Baron sprawling into the abyss.

Chéri-Bibi and the Dodger came to a stand in some excitement. Soon they caught below them the sound of a crash!

"He was a great rotter," said Chéri-Bibi. "Let's go to bed Dodger. Take my word for it, we mustn't come here again for a stroll, the cliff offers too many temptations!"

CHAPTER V

At eight o'clock in the morning, for the duel was fixed for nine o'clock, Chéri-Bibi and his secretary were walking in the main avenue of the Bourrelier grounds waiting for their principal second, Maître Régime.

Chéri-Bibi was certainly good to look upon. His splendid composure before the combat, the perfect serenity of his manner, his quiet language, in a word his dignified bearing, would have astonished the most casual person, for it is seldom given even to the bravest man to be complete master of his nerves a few minutes before hazarding his life.

In the shadow of a window blind on the first floor a feminine form was watching the heroic spectacle.

It was Cecily, who had not slept during the night and who stood gazing with increasing agitation at this husband who was about to fight and perhaps die for her. . . .

For her! Since his return to Dieppe the Marquis's behavior had completely revolutionized the mind and perhaps the heart of the adorable Cecily. Was it indeed possible that the same man who had made her cruelly suffer was now giving her such grounds for satisfaction? Two days before, he had forced back the Baroness' horses, the day before he had turned the creature out of the Château du Touchais which was

108

desecrated by her presence, and to-day he was to fight
for his wife!

With one hand on her heart, whose unwonted throbbing she had some difficulty to restrain, Cecily began to
reproach herself; for in the main she was the best person that ever lived, and if she had treated the repentant
Marquis with disdain, it was because the past had unfortunately given her only too much reason to doubt
the reality of such a transformation in his character.
Thus she reproached herself. She thought that she
was partly to blame for his conduct which was, perhaps,
brought about by her coldness to him in the early
days of their marriage. If he now bestowed on her so
many marks of his love, it was doubtless because he
loved her then. And she had never guessed it! . . .
Yet it was the explanation of many things . . . the
licentiousness of his life, the scandal of the "Belle of
Dieppe," and all the incidents which came after, even
up to the terrible night of his departure for Norway
in which he now tried to see less the desire of revenge
than the irresistible love of a man whom, when all was
said, she had scoffed at.

And thus it is with the heart of a woman—always
in extremes, passing from love to hate and hate to love
with a celerity that nothing can stop.

And the Cecily who was concealed behind the window blind was not far from being in love with Chéri-
Bibi.

To begin with the step that she had taken in the
night, the kiss that she had given him, the encourage-
ment that she had held out to him by burning his will
before his eyes, were so many proofs, clearer than the
soft light of that morning, that her heart was opening

to the tenderest feelings, the feelings of forgiveness and love.

She admired his strength of mind in the face of danger and, in truth, she trembled for him. She dreaded the result of the duel.

She shivered at the reflection that his lifeless body might presently be brought back to her. She who a few days before had every right to consider that the death of the Marquis would be a deliverance, no longer struggled against a feeling of anguish at the thought of it. She wanted him to live, and since she was a good Catholic she prayed for him.

Meanwhile Chéri-Bibi began to lose patience for such is the stuff of which real heroes are made; they always desire to be the first to reach the field of battle!

Chéri-Bibi feared to be late. Maître Régime had not yet put in an appearance.

"This man of law will bring disgrace on us," the Marquis said aloud, "I shall never forgive myself for keeping the Baron waiting."

He had no sooner uttered those words than a carriage stopped outside the gate, and Maître Régime alighted; but he was not alone.

On recognizing the person who accompanied his principal second, Chéri-Bibi could not repress a gesture of disagreeable surprise. This man, short but well-proportioned, with a small head on broad shoulders and shrewd eyes, was his most deadly enemy. It was the famous Costaud, at one time secretary to the Commissary of Police at Dieppe, and now a Detective-Inspector in the criminal investigation department, the infernal individual who had pursued him from the beginning with such relentless energy.

The new Marquis du Touchais was already on the defensive. He caught a glimpse of Cecily's sweet face behind the blind, and the thought that she was beginning to show a sympathetic interest in him, inspired him with more than sufficient resolution to confront a man like Costaud.

Moreover, he had no fear of being recognized. In so far as his voice was concerned he had never held much communication with Costaud, whose part had consisted chiefly in putting the handcuffs on; and that was some considerable time ago.

His voice had altered since. Then again Costaud never used to visit the Marquis du Touchais, and was it not absurd to suppose that he would suspect Chéri-Bibi of masquerading in the Marquis' skin?

The Dodger had nothing to fear from Costaud in particular any more than from the police in general, for since Chéri-Bibi's first escape he had lived in the shadow of his notorious friend without being directly concerned in any of his enterprises. Never caught in the act, never arrested, he had a clean sheet in police records. Moreover, was he not the Marquis' secretary?

They stood their ground ready to receive the representative of authority who came forward in silence with Maître Régime. The solicitor seemed to be in a state of even greater excitement than on the previous day, but his plump person was brimming over with a certain air of cheerfulness. And when Chéri-Bibi reproached him, as he came up, with his lack of punctuality in keeping the appointment, he explained, waiving his arms enthusiastically, that the fault lay with Detective-Inspector Costaud who had detained him at Le Pollett to give him an extraordinary piece of news,

namely that shrimpers had found Baron Proskof's body
at the foot of the cliff.

"Do you mean to say that the Baron is dead?" exclaimed Chéri-Bibi falling back a step in astonishment.

"Dead! . . . But he can't be," added Hilaire. "We
are fighting a duel with him this morning!"

"I know that," said Costaud whom the solicitor now
introduced, "and I know also that Maître Régime was
the Marquis' principal second. I happened to be staying in Dieppe—where I began my career by investigat-
ing a celebrated case which made a great sensation in
the world—and one of my colleagues informed me this
morning of the grim discovery made by shrimpers. I
at once started off for the cliff, and I discovered the
body of Baron Proskof at the very spot where, many
years ago, we found the body of M. Bourrelier senior,
who was murdered by Chéri-Bibi."

"At the very spot?" echoed the Marquis in a voice of
obvious stupefaction.

"Yes, at the very spot, I assure you. The body was
lying on its face like M. Bourrelier's with arms outstretched. I could have imagined, had I been a few
years younger, that Chéri-Bibi had once again passed
that way. . . .

"Always presuming of course, that Chéri-Bibi was
still alive," went on the Detective-Inspector. "But as
a matter of fact you were present when the notorious
miscreant died on board the 'Bayard.' I confess that
I read with tremendous interest the interviews with you
which were published in the daily papers. Up to then
I had doubted the ruffian's death. But, in the end,
your evidence, the evidence gathered from other survivors of that amazing adventure and the return of

Sister Mary of the Angels after her brother's death, convinced me; although I don't deny that deep down within me, I have a sort of presentiment that we shall hear something more of that terrible man. . . ."

"Even now that he is dead?"

"Well, Monsieur le Marquis, I can't reconcile myself to the idea of his death. . . . I can't believe that Chéri-Bibi would die of an illness like an ordinary mortal, and leave the world so simply as that, at the moment when he had made himself supreme, and had only to gather the fruit of his immeasurable audacity and receive your millions. . . . No . . . no. . . . The thing doesn't sound feasible."

"All right, Monsieur Costaud," returned Chéri-Bibi in the calmest of tones, seemingly taking no further interest in the matter. "We will assume that he is not dead, that's all."

"Oh, I won't go so far as to say that. But the thing astonishes me more than I know how to express. He has played us so many tricks! Has he not faked up a last one in his own particular style? Are you positive that you saw him dead?"

"I saw him dead, as plainly as I see you living."

"Ah, I wanted to hear your evidence before making up my mind. I was longing to have a word with you on the subject. Baron Proskof's death gives me the opportunity, and it's just as well. You will excuse me for troubling you, Monsieur le Marquis. . . . Now I can continue my investigations into the poor Baron's death. "

"It's a queer sort of death," observed Chéri-Bibi. "It has done me out of a very fine duel! However that may

be, gentlemen," he added turning to his seconds, "our
duty is to go to the meeting-place. It's quite time."

"Permit me to come with you," suggested Costaud,
"I shall have a few questions to put to you on the way,
as man to man, in the interests of justice."

"I am entirely at your disposal, Monsieur."

They went off. As he opened the gate Chéri-Bibi
turned to the window and saw a handkerchief fluttering
behind it. Cecily had not heard the conversation between the men, and consequently was under the impression that her husband was on his way to the duel.
Moreover, it was with a sense of dread that she caught
sight of a heavy case of pistols which Maître Régime
was carrying, as a lawyer carries a portfolio, but with
an easy assurance due to his certainty that there would
be no occasion to use them.

The Marchioness assumed that M. Costaud, the
fourth person, was a doctor staying in the country,
whose services had been requisitioned by the seconds.
The truth was that the doctors were to go direct to
the spot chosen for the duel, which was on the cliff on
the far side of the Château du Touchais. It was no
great distance. They went on foot by a short cut.

Costaud drew nearer the Marquis.

"I have a few rather delicate points to put to you,
Monsieur le Marquis. Don't say anything if they are
inconvenient to you. But if you are able to answer
me, it would be of great service. It's like this: Before
my return to Dieppe this morning I went, as you may
imagine, to see the Baroness. It was I, in fact, who
broke the bad news to her while the Commissary of Police had the body removed to the town for the purpose
of the post-mortem examination. The Baroness has a

cool head. When she learnt that her husband's body had been found underneath the cliff she said: 'What a fool!' "

"Oh really. . . . She said, 'What a fool!' "

"She said: 'What a fool!' and the words were, to me, a revelation. I imagined that it was an accident, but now Monsieur le Marquis, I do not believe that it was an accident."

"And what do you think it was?" asked Chéri-Bibi displaying keen interest.

"To tell you the truth, I believe it was a case of suicide. It was common knowledge that the Baron and Baroness' affairs were in a very bad way. They were waiting with constantly increasing impatience for you to come back, to get them out of their difficulties. Now it appears, if one may trust the gossips of the place, that you did not fulfill any of the worthy couple's expectations. It seems that you gave the 'Belle of Dieppe' notice to quit. I say again, Monsieur le Marquis, that I am putting these points to you only with the desire to elucidate, at the earliest moment, the facts of the tragedy which seem to me to be perfectly simple."

"But Monsieur Costaud, I don't consider that you're in any way indiscreet. One arrives at an age when one must settle down. I have had my fling in my youth, but youth passes. That is what in point of fact I endeavored to convey to the Baroness Proskof and her husband. They received my declaration in a very unpleasant spirit . . . hence the duel."

"Hence the suicide. . . . The Baron expected you to pay his debts, but you knocked him down instead. He lost his head, and the 'Belle of Dieppe,' who has not entirely given up all hope of you, regards him as a fool. That's the whole story. What is your opinion?"

"My opinion, Monsieur, is that your arguments are convincing. We'll take it for granted that the Baron committed suicide. I prefer that it should be so rather than to kill him with my own hand seeing that he and I and his wife were on such friendly terms."

And thus the suicide of the Baron from the cliff at Puys was established in a circumstantial report drawn up by the Detective-Inspector of the Criminal investigation department who demonstrated his powers of psychological deduction. Chéri-Bibi's first encounter with the redoubtable officer filled him with unspeakable delight. He secretly reveled in the joy of being treated with great deference by one of the police from whom formerly he had been subjected to the worst brutalities.

"It's certain," he said to himself, "that if you are rich you succeed in everything. It is as though the whole world combines to save you from the least annoyance, and Costaud takes upon himself the burden of sweeping out of my path all those whom I might have feared as a result of that movement of my shoulders on the cliff."

He considered that the basis of society was a sound one, and he began to have a liking for Costaud. He shook hands in great good humor with all the men in the park near him, and when the Baron's seconds gravely conveyed the sad news to him, it was with great difficulty that he forbore to congratulate them on their principal's death. He thanked the doctors for their zeal, and regretted sincerely, as he said, that "they had all their trouble for nothing." Finally he asked to be allowed to present his respects to the widow.

The Baroness did not refuse to receive him. Hilaire watched him enter the Château in terror. He said to himself that the "Belle of Dieppe" would be his undoing. He was not easy in his mind until he saw him come out, some minutes later, with a smile on his lips, seemingly well pleased with himself. Chéri-Bibi at once dragged Hilaire off with him after taking leave of M. Costaud, Maître Régime, and the rest of the party.

"That woman," he said to Hilaire speaking of the Baroness, "seemed to me to be delighted at the thought of her husband's death, although she deemed it advisable when she saw me to make a show of gloomy despair. I soon put an end to that farce by presenting her with a check for a substantial amount. Though I'm not fond of unnecessary expenditure, Hilaire, I don't hesitate to "make sacrifices" when the circumstances concern the honor of the Marquis du Touchais or the dignity of his wife. We shan't hear any more of the Baroness Proskof. . . .

"After the funeral at which we shall be present as country neighbors, she will leave this place for good and all. Let us hasten with the news to our Cecily. I am very grateful to this duel which has ended so happily. But for the duel the Marchioness would never had soothed my mind last night by her generous impulse. She allowed me to kiss her. But for the duel she would never have stood behind the blind watching my departure. Gentle, lovable Cecily! . . . She waved her handkerchief to me. She thought that I was going off to fight. Hilaire, I tell you that she loves me or is not far from loving me. Let us hasten to calm her fears and put an end to her anxiety. If I have at last touched her heart, as I hope, she must be in a state of terrible suspense."

They hurried along without exchanging another word. Chéri-Bibi reached the gate first, and could not repress an exclamation, a very violent exclamation, for he caught sight of Cecily in a covered walk talking in a somewhat intimate manner to de Pont-Marie.

After giving expression to his feelings, Chéri-Bibi opened the gate and went towards the couple with clenched fists, while the gentle Dodger held on to the skirts of his coat whispering in supplicating tones:

"Don't be rash, Monsieur le Marquis. And above all no more duels for the love of Heaven."

The conversation in the arbor was an animated one and neither Cecily nor de Pont-Marie had yet noticed Chéri-Bibi's arrival. When they saw him he was quite close to them, and they both rose embarrassed, changing color in their confusion.

What were they saying? From all appearance they feared lest they had been overheard. But Chéri-Bibi to his great regret had been unable to catch a word of their conversation. He rolled his eyes fiercely. Cecily was the first to recover her composure.

"M. de Pont-Marie came to tell me of the Baron's death," she said. "The news greatly reassured me, dear."

At these words Chéri-Bibi's anger fell away. They were spoken so simply and sweetly and at the same time so significantly, that he would have been a monster of ingratitude had his heart not been softened. But none the less he continued to entertain a feeling of resentment against de Pont-Marie for his presence there.

But for M. de Pont-Marie he would certainly have enjoyed a different sight, a sight that he had already tasted in anticipation. He imagined Cecily's delight when she heard of his escape from danger in the duel, and in a mental picture he saw her throw herself into his arms, and forget the past in a sob of love.

Thus doubtless matters would have come to pass and completely satisfied his love and pride. Time enough, he had thought, to tell her that there had been no duel; the ice would none the less have been broken. And here was the intolerable de Pont-Marie thwarting his plans for so happy an issue.

He loathed the man. It was a veritable misfortune that he was prevented from ridding himself of him in some duel because of the miserable piece of skin which the Kanaka had left on his chest, and which it was expedient to hide from every one, even and above all in case of an accident, which must needs be provided for in dueling.

In any event it would not be long before he closed the door of his house to him. And meanwhile, that very day, he would politely inform him that he wasn't wanted. Chéri-Bibi longed to be alone with Cecily, face to face, and to pursue the work of winning her troubled heart which he had so well begun. Thus he opened his lips in order to tell M. de Pont-Marie that the "Belle of Dieppe" was expecting to see him at her place when Cecily, with her most charming smile, said to him:

"I asked you to invite M. de Pont-Marie to lunch to-morrow, but since he is here, I will keep him with us to-day. We have a great deal to talk about. M. de Pont-Marie is the secretary of the Poor Seaman's Fund and I am the president. We have to make up the accounts. We shall finish them to-day—at least I hope so. Meantime, would you mind excusing us? We are going to steep ourselves in figures. Good-by for the present."

She held out her hand. He took it in his own scarcely knowing what he was doing. It was he who was being told that he wasn't wanted! He bowed over the hand that he adored, feeling a lump in his throat. But Cecily had already turned her back on him, and reached her boudoir, near the veranda, in which she shut herself up with de Pont-Marie.

Chéri-Bibi uttered a groan like the horn of a motor car and fled across the country. Behind him ran the Dodger out of breath. At length he came up to him on a sloping bank on which Chéri-Bibi had sunk. His face was covered with his hands in an attitude of extreme dejection.

The Dodger respected his grief until it was time for luncheon. Then he ventured to speak:

"It's twelve o'clock," he said.

Chéri-Bibi got up. He was now calm. It was as though he had made up his mind, and the Dodger at once felt a certain anxiety.

"What's he going to do now?" he asked himself, always ready to anticipate and to prevent as far as possible untoward accidents.

As they drew near the villa, Chéri-Bibi recovered his self-possession as a man of the world. He strove to maintain it notwithstanding the shock that he received when the man servant told him that the Marchioness and M. de Pont-Marie were still in the boudoir. He was inclined to break in upon their duet, which, indeed, had lasted a little too long even in the cause of charity.

Was he not the master? Was he not in his own house? . . . But the door before him opened and the two persons came out. De Pont-Marie wore a slightly satirical expression which was not pleasant to see. Cecily, on the other hand, did not show to advantage for she was of extreme pallor, and there was a look of anxiety in her eyes which she dared not raise to her husband.

"Come, let us have lunch," she said in a peculiar voice, taking Chéri-Bibi's arm.

Chéri-Bibi, whose agitation had reached its culminating point, was conscious of the trembling of her hand. De Pont-Marie remained behind, caught up by young Bernard who was playing with him, and Chéri-Bibi said to Cecily in a voice as deep as self-sacrifice, as secret as revenge, and as swift as love:

"This man is making you suffer. I don't wish to know the cause, but do you want me to get rid of him once for all?"

"You are dreaming," she replied quickly. "What are you thinking of? We have had some dispute in connection with the accounts. I will tell you the story later on. It's of no importance . . . none whatever." Her hand trembled more and more. I entreat you to be civil to him during lunch. See for yourself, he has already forgotten our difference of opinion. He is amusing himself with Bernard . . . with your son."

Chéri-Bibi gave a cry, for Cecily had fallen in a dead faint in his arms.

He carried her as though she were a child into her room. The servants came hurrying in, and gave her smelling salts. Her pale face was reclining on his shoulder. He was wild with anxiety and love. They

unloosened her corsage. Chéri-Bibi closed his eyes, and
Cecily chose that moment to open hers. She gave a
sigh and caught sight of the Marquis' distraught
features. "How he loves me!" she said to herself; and
she shuddered as she thought of the terrible battle in
which she was engaged with de Pont-Marie and in which
she might, perhaps, in the end succumb. Meanwhile
Bernard came in and she took him in her arms and
covered him—the object of so much love and sorrow—
with passionate kisses. She pressed the price of her
suffering to her heart with such a wild outburst of
emotion that she failed to notice that the father's
ardent gaze was now fixed upon her. At length, greatly
concerned, he left her in the servants' hands, stumbling
against the furniture on his way from the room like a
man possessed.

In the garden he at once encountered the eternal de
Pont-Marie, who inquired after the Marchioness.
Chéri-Bibi asked him to come with him to his study.
And here he carried into effect his determination to tell
de Pont-Marie, openly and frankly, that his presence
was no longer welcome. In his excitement he did not
mince matters. The Dodger with a beating heart was
listening behind the door. And this is what he heard:

"You must excuse us for not being able to keep you
to lunch in view of the Marchioness' condition. My
car will take you back to Dieppe if you wish it. Personally I have a slight request to make to you: don't
set foot in this place again. . . . Oh, please let me
have my say, it won't take long. We have been the
closest friends. We are friends no longer. You know
the reason. I am not a silly ass. You have been
making love to my wife. You were, perhaps, entitled to

do so in the days when I was not in love with her myself, but now I adore her. I dislike your conduct intensely. Let us understand each other. I have no grudge against you. I don't want to quarrel with you. I have the greatest confidence in the Marchioness, and I know that in spite of all that I have made her suffer she is incapable of deceiving me. Only you understand the position is changed. I have now come to take up the place here that I used not to care about. I want it, and nothing remains for you to do but to pass out of sight. Let's shake hands and say good-by."

M. de Pont-Marie ignored the hand that was held out to him and took a seat without being invited.

Amazed and out of all patience with this unexpected development, Chéri-Bibi made a step forward, his whole body expressing menace, and the Dodger, who was peeping through the key-hole, expected to see his master throw the foolhardy de Pont-Marie out of the window. But a few words dropped by him stopped Chéri-Bibi short in his sudden impulse.

"Have you entirely lost your memory?"

Chéri-Bibi stood aghast.

"Memory . . . What memory?" he stammered.

"Yes," returned the other in the calmest of tones, crossing his legs, "because let me tell you that if you've lost your memory as a result of your illness, which after all is quite likely, I will undertake to bring it back to you. That's a slight service which one cannot refuse between old pals like ourselves. And I shan't need the help of a doctor for that!" went on de Pont-Marie in a hissing voice while his knitted brows and his thin lips gnawing his mustache, betrayed the inward rage which consumed him and which he could scarcely control.

Suddenly he rose and stood erect before Chéri-Bibi, whose face was like stone, looked him straight in the eyes, and slapped him with authority on the shoulder with his right hand.

"Come," he said, "admit that you have forgotten nothing. I insist on it! . . . Do you understand? . . . I want to hear you say it to-day. It's absolutely necessary."

Chéri-Bibi was greatly embarrassed, but he gathered from the flash and fury in the eyes of this man that it was not the moment to thwart him, and dreading some mysterious scandal, he knew not what, he submitted, murmuring:

"No, no, I have forgotten nothing. . . ." And he hung his head, flung into consternation.

"Then hand me over a hundred louis, that will suit me better."

"A hundred louis? . . . Here you are. And, you know, if you want any more to keep away from here. . . ."

"Not a bit of it! I value above all your friendship," returned de Pont-Marie as he pocketed the two bank notes, "and instead of showing me the door, remember that we must meet frequently! My kind regards to the Marchioness. Tell her that I shall call and see her about two o'clock to-morrow or the next day."

He left the place whistling.

Chéri-Bibi sat at his desk in a state of stupefaction. It was thus that the Dodger found him.

"Well, that's another nice story! What can I have

been up to with that brute?" he asked as he folded his
arms.

"Nothing very seemly, that's certain," said the secretary in a diffident voice. "Monsieur le Marquis must
have had a riotous youth. . . ."

Chéri-Bibi did not see Cecily again during the day.
She sent him word that she was still indisposed and
begged him to excuse her. He bore the disappointment
patiently, hoping that the next day would set things
right; in other words, take him back to the point at
which they stood a few minutes before the hour fixed
for the duel when Cecily's attitude towards him gave
him every reason to hope.

But next day the Marchioness' indisposition continued. She did not leave her room: and in fact she was
feverish. Chéri-Bibi, who was admitted at the same
time as Bernard into the privacy of this elegant and
perfumed nest in which lay the being whom he most
loved on earth, was so moved that he did not know
what to say. He could mutter nothing but that they
must send for a doctor.

But Cecily set her face against it, declaring that
what she wanted was a little rest. Moreover, she could
not endure any doctor but Doctor Walter, an Englishman, who sometime before had settled in the district
and, as it happened, had left for Marseilles on the day
of the Marquis' arrival, in order to meet his wife
who was on her way home from the Indies.

This particularly clever man had managed in a short
time to acquire a practice among the principal families
in the district. The Dowager Marchioness had been
tended by him with incomparable skill and devotion,

and Cecily herself had nothing but praise for the accuracy of his diagnoses and his perfect tact.

Chéri-Bibi did not give ear to the eulogies which Cecily, with a view doubtless of having something to talk about—for she seemed not less perturbed than her husband—showered so lavishly on the doctor whom Chéri-Bibi thought that he "did not know from Adam." To his thinking Cecily's voice made sweet music, but so long as that voice did not utter the words, "I love you," the meaning of what she was saying was as indifferent to him as was Dr. Walter himself.

Meanwhile he watched her and the sight of her in a charming loose robe accentuated his memories of the night before and fired his imagination. Dark rings had formed round her great eyes from the fever and sleeplessness of two anxious and perhaps tearful nights, but she had never seemed so attractive to him nor so beautiful.

He diffidently and clumsily pressed a kiss upon her hand but she was all indifference.

He fled once more. *Fatalitas!* In the garden he again encountered the intolerable de Pont-Marie.

"The Marchioness is ill and it is impossible for you to see her, old man. She isn't receiving any one to-day," he said. But he had no sooner spoken than a lady's maid came up.

"The Marchioness hopes that M. de Pont-Marie will not leave without seeing her. She will receive him in a few moments in the drawing room."

Chéri-Bibi was struck like a statue. He could not say a word and silently his hand grasped a young elm and crushed it. De Pont-Marie had turned away and was slashing the grass with his stick. Chéri-Bibi ground his teeth and left him without committing the crime for which his fingers itched. He was never so crestfallen.

At the gate he met the Dodger who was beaming, for he had just returned from Dieppe where he had seen the handsome Virginie, the young waitress from the restaurant who had made from the first a great impression on him.

"Oh Monsieur le Marquis," he said full of his subject and failing to observe the agitation which shook his master from head to foot, "I can understand you now. What a splendid thing love is!"

"Are you in love my dear Hilaire?" asked Chéri-Bibi.

"I am indeed," returned the Dodger with enthusiasm, clasping his hands.

"If you're in love, poor fellow, a day will come when you'll know the pangs of jealousy. It is the most desperate of evils. It is consuming me. You see that man?"

"M. de Pont-Marie?"

"Yes. Well, I suspect him of being in the good graces of the Marchioness. But I want to be certain. He is to see her presently. I shall be glad if you will listen to them behind the door, and come back here to this path and tell me what they say. I shall be walking about waiting for you. Off you go!"

Hilaire bowed and left to carry out the order while Chéri-Bibi threw up his arms to the inviolable blue of the heavens calling for the storm. He was back again to the time when he longed to surround his actions with the tempest.

From the place where he stood he watched the entrance to the Villa. In less than a quarter of an hour he saw de Pont-Marie come out twirling his mustache with a sprightly air. The Dodger soon followed with a look on his countenance which to Chéri-Bibi's mind was pitiful. Doubtless he was the bearer of bad news and was already assuming a special face for the occasion.

Chéri-Bibi's heart throbbed wildly. As the Dodger drew nearer he put on an increasingly funereal expression. The other could not contain himself but made a few steps to meet him and before he came up to him cried in a choking voice:

"Well?"

"Well," returned the Dodger, ill at ease, "it was rather difficult to listen behind the door because I was in constant fear of being caught by the servants."

Chéri-Bibi seized the Dodger's wrist in an iron grip making him groan with pain.

"Tell me what you heard."

"Yes, yes," whimpered the Dodger, "but let me go. You're hurting me."

"Speak. . . ."

"De Pont-Marie is a blackguard. I didn't hear much, but he's a blackguard. . . ."

"Come to the point I tell you. I'm listening."

"Monsieur le Marquis, . . . he is playing you false."

"Oh!"

Chéri-Bibi flinched when the blow fell upon him and did not disguise his discomfiture from the Dodger who would have liked to prevaricate to avoid complications but lacked the courage. He was careful not to mention Cecily's name, but if de Pont-Marie were playing

him false it was with Cecily. That was a self-evident
truth which needed no demonstration.

Chéri-Bibi turned livid.

The Dodger, who feared lest he should straightway
breathe his last, murmured to himself, "Oh dear, oh
dear." Silently he followed his master who walked
with bent back, his legs shaking under him like a man
who had suddenly become twenty years older.

They continued their way until they came to the
beach and Chéri-Bibi dropped rather than sat upon a
rock. The sea was smooth; the sky cloudless; an ag-
gravating peace held sway over all living things.

"So she has a lover?" said the Marquis in a hoarse
voice.

"Why, yes," sighed the Dodger. "You see, you've
been away so long."

"Spare me your comments. Don't try to find excuses
for her if you don't mind. . . . She's a wretch!"

He gave full rein to his grief. The Dodger was not
unmoved.

"But I say what did you hear?"

"The servants were coming and going all the
time. . . ."

"Now don't start that over again. . . ."

"I couldn't hear more than two or three sentences.
He told her that he loved her. She was the dream
of his life . . . a lot of nonsense."

"What next?"

"Next it would be better perhaps if I held my tongue
for if I speak, which is unnecessary now that you know,
some great misfortune might happen."

"The greatest misfortune that can happen Dodger
is for you not to speak . . ."

Chéri-Bibi became so threatening that the Dodger began to quake.

"Monsieur, monsieur, we were so peaceful. . . . Yes, yes, I'll tell you. . . . He made an appointment with her. . . ."

"Oh! . . . When?"

"The day after tomorrow . . . in the afternoon," said the Dodger with chattering teeth.

"Where?"

"I couldn't hear where. . . . I tell you . . . I swear. . . ."

Chéri-Bibi glared at him with a fury which the poor fellow made no effort to withstand. He blurted out:

"The appointment is for three o'clock in the afternoon in a villa called 'Sea Mew' at Pourville. She promised to go. That's all. I don't know any more. I only just had time to get away after hearing that. . . ."

That very evening the Marquis du Touchais announced that he was obliged to go away for a few days. Of course he took his secretary with him. The second day after his departure a closed carriage was waiting for the Marchioness outside the Villa on the Cliff. She stepped in after wildly kissing her son without lifting the thick veil which concealed her pallor and despair.

The brougham put her down before the main door of a church in a narrow street in Dieppe, and drove off as soon as she had entered. However sincere and emotional her prayer may have been, it was none the less short, for a few minutes later the Marchioness left the church by a small door and turned to steps towards a closed motor car which was waiting for her a few yards away.

Cecily had no need to speak to the chauffeur for he at once set the engine going and drove off in the direction of Pourville.

The car and the unknown chauffeur, thus placed at the Marchioness's disposal, were a delicate attention from that perfect man of fashion the Vicomte de Pont-Marie. He had taken upon himself to settle the details of the proceedings so that Cecily's reputation might not suffer from an adventure into which he had driven her with a patience and determination which were now about to reap their reward.

At the time when he was looking for a chauffeur—who must be a stranger to the country—to drive his beautiful victim secretly to "Sea Mew," it so happened that by the good fortune which smiles only on lovers, a man came forward, whose master, a visitor to Dieppe, was away for a few days. De Pont-Marie thus had at his command motor car and chauffeur. The chauffeur's name was Cadol and, for a certain payment, he promised to act with discretion.

The car climbed the hill at Pourville at top speed but at once slowed down when it entered a private road leading to an iron gate which was open.

They drove into a courtyard and stopped at the front steps of a villa which stood in the heart of a little wood after the manner of a Swiss cottage.

The windows of the châlet were closed and the Venetian blinds drawn. It looked as if the house were empty. Nevertheless at the noise which the car made in drawing up alongside, the door was partly opened.

Cecily quickly alighted and mounted the steps excitedly, like a terrified animal that is being hunted down and is eager to rush into some dark hole and hide itself. Only she felt as if she were going to her doom.

She found herself in the partial gloom of a passage, dazed and with throbbing temples. A man closed the door behind her, took her cold hand in his and led her to the staircase. She allowed herself to be guided by him as in a dream, powerless to resist, faltering, leaning heavily on the arm which supported her and closed in upon her as on a prey. She was taken to a bedroom illuminated by candles in a sconce; like the lights which burn round the dead in daytime. It was a sinister, a dismal, a funereal sight. She started back in horror. The wretched man had not shown her the delicacy of first taking her to a drawing room or a boudoir.

"You are in your own house," he said.

He made a step to the door with the cynical remark that it would not be long before he returned. She called him back. She was stifling in that mortuary chamber. She leant for support against the dark wall. She asked for air. He moved his head to signify a negative. The room was closed and thick curtains were drawn across the windows. He did not explain, but it was easy to gather that he had taken every precaution to prevent a last resistance, a final revolt. He determined not to incur the risk at the eleventh hour that in her frenzy she might cry for assistance and be heard from the outside. And then, perhaps, he preferred to see his victim half-dead in this tomb.

"I am coming back. I will bring the letters. You understand," he said and left the room.

She sank on to a couch staring wild-eyed at the tragic setting, the ominous bed, the two pale lights reflected in the mirror, revealing the ghostly image of her ivory cheeks beneath the veil which she had raised to enable her to breathe.

She remained without moving until he returned.

Doubtless he hoped that confronted with the inevitable she would be eager to have done with it, and he would find her submissive. He could not repress a gesture of impatience.

"You are unreasonable," he said.

She turned her haggard eyes to him as if she were amazed to see him there, as if she had not expected to see him, as if she were asking herself: "What does this man want with me?"

"You are unreasonable, Cecily," he repeated. "I see that I've got to talk to you again although at the point at which we stand and to which you yourself are a consenting party, words between us are useless. But anyway make yourself at home. Take off your hat and veil if you don't mind."

He went up to her.

"Don't touch me. . . . Don't touch me," she cried.

She threw out her hands shaken by an uncontrollable tremor. The hardest heart might have been softened in pity of her. He was calm, sure of himself, almost cold in the presence of this woman whom he was torturing and whose sufferings he silently reveled in. Thus they remained for some moments. Only Cecily's quick breathing could be heard.

"Am I so distasteful to you?" he asked sneeringly.

She did not answer him.

"Why did you come?" he went on. "You ought not to be here if you don't want to save your son . . . your son's honor and good name. See, here are your letters."

She held out her hand with a fierce gesture and clutched the packet which he offered to her and allowed her to take. She gave a cry of triumph.

"You may count the letters," he grinned. "They are all there. When I make a promise I keep it. I am a man of honor. In view of the deplorable fluster in which I find you, I might have kept for my own purposes one of those scraps of paper in which you express, with so much enthusiasm, your secret joy in bringing up a child who hasn't a drop of the du Touchais blood in his veins, and consequently has a chance of becoming an honest man like his father Marcel Garavan. I might have torn out for my personal use, one of those pages in which you describe with so much discrimination the coming of those marks of resemblance in the child's features and ways which led you to say: 'He's the very image of his father. Don't let the Marquis du Touchais ever see you, my dear Marcel.' Nothing could have prevented me, after making a few extracts from those letters which were returned to you on the death of the worthy sea Captain, nothing could have prevented me, I tell you, from taking to myself a few loving lines —there are so many of them—written by your lover himself in which he celebrates the memory of certain exciting hours which you passed together."

He drew nearer and continued:

"Why do you hide your face? Why do you turn away? Don't be ashamed of having given a few hours of your unhappy life to love. It was your only consolation. I venture to hope that it will continue to be so, for as you may readily imagine, dear lady, it is not for a casual meeting that I have worked so hard to bring you here. We shall be lovers. I shall make you

love me, and though I have been rough with you, owing
to your unwillingness, I shall have time to show you
that I am a gentleman and you will forgive me. You
will see. . . . You will see. . . . So don't begin by
holding aloof from me. It's absolutely useless. You
belong to me . . . and will belong to me for a long
while, for as long as I like. You must resign yourself
to that. If you assume that because I have returned
those letters to you—all of them mark me—if you assume that because I have restored them to you, you
will be relieved of me, once the price has been paid, you
strangely misunderstand my character and the strength
of my love. I am not prepared to say good-by to you.
You don't know me!"

He paused for a moment after indulging in this
diatribe to enjoy in silence the effect that he had produced, and the fresh anxiety which he could read in
Cecily's expression, for since she had got back her
letters she was wondering in horror by what unsus-
pected and infernal artifice the miscreant proposed to
"hold" her for the rest of her life.

At length he condescended to show her the full extent of her misery.

"You have your letters but I have photographs of
all of them. So you understand that you will never
be set free and you have to buy, not a few scraps of
paper, but my silence. Come, Cecily, be reasonable
. . . and 'make yourself at home.' "

She lay in a huddled heap on the couch, more dead
than alive, unable to see any way of eluding her tormentor. She might go mad.

Passively and without moving as if she was unconscious of his presence she allowed him to take out the

pins from her hat, and to remove the hat and veil from her glorious hair.

It was then that her son's name slipped out from her colorless lips: Bernard. How dear he must have been to her! At that dreadful moment when the man's arms were already about her, there rose a vision of her son Bernard: the fruit of her sin. How bitterly she was to pay for that sin. And her punishment was only about to begin. It would be renewed whenever that man liked, whenever he held up a beckoning finger. Would that she were dead! Her death, alas, would avail her nothing, nor save the boy from the fate with which de Pont-Marie threatened him. Moreover he had charitably warned her that if at a time when she hardly knew what she was doing she endeavored to escape from him by such fatal means, he would at once furnish the Marquis with the proof that the boy was not his son.

Suddenly she gave a cry and slipped out of the arms that held her:

"No, no," she said in a stifled voice. "Not that, not that. Money, money. Any money that you want but not that. . . . My entire private fortune. . . . Anything you like but that."

"Oh," cried de Pont-Marie grinding his teeth in rage, for he had believed a moment ago that she was about to yield. "Oh, we're not going to have the whole thing over again. Money? You know that I don't need it. If I want any," he grinned in ominous fashion, "your husband will provide it! But as to you, I want you . . . yourself. What do you take me for, Cecily? You know very well that I don't mix up questions of money with questions of love. . . . I love you Cecily."

"Scoundrel!"

He drove her into a corner. His arms were about her. She struck him and slipped away once more. He rushed at her infuriated. She fell on her knees, raised her hands, and moaned:

"I'm not a bad woman."

"You lie," he threw at her, exasperated, his features inflamed. "You always have lied. You lied to your husband and everyone else. . . . You pretended to be a good woman and you were not so. If you don't stop this farce before the evening, all the world shall know the sort of woman you are. You have had one lover. You may as well have a second. The first step over, the rest is easy."

Still on her knees she clutched the hands that threatened her, and succeeded in placating his rage and in making him listen to her as, shaken with sobs, she tried once more to arouse his compassion. She told him a pitiful story and de Pont-Marie bent over her for a while to hear it.

She told him how it was that she had become Marcel Garavan's mistress, and of the frightful incident which preceded the one fault of her life. The Marquis until the famous night before his departure for Norway was her husband only in name. She had married him in obedience to her dead father's wishes and not because she loved him. The Marquis adhered to the conditions of this strange marriage though he attempted on more than one occasion to induce her to change her mind.

The Marquis' pride suffered a rude rebuff and he determined to take a mean revenge. The evening before he sailed for northern waters he administered a sleeping draught which placed her at his mercy. . . . And then he left her. Some days later Marcel Garavan arrived. She had always been in love with him. . . . Thus the Marquis' conduct has its sequel.

The cries, tears, entreaties by which the story of this disgraceful incident was accompanied did not move de Pont-Marie. He saw in the recital only another reason for carrying his passions to the bitter end.

"What you tell me," he said, "doesn't surprise me in the least. Your husband would stick at nothing. You were quite right to revenge yourself with Marcel Garavan, and now that Garavan is dead, you have only to revenge yourself on him once more with me! . . ."

She sobbed as if her heart would break. He took her in his arms again, and she gave herself up for lost when suddenly it was de Pont-Marie's turn to utter a cry of terror. His arms unclosed and Cecily sank to the floor. De Pont-Marie was being throttled by the grip of an iron hand. A man had jumped out of a cupboard like a jack-in-the-box and was quietly strangling the Vicomte. It was the terrible Chéri-Bibi. Cecily rose to her feet overwhelmed with horror, and Chéri-Bibi more from pity for her than mercy for the wretched de Pont-Marie spared his life but told him savagely not to cross his path again. He threw him out of the room with such violence that he fell sprawling down the stairs on his back making a considerable noise, so that Cadol, the chauffeur, who was waiting patiently in the courtyard until he was wanted, ran up to see what the trouble was. He pushed open the door—a sight witnessed by de Pont-Marie with consternation for he had himself locked it—and asked de Pont-Marie, who had picked himself up and was rubbing his sides, the cause of the disturbance.

Scorning to reply to the impertinent question, M. de Pont-Marie ordered the chauffeur to set his engine going at once, but the man replied, with the greatest coolness, that his master had just returned to Dieppe, and, as it happened, was in the house so that he could not take any further orders from his temporary employer.

"I am the Marquis du Touchais' chauffeur," he said.

That was enough for M. de Pont-Marie, who slunk away on foot, with rage in his heart, threats on his lips, meditating schemes of revenge.

Chéri-Bibi and Cecily were left upstairs face to face and looked at each other in silence, the former with eyes filled with the tenderest love and the latter showing signs of profound dismay. The Marquis' arrival, while it disposed of de Pont-Marie's hateful purpose, had by no means saved her. Far from it; for his intervention had acquainted him with a secret of which he ought to have remained ignorant throughout his life and to guard which Cecily had been on the verge of making the greatest sacrifice. The Marquis, hiding in the cupboard, had doubtless heard everything. He knew that Bernard was not his son. At the terrible thought that henceforth her son would bear the whole brunt of her sin she gave a sigh and fell in a dead faint.

When she came to herself she was in her own room in the Villa at Puys with her maids, her husband and her son standing round. The child, rejoiced to see his mother come to life again, heaped kisses on her. She returned his caresses in an unspeakable state of alarm.

She submitted to the attentions that were lavished on her but all the same dared not lift her eyes to the Marquis who spoke to her with a gentleness which unnerved her. In her innermost conscience she dreaded his attitude more than his anger or contempt or an immediate act of revenge. She knew the Marquis' immense pride, and did not question that he had already settled in his own mind the plan of the catastrophe which by inevitable necessity was about to burst over her. So much play-acting was only the forerunner of the greater display of cruelty. Apparently he had determined that she should completely recover her strength in order to bear the blow that he had in store for her. She gave a shudder.

"Are you cold?" asked Chéri-Bibi gently taking her hand.

She looked up at him this time.

Was it true that he knew nothing? Was it possible that he had heard nothing? She read in his face so much real kindness that she might well believe in his ignorance. She saw him kiss Bernard with such obvious affection that she was mistaken. But at the very moment when he kissed him he asked the boy to leave the room so that his mother might have rest, and he sent the maids away, and she was seized with a new terror. He remained behind. He wanted to be alone with her. What was about to happen?

He still held her hand which trembled in his while an unutterable anguish overspread her features.

"Cecily," said Chéri-Bibi in a deep voice, "I heard everything that passed between you and that man in the Villa at Pourville, but I swear to you on the life

of the boy whom I kissed just now, that I have decided
to let bygones be bygones."

At first she was at a loss. She did not understand
him. She was dazed by the shock of the tremendous
announcement. She had to repeat to herself his words
before hope dawned in her. The immensity of his forgiveness staggered her. When Chéri-Bibi saw her agitation he thought that she still doubted him, and he
did not hesitate to show her the full measure of his
generosity.

"You need not be afraid for yourself or our son.
I shall continue to love the child. He will still bear
my name. Bernard is innocent of the fault which it
would ill become me to reproach you with. The real
sinner is myself. After the manner in which I treated
you I deserve every misfortune, but misfortunes are
as nothing compared with the delight of seeing you
perfectly happy. You deserve to be happy."

While he was speaking Chéri-Bibi was good to look
upon. His eyes gleamed brightly; his expressive features were animated with the joy of sacrifice; the light
of a good action shed a crown upon him. He was no
ordinary man. It was as though he had really assumed the form of an ideal marquis who rose above
the prejudices of name and family pride, and consented,
in spite of the most deadly injury, to treat as a son
a child who was not his child. Not for a moment during this scene did he entertain the unworthy or base
thought that it was easy for him to be magnanimous
inasmuch as he had everything to gain and nothing to
lose, not even honor. Not for a moment did he say to
himself: "Whether the boy is the son of the Marquis
du Touchais or Marcel Garavan is a matter of indiffer-

ence to me since he is not my son." On the lofty pin-
nacle on which he stood he was, in very sooth, the
outraged husband who accomplished the superbly Christian act not only of forgiving the sin but of taking
under his protection the sinner and the fruit of the sin.

"You are splendid," cried Cecily, bursting into sobs.
And she threw her arms round his neck and drew him
to her heart which was at last his.

"True, I am splendid," thought Chéri-Bibi in the
delirium of his wife's first kiss; and he needed nothing
less than the consciousness of his greatness of soul to
prevent him from giving way to exaggerated demontra-
tions of gratitude for a love which had at length been
won after so long a pursuit.

Chéri-Bibi knew how to retain his magnanimity in
that supreme moment. He knew how to yield to love.
. . . The soft shadows of twilight fell over the happiness of that home. . . .

CHAPTER VI

THE following morning Chéri-Bibi was walking in his garden with an air which betrayed his satisfaction.

The Dodger came up to him and heard him talking to himself.

"What's the matter, Monsieur le Marquis? You're talking to yourself now."

"I'm in the mood to make it up with Providence. What splendid weather and how beautiful the world is under this azure sky, how sweet the flowers smell, how fresh and invigorating the morning air is, and how freely one can breathe facing this calm sea. I am a happy man, my dear Dodger, and I ask forgiveness of the good God for having ignored until today the greatness of his blessings."

"I love to hear you talk like that. I assure you that when I saw you start off for Pourville with that ominous look on your face, suggestive of the worst calamities, I thought it was all over with our safety and happiness. Fatality still pursues him, I said to myself, and will always pursue him. Chéri-Bibi is returning to a life of crime."

"I was going forward to love," replied the Marquis while he lifted his arms above his head corbel-wise in a gesture of enthusiasm which greatly impressed the Dodger. He drew still nearer and gazed at him with a

143

slightly impertinent curiosity and asked him with un-
compromising frankness:

"What is it that has changed you so?"

"I have changed because Cecily loves me, my dear
old Dodger."

In order to show his absolute and eternal friendship
the Marquis shook his secretary by the hand with a
warmth that crushed the poor fellow's fingers and
brought the tears to his eyes.

"You're hurting me," he ventured to whisper, his
face white with pain.

"That's a punishment, my dear Dodger, for the unfortunate habit you have of listening behind doors.
Apart from the fact that one doesn't do such things in
decent society, it leads you, as your hearing is bad, to
misunderstand what is said, and that is why I believed
for a moment that the Marchioness, who is goodness
itself, was in love with de Pont-Marie when, in fact,
she loathes him. Bear in mind once for all that the
Marchioness loves no one but me."

Chéri-Bibi's features were lit up with so much pride
and delight, and he was overflowing with such high
spirits, that Hilaire felt confident that his victory was
complete.

"I congratulate you," he said. "For that matter I
never doubted that you would win the day. Your
qualities . . ."

"I say, Dodger, you needn't pile it on too thick
you know. . . ."

"I assure you that I say what I think and that I
am far from expressing all the esteem and confidence
and . . ."

"All right. . . . All right. What about yourself,

Dodger? Are you satisfied? You mentioned a certain Virginie. . . ."

"Monsieur, I can tell you that it looks as if everything would turn out well. . . ."

"That's a good thing. I'm not selfish, and when I'm happy I like everyone around me to be happy too. And now be off, old man, because I see the Marchioness coming in her charming early morning dress."

The Dodger did not wait to be asked a second time but hurried away bowing from afar to Cecily who was coming down the front steps, a white and graceful vision on the threshold of that happy household.

Chéri-Bibi hastened to meet her, holding out both hands, a smile of welcome on his face.

Cecily, flushing slightly, bent her forehead towards him that he might kiss it, but Chéri-Bibi drew her to him and tried for a moment to hold her prisoner.

"Mind the servants, Maxime," she said gently.

"You are quite right," acquiesced her husband submissively. "Our happiness has nothing to do with anything or anybody and we must keep it to ourselves. Therefore to avoid the crowd, I propose, darling, after careful consideration, a little honeymoon. If we go among strangers and travel under another name, we shall be able to live for ourselves. No society duty will interfere with our enjoyment because for me, and I hope for you, we are like a young couple who were only married yesterday."

"I will do as you please, dear," returned Cecily with a sweet smile. "Wherever we may be, as long as I am with you I shall be the happiest of women."

They determined to go to Paris.

Chéri-Bibi began to show off and pretend to know

all about Paris. In his fear lest he might not be considered sufficiently the marquis, he exaggerated the pleasures of Paris, of those melancholy and fleeting joys to which he had submitted with indifference on his return from America, and of which he spoke, without suspecting it, like a provincial. The thing that saved him was that Cecily's mind was even simpler and less informed than his own.

In the train on their way to Saint Lazare, the great Paris terminus, Chéri-Bibi thought it well to return with a certain forced enthusiasm and what he deemed to be good taste, to the enumeration of the attractions that were in store for them, but Cecily nestled coaxingly up to him and said lifting her beautiful eyes to his:

"If Paris is going to take you away from me again, I shall never get over it."

"No more shall I," returned Chéri-Bibi, "because I assure you that I am tired of the empty life of a great aristocrat. So you have no cause to fear my love. There's no one in the world for Maxime but his Cecily."

Love delights in sweet nothings and in a form of speech which is all the more childish the further the lovers are from the days of the nursery.

The train arrived at its destination. First they went to the telegraph office and sent a message to the governess and the Dodger who had been entrusted, between them, with the care of young Bernard; and then they started on foot to see Paris, at Cecily's wish, for the idea of walking along the streets and stopping before the shop windows attracted her.

The first thing which Chéri-Bibi's eyes encountered as he stood on the asphalt of that Paris in which he had led so astonishing a life, was the omnibus-shelter in which Detective Inspector Costaud had so roughly tackled him in consequence of some, he knew not what, crime. He turned his head away.

They went up the Rue Auber and reached the Opera House which Cecily greatly admired under Chéri-Bibi's guidance, and he did not forget to mention that in the old days he had a box.

"We'll go to *Faust*," she said, "*Faust* at the Opera and *Œdipus the King* at the Comédie Française are what I want to see first."

"And then the Emperor's tomb," added Chéri-Bibi.

"You're making fun of me," said Cecily pouting. "I know that I'm not a Parisian but I'll become one if you wish it."

"Not I, my Cecily. Keep as you are. You're a dear, and the most beautiful, the cleverest and the best of women. Not for the world would I see you become like one of those dolls with whom I wasted the best years of my life. They've neither heart nor brains and spend their time changing their clothes and powdering their faces."

"What a miserable life," said Cecily.

"Yes, what a life for them and their husbands and their children if they have any. When I think of the way you have brought up our Bernard . . ."

"Our Bernard. . . . How good you are to me, Maxime."

"Well if I'm as good as all that, we'll see if there's a performance of *Faust* this evening, and if there is, you shall have your wish straightaway."

The Marchioness hummed the first two lines from the song in Margarita's garden:

Gentle flow'rs in the dew
Be message from me. . . .

It seemed indeed as if she were like a young bride easily and artlessly delighted in the veriest trifles, such as in a hat in a shop window which took her fancy, and which Maxime bought for her without haggling though it cost one hundred and fifty francs.

"What does the price matter since it suits you to perfection?" he said.

Faust was not in the bill for that evening, but they discovered when they reached the Place du Théâtre Française that they were traveling under a lucky star, for the advertisements at the Comédie Française announced for that evening *Œdipus the King* with the great Mounet-Sully in the title rôle.

Chéri-Bibi called a taxi.

"We will go back to our hotel to dress, dearest, and dine out, and then we'll go to *Œdipus the King* since you want to see this piece. Let the fun begin."

Chéri-Bibi had sent their trunks to the Grand Hotel in the Rue de Rivoli. He had engaged a suite of rooms whose windows fronted the gardens of the Tuileries. Cecily was enchanted.

"How pleasant are the trees, the foliage, the grassy slopes, the singing birds, the jolly shouts of children, after the din of the streets and the block of the traffic in the great crossroads," said Cecily. "One could imagine one's self in the country."

"Already," said Chéri-Bibi with a laugh. "Do you want to go back?"

"Not yet."

She put her arms round his neck and they forgot the country and the town in a kiss.

Cecily rang for the maid and Chéri-Bibi went into the sitting room. He picked up a paper that lay on the table and read:

"It is stated that twenty-eight healthy young women from the Departmental prison at Clermont have sailed for Cayenne. Some of them are strikingly handsome. It is proposed to marry them to convicts who have distinguished themselves by their good conduct. It is evident that since the affair of Chéri-Bibi the authorities at the penal settlements cannot do too much to make themselves popular with messieurs the convicts. Having learnt to their cost that iron bars mean little for such sturdy fellows, they intend to replace them by the softer chains of a compulsory but respectable marriage. Before he died Chéri-Bibi did a great deal for the hardened criminal. We hope that the latter in their gratitude when they have made themselves masters of our convict prisons, which under the present humanitarian system cannot be long delayed, will not hesitate to erect a monument to him in the public square in Numea in Cayenne."

Chéri-Bibi flung aside the paper with a gesture of disgust as the Marchioness opened the door of her room and gave him one of her sweetest smiles. She wore a light wrapper negligently thrown over her shoulders. Chéri-Bibi looked askance, but Cecily with a swift and graceful movement darted forward and picked up the newspaper and searched for the passage which was the cause of his ill-humor.

"It's nothing," he protested. "Please, Cecily, don't read it. Writers in these days have no brains, and

newspapers are driven to make a fuss about nothing
so as to fill their columns. Dress as quickly as you
can, for if you want to go to the theater we haven't
much time to spare."

But she would have her way, and she read the
paragraph. She, too, threw down the paper in horror.

"That name again," she cried. "I can't get away
from it; it follows me everywhere. In vain I try to
forget the monster who murdered my father and yours.
To think that I was nice to him when I was a girl
and treated him as a friend though he was only our
lodge-keeper's son. Oh, I should like to have my life
over again simply to wring his neck for him! What a
number of disasters we should have been spared! And
he wouldn't have terrorized the world."

Suddenly she went up to the Marquis who had sunk
back in a chair.

"What's the matter? How pale you are. Aren't
you well?"

"Give me a glass of sugared water," he murmured
with white lips. "I'm not feeling at all well."

"It's my fault," exclaimed Cecily in a distracted
voice, as she crushed a lump of sugar in a glass of
water, and with a trembling hand gave it to her im-
pressionable husband. "I ought not to have revived
those frightful memories. . . . How do you feel now?"

"I feel much better, but you see, dearest, whenever
any one speaks of Chéri-Bibi in my presence . . ."

"It shan't happen again, I promise you, Maxime.
Forgive me this time for recalling the past, as I forgive myself because I have at least had another proof
of your kindness of heart. Like a good son you are
fond of your parents."

"I am indeed," sighed Chéri-Bibi lifting his eyes to heaven.

"Well, if they can look down upon us now," said Cecily with quiet faith, "they must rejoice to see our happiness."

She bent over him to kiss him on the forehead and but for the impatience of the maid whose presence in the other room had been overlooked, they would have forgotten that time creeps on apace whether one laughs or cries or kisses or kills.

They entered a restaurant in the Boulevard des Capucines. The head waiter came running up and gave them a hearty welcome as he took them to a table "for Monsieur le Marquis."

Cecily as she left her cloak in the hands of an attendant, experienced a legitimate pride in being seen in the company of a gentleman "so well known in Paris"; while Chéri-Bibi feared some blunder on his part, and regretted coming to a restaurant where the head waiter appeared to know him so well while he knew so little of the head waiter.

The man's face beamed in a manner that filled him with uneasiness. His expression of satisfaction in seeing "Monsieur le Marquis" was dangerous because he talked so much. He inquired after the Marquis' health, lamented that he had not seen him for so many years, alluded to distant services, and dragged out from the dim recesses of the past the names of old friends and carouses which Chéri-Bibi heard of for the first time.

He determined to cut short the man's exuberance which, not without reason, he considered in bad form, and which was a torture to him because he felt some

difficulty in taking part in it, and he ended by saying
drily, at haphazard:

"That'll do, Henry, give me the menu."

The head waiter at once became serious and correct
and extraordinarily reserved, waiting for the order,
after however, remarking that his name was not Henry
but Emile.

There was an air of depression over them owing to
the frigid manner in which Emile—not Henry—hovered
round the table watching the service with a jealous eye.
It was as though he feared lest Chéri-Bibi should make
off without paying. The latter, perhaps, felt in-
tuitively as much; for he called for the bill without
waiting to order liqueurs and cigars.

He left prominently on a plate a "tip" which to his
mind was extravagant, but which was barely adequate,
and the harsh figure of the head waiter bent towards
him and he said in low tones:

"Monsieur le Marquis, I have not seen you for some
years, and you have apparently forgotten that you
owe me twenty francs."

Chéri-Bibi turned pale for Cecily had heard him.
Nevertheless without hesitation he put two fingers in
his waistcoat pocket and drew forth and threw down
a louis which Emile picked up with the remark:

"Thank you for the interest! Bring Monsieur le
Marquis's coat and hat. . . ."

Chéri-Bibi was furious. From pale he had become
white with rage, and he was glad to find himself in
the open air for he needed all his self-possession.

"The idiot borrowed money from servants," he could
not help exclaiming as he stood on the pavement.

"Whom do you mean, dear?" asked Cecily alarmed to see him in such a state of suppressed fury.

"Oh, a friend of mine whom I told to pay my accounts in town and who, as you see for yourself, has been unscrupulous enough to leave debts all over the place!"

"Good gracious, my dear Maxime, that's not very serious; and between ourselves you ought to have rewarded the head waiter's civility seeing that he did your friend a service, thinking he was doing it for you."

"The fellow didn't deserve a sou," said Chéri-Bibi emphatically. "And besides if I am generous and even extravagant"—an allusion to the hundred and fifty franc hat—"confiding and even unselfish, grateful and even self-sacrificing, I can very readily be economical and even parsimonious with servants who are only too eager to rob you. If needs be I can be resentful and spiteful and vindictive, and I can hate and lay traps and betray."

"You are libeling yourself," cried Cecily. "You have given me proof that you know how to forgive."

"You forgave me first, dearest," returned Chéri-Bibi pressing her arm.

"But in that case why do you use such terrible language? Whom do you hate? Whom do you want to be revenged on, and lay traps for and betray?"

He wiped the perspiration from his forehead. He was himself again.

"The friend who borrowed twenty francs from Emile as if they were for me."

"Well, Maxime, it all happened so long ago. Promise

me that if by chance you meet this old friend in Paris, he shall come to no harm."

"I can promise you that, and don't let my fit of anger upset you for the old friend is dead."

They reached the Place du Théâtre Français and as they entered the stately building were exchanging the prettiest speeches and the softest glances, entirely unconscious of the interested gaze of two persons who were the next to take a box at the box office and who, as if by chance, came face to face with them in the auditorium.

It was Cecily who first recognized them.

"Look," she exclaimed, "Monsieur and Madame d'Artigues."

"Where are they?" asked Chéri-Bibi suddenly remembering the society couple who had been introduced to him when he was Captain of the "Bayard."

"Don't you see them in front of us? They see us and are bowing. Acknowledge the bow, Maxime."

Maxime grudgingly bowed to them.

"I must tell you, dearest, that I don't much care for those people. There's been a coldness between us since our last voyage. They are annoyed with me and put down all their troubles to me, and I, for my part, have noticed that notwithstanding their society manners they are not quite what they pretend to be."

"I am very pleased to hear you say so, because I must confess to-day that I always had a feeling of repugnance when I received them at our table, but you brought them, and even in those days I had no wish to thwart you in anything. I tried to be as nice as I could to them."

"You are a model wife, Cecily. You are, shall I say, 'a saint.'"

"Saints wait for their reward until they go to Heaven," retorted the Marchioness quickly, "but I've had my happiness on earth."

She took his hand and pressed it fondly and he left his big paw in her little white perfumed glove and enfolded her with a tender look. He forgot all the d'Artigues in the world when the curtain went up on the tragedy of Œdipus:

> *My children, fruit of Cadmus' ancient tree*
> *New springing, wherefore thus with bended knee*
> *Press ye upon us. . . .*

He gradually became absorbed in the piece. The destiny which overhung the life of the son of Laius and Jocasta was familiar to him. He knew from his own experience how relentless fate could be with men. He knew that this was no story, no work of fiction, no figment of some poet's imagination. He loved and pitied Œdipus like a brother.

During an interval he left the box without saying a word to Cecily much to her astonishment.

He paced to and fro in the gallery of statues, and took a turn in the crush-room under the portrait of Voltaire, muttering incoherent words so that people near him looked at him as if he were out of his wits:

When he came back to the box Cecily said:

"M. d'Artigues has just left me. He was extremely amiable. You had better go to their box in the next interval and be polite to Madame d'Artigues. Tell them that we're only passing through Paris and are leaving to-morrow, and above all take care not to accept any invitation since you dislike these people as much as I do."

Chéri-Bibi nodded his head in acquiescence and became immersed in the terrible story of the Theban hero. The more the king was emmeshed in the deadly toils of disaster the more Chéri-Bibi's excitement increased. Occasionally he uttered exclamations in a muffled voice that surprised Cecily. He mumbled, "That's it. . . . That's it" with an approving gesture, and displayed so much emotion that the Marchioness was at first amused and at length touched.

She had to tell him more than once, at the end of the act, that it was his duty to pay his respects to Madame d'Artigues. He went to her box much against his will, determined to be so disagreeable and to show so little inclination to renew their relations, which worried him, that they would regard the friendship between them as definitely at an end.

When he entered the box Madame d'Artigues turned to him with a somewhat haughty demeanor and held out her hand like a queen condescending to a subject.

Chéri-Bibi was taken aback. He expected to find Monsieur d'Artigues with his wife but he had vanished. He recalled to mind the flirtation between the Marquis du Touchais and her which he had noticed on the "Bayard," and he regarded the position as somewhat disquieting. Unconsciously, perhaps, he had behaved like a "mug" to a woman of the world who seemed to him to have been on the closest intimacy with her dear Maxime, and Maxime had completely ignored her since his return to France.

She asked him to sit down and she stared at him in a peculiar manner through her lorgnette.

"It's very queer," she said, "but when I see you quite close I can hardly believe my eyes. From the distance it's you; when you are near, I have my doubts. Besides it's not the first time that you have produced this effect on me. When, in the end, we were able to see you on the "Bayard" after your illness, I found you, somehow, changed. I knew that an illness could alter a man but not to such an extent."

Chéri-Bibi listened to her in stupefied silence, his whole being demoralized. How unfortunate that his evil star should still pursue him, and at the beginning of his honeymoon, which in his dreams he pictured as a path bestrewn with roses and free from any unpleasant complication, he should come upon this crafty woman whose every word made him shudder!

Madame d'Artigues's eyes which he could discern behind her lorgnette frightened him. He who had braved the worst dangers, who had not feared to meet Cecily, asked himself, his heart rent with anguish, whether the miracle which had made him a marquis was about to lose its potence under her penetrating gaze.

She went on:

"You have changed completely for others as well as for me. As soon as you were able to get up from your sick bed on board the ship you shunned us. Why? What had we done to you? Were we not your principal victims? Had we not followed you through thick and thin? And when a certain person left you, did I not remain at your side, facing death with you? Oh, Monsieur I can never forgive your attitude towards

us . . . towards me. You left us to ourselves, you
sailed for Europe without paying any more heed to
us . . . to me . . . than if we had never existed. And
yet . . . and yet, Maxime, do you remember that terrible night, that last night, which we spent on the
'Belle of Dieppe' when she was but a wreck, and you
lamented that the Baroness Proskof had deserted you?
Who was it that comforted you?"

"Yes, yes I remember," whispered Chéri-Bibi anxious above all to check this exuberant flood of remi-
niscences. . . . And he thought: "Absurd! Here's
another to whom I owe gratitude and who won't leave
me alone until I have proved it to her." But in so
saying he began to "breathe freely" once more, because
those violent reproaches demonstrated that his secret
was safe; and he realized that his impression that she
was subjecting him to a dangerous scrutiny was false,
and came from the lorgnette that she still leveled at
him.

"Madame," he said, "I like you better without your
lorgnette."

She lowered it and condescended to smile at him.
Stranger still she placed her hand in his and bent over
him, but with the fidelity of a Hector and the purity
of a Joseph he started back. She gave expression to
her irritation.

"You are very particular."

"Upon my word," he said rising, "I believe that this
is the end of the interval and I must return to my
wife."

"Give her my kind regards," Madame d'Artigues
threw at him in exasperated accents. . . . "My dear
Maxime, you won't be astonished to hear that since you

treat me as a woman of no importance, I shall revenge myself like one. The Marchioness will, I am sure, read certain letters with great interest. . . ."

"What letters? . . . What letters?" stammered Chéri-Bibi.

"I say, you have a very short memory! . . . The letters you wrote to me on the 'Belle of Dieppe' when you promised to give up Baroness Proskof, and even to divorce your Cecily so as to marry Madame d'Artigues one day when she also was free."

"How complicated the brute's love affairs are," thought Chéri-Bibi with increasing rage and dismay. "I shall never manage to get out of them."

Madame d'Artigues observing his bewilderment went on pitilessly:

"Well, my dear man, if your memory is short your letters are long. Your wife will certainly be delighted to see what you thought of her in those days, how you appreciated her, and how you spoke of her. A woman can forget ill treatment, infidelities, humiliations, but there are certain things, little things, which she can never forgive. The most painful things are those which turn her into ridicule."

Chéri-Bibi felt that he was stifling. He drew back to a corner of the box. It seemed to him that the du Touchais family had no luck in the matter of letters.

"How much?" he said in a choking voice.

But Madame d'Artigues burst into a fit of laughter which set off her beautiful teeth. She realized that he was at her mercy and she pitilessly played with him.

"Good gracious, you have become very blunt, my dear Marquis," she said. "Have you forgotten that a present loses in value by the manner in which it is given? I decline your gifts unless you offer them with good grace. Wait a bit . . . there's the signal for the curtain to go up. Return to the Marchioness and say nice things to her on my behalf."

"When shall I see you again?" asked Chéri-Bibi in trepidation, humbly kissing the hand that she held out to him though he would have liked to bite it.

"This very evening."

"This very evening," cried Chéri-Bibi more and more perturbed. "This very evening. . . . But that's impossible. . . ."

"I insist on it," she replied stubbornly. "Charles and I are going to supper at the 'Abbaye de Bedlam.' There are still a few things I want to say to you which will not brook delay. Good-by for the present. . . . I am relying on you."

M. d'Artigues appeared, and Chéri-Bibi who had a wild longing to throw himself on the pair of them, and to reduce them to nothingness, hurried away, his ears buzzing, his temples throbbing, and his mind in a tumult.

He rejoined Cecily who was engrossed in the play.

The woes of Œdipus continued. And Chéri-Bibi could not help drawing a curious comparison between the fate which had so relentlessly stricken the hero of ancient times with the fate which pursued him even in that theater.

After all, what were the crimes of Œdipus who had killed his father and married his own mother, in ignorance of his parentage, beside the innumerable crimes of Chéri-Bibi all of which had sprung one from the other, and all of which were the consequence of a generous action—the action of killing Cecily's father when he was in reality trying to save him? And now when he believed that he had at length shaken off the necessity of committing crime—after taking another man's skin—calamity was prowling anew round him, was stealthily preparing its blows, and was lifting up before him its hideous blood-stained face.

Chéri-Bibi crushed the shelf in the box on which Cecily had placed her opera glasses, her wrist bag and the trifling odds and ends which a beautiful woman is never without. He had to wreak his passion on something.

The shelf gave way. The things which lay on it fell with a clatter. Cecily uttered an exclamation. The audience moved restlessly in their seats. There was a general protest. At that moment Œdipus, who had put out his eyes, was descending the steps of the temple, his blood-stained hands stealing over the young and innocent faces of Eteocles and Polyneices.

The scene itself, the excitement in the house, Cecily's exclamation, the fury that possessed him, all contributed to make Chéri-Bibi lose his head, and in a savage gesture pointing to the son of Laius, forsaken of the gods, he cried: "There's a man after my own heart! . . . A man after my own heart!"

The Marchioness, filled with dread, thinking that her husband had suddenly taken leave of his senses, implored him to be calm, and placing her trembling arms about him, defended him from two policemen who had come up, intending to eject the person who had created the disturbance.

"All right, all right. Don't make a fuss," said Chéri-Bibi. "We're going. And whatever you do, don't touch me. I am the Marquis du Touchais."

The policemen when they heard the title bowed respectfully like good republicans.

Chéri-Bibi helped the Marchioness with her cloak, put on his own overcoat, and left the theater with dignity while regretting, within himself, that he had not been able to maintain his composure. Persons near him muttered "The man's mad," loud enough for Chéri-Bibi to hear, but he turned a deaf ear to them, and hastened to assist Cecily who was trembling like a leaf into a taxi.

As soon as he had given the address to the driver and they were alone, the Marchioness burst into a fit of sobbing. Chéri-Bibi put his arms round her and said:

"Don't worry, dearest. I had a nervous attack. I have often had these attacks since that dreadful experience in the Malay Archipelago, but as you see the attack is soon over. I have not suffered from them for some eighteen months. As a matter of fact the doctors whom I have consulted assure me that in course of time I shall be free from them. Don't let them interfere with our happiness."

"I was dreadfully alarmed," said Cecily who had indeed feared for her husband's reason.

When they reached the hotel she was the first to insist on the necessity of rest. Chéri-Bibi was as quiet as a lamb, and allowed himself to be put to bed and tucked in like a child. But at midnight he clandestinely left his room, and did not return to the hotel until daybreak.

When Cecily saw him in the morning his features were still distraught but he wore a look of satisfaction.

"It's very strange," she said, "you look ill and yet pleased with yourself."

"Well, dearest, if I look ill it is because the air of
Paris doesn't agree with me, and if I look pleased it is
because, with your permission, I have decided to go
elsewhere."

"We ought not to have left Dieppe," sighed the
Marchioness.

"Let us go back home," exclaimed Chéri-Bibi.

It did not take them long to pack up. As they left
the hotel a newsboy passed them shouting:

DOUBLE MURDER IN THE ISLE DE PUTEAUX
TRAGIC DEATH OF M. AND MME. D'ARTIGUES

The Marquis and Marchioness uttered a simultane-
ous cry of horror. Their eyes fell on a few lines in
the stop press news:

"It was at first thought that M. and Mme. d'Artigues
had met with an accident and were drowned last night
in crossing the Seine to reach the Isle de Puteaux
where they owned a lodge which was the scene of considerable hospitality . . . but an examination of the
bodies shows that both of them were the victims of a
terrible aggression. Their throats bear the marks of
strangulation. It is supposed that the motive of the
crime was jealousy or revenge. . . ."

"Oh this Paris, this Paris," cried Chéri-Bibi. "I
shall never set foot in it again. One day you meet
your friends in the best of health, and the next day
nothing remains of them, but an article in the newspaper which shows disgrace upon them!"

Cecily shuddered, struck dumb with terror.

"To Dieppe. . . . To Dieppe," cried Chéri-Bibi,
"and at top speed."

CHAPTER VII

CHÉRI-BIBI was a father. It was an event which was received with great joy. Though it was notorious in Dieppe and the district that since his return from his adventure the Marquis du Touchais did not "throw his money about," there was, on this occasion, a great distribution of alms to the poor. The Dodger's salary was doubled. Happy Chéri-Bibi! Happy Dodger!

In brief, they were living in an earthly paradise. No cloud seemed to threaten their security. De Pont-Marie had disappeared from their horizon. They loved and were loved. Virginie had not been able to resist the Dodger's blandishments. The two men allowed themselves to be pampered and made much of by their women folk, and they lazily enjoyed life.

They discussed the causes of happiness among mankind. Often as they breasted together the hill at Le Pollet, they conversed like wise men. Chéri-Bibi had changed mentally as well as physically. And now the transformation was complete. He knew that he was handsome, strong, rich. Thenceforward he became kind-hearted while husbanding his fortune which is the acme of wisdom. His case does not prove that all men who are handsome and strong and rich are kind-hearted, but it does prove that his former wickedness was but an accident. It was an argument that satisfied him

164

whenever his thoughts recurred—which was as seldom as possible—to certain events of the past for which he desired to discover some excuse.

On one occasion Chéri-Bibi stopped the Dodger outside a fisherman's modest cottage. It was evening. The man had returned from his arduous labor and was smoking his pipe on the doorstep while his wife was mending the nets, and their children were playing in the gutter.

"Look at that picture," he said. "Those people are poor but honest. They are happy. Money might ruin them. Don't seek any other explanation, Dodger, of what, out of politeness, you call my economy. Nothing pleases me better than to assist 'those who are in need,' but you must prove to me first of all that they do need something."

Thus in philosophizing they reached the Villa on the Cliff. And Chéri-Bibi caught sight of a white veil which Cecily was waving and he hastened his steps.

"She's waiting for me, the dear girl."

She was waiting for him with her latest born in her arms, and the meeting of father, mother, and son was a moving sight. It was a moment for affectionate kisses, and the pleasing joys of family life.

Chéri-Bibi's heart melted in the warmth of that delightful hearth. The Dodger's eyes were bedewed with tears. Young Bernard, an adorable rascal who was up to all sorts of mischief, lent an air of gaiety to the rustic scene. His "father" spoilt him, for he could refuse none of his whims, and the little fellow played the tyrant in the house, while Cecily, realizing more every day her husband's perfect behavior towards the boy who occupied a place to which he was not entitled, felt her love increase for the extraordinary man who had once made her greatly suffer, but who now gave her unhoped for cause of rejoicing.

She was naturally anxious, now that happiness had so bravely and unexpectedly entered under the conjugal roof, that the child should be baptised in the name by which she herself called the Marquis. But by a strange obstinacy the Marquis set his face against the name of Maxime, and the child was christened Jacques. He declared that, to his thinking, it was a nice name; and the Dodger who was fully aware of Chéri-Bibi's real name surpassed himself in dilating on its charm. Cecily gave way, and Jacques was now a lusty baby of three months old who bore no greater resemblance to his father than his brother did.

It was impossible to recognize any trace of the Marquis in him, but there was a certain harshness in his features, unknown in the family, which delighted Chéri-Bibi whilst it somewhat alarmed the mother. He was not easy to please, the imp! He already showed that he had a will of his own.

Chéri-Bibi no longer uttered the word *Fatalitas*. And he was inclined to think that, in the main, men were impatient beings who did not allow divine wisdom time to counterbalance the bitter experiences through which it pleased Providence that they should first pass, in order that when a definite share of pleasure was bestowed on them, they might appreciate all the more, by contrast, the blessings of earthly happiness.

"When you marry Virginie I shall make you a present of ten thousand francs," said Chéri-Bibi to the Dodger.

"Oh Monsieur le Marquis, you are a better man than

any of us. . . . You are quite right. Virginie is in love with me and I am with her. I had hoped to make a good marriage. But why should I seek riches when I can find happiness? One must not be too ambitious."

"Well done. I like to hear you talk like a decent fellow. A good marriage! Whom did you expect to marry! . . . Don't forget that I raised you from nothing. . . . You were a baker's man and I made you secretary to the Marquis du Touchais."

"I shall always remember it, Monsieur le Marquis, always. So I'll be off and tell Virginie the good news. As it happens it will come at the right moment, for she's leaving the restaurant in the harbor to-day or to-morrow. The new proprietor, it seems, is bringing a new staff."

"Is the restaurant always changing hands?" asked Chéri-Bibi who recollected that the Dodger had told him about a year ago that M. Oscar was giving it up.

"They've been waiting a year for the new proprietor. He was to have come in between one day and the next, and that's been going on for a year. . . . It beat's everything! . . . During this time a chap from Paris has been running the show with the help of Virginie. . . . Luckily for him, the manager had to do with an honest girl for he knew nothing about the restaurant and café business. And to show his gratitude to Virginie he has given her the sack."

"You can bring her here and she can enter our service to-morrow," said Chéri-Bibi.

"Oh Monsieur le Marquis!"

"That's all right, you can thank me some other time, you rotter."

"Let me shake hands with you."

"Well, shake hands. And whatever you do, always try to be a decent fellow. It is the best way to be happy, Dodger."

Hilaire left the Marquis and hurried to Dieppe, tearing down the hill at Le Pollet, and reaching the bottom out of breath and bathed in perspiration. When he got to the bridge he was almost run over by a carriage which was going at a smart pace towards Puys.

It was a private carriage, a fashionable buggy, driven by a man who inveighed against the incautious Dodger in somewhat rough language.

The Secretary started at the sound of that voice and looked round. But the little turn-out had passed him with the speed of a train.

"What a brute!" muttered the Dodger.

A man standing on the pavement who witnessed the incident came up to him.

"I say, you had a narrow escape. He's in a hurry, is Dr. Walter," observed the chance wayfarer in whom the Marquis' secretary recognized Detective-Inspector Costaud of the Criminal Investigation Department.

Hilaire bowed and shrugged his shoulders without replying. He was not fond of talking to gentlemen of the police in general nor with Costaud in particular whose face had never possessed any attraction for him.

Five minutes later he pushed open the door of the restaurant, and was welcomed, half laughing and half crying, by the handsome Virginie who beckoned him to sit in a corner near the cash desk.

She was as rosy as a bunch of cherries, her hair was rumpled and her cap awry, and she confided to him, out of breath, that she had had a passage of arms with the new proprietor who had just arrived.

She had managed to make him keep his distance, and had demanded the amount due to her, and she was waiting for the fellow to come down from the first floor where he had gone to obtain the money with which to pay her.

"I am very glad that I'm leaving," she said, "because that man frightens me. He's like a barrel in appearance, and pierces you with his little weasel eyes. To look at him you can't tell if he wants to laugh at you or murder you. When he comes near you, you instinctively draw back as you would from a wild animal. When I saw that he wanted to kiss me, I gave a terrified cry and struck him. I thought he was going to kill me. And then he laughed in an ominous manner."

As Hilaire listened to the story he was filled with righteous indignation.

"I've come in the nick of time," he said gravely. "First of all, Virginie, I have a piece of good news for you. I'm going to marry you. The Marquis has promised to give us ten thousand francs to enable us to set up housekeeping. You will be lady's maid to the Marchioness who is one of the best. We shall be nicely settled for the rest of our lives."

"Good gracious, you don't mean to say so," cried Virginie who when she heard of her unexpected good fortune changed color; that is to say her face which was as rosy as a bunch of cherries became as white as an orange blossom.

"To show you that I mean it, I'm going to take you away at once, and woe betide the wretch who dares to insult you. I shall be man enough to see that you are respected. And, as a start, you shall see how I deal with the proprietor. Have you packed up your trunk?

Then go and do it, and have it brought down by the scullery maid. I shall stay here and give that blackguard a piece of my mind."

"Oh, my dear, whatever you do, be careful. He looks a man that would stick at nothing. Wait until we get outside before you tell him what you think of him," advised the prudent Virginie.

"Don't be afraid. I don't want you to tell me what I must and must not do. I'll teach that barrel how to behave to respectable girls even if I have to tap him!"

Virginie went off quickly to fetch her trunk and almost at the same moment the proprietor appeared at the other end of the café. The light from the door fell upon him and Hilaire was able to see his full face.

Hilaire, who was seated, rose in the air as if he were propelled by some mechanical device and fell back in his seat an inert mass. The newcomer, who had observed his peculiar movement, did not seem to be unduly astonished. He continued to roll his pot-belly towards his only customer, and when he came up to him held out a short arm at the end of which was a horribly flabby hand.

"Good morning, Dodger," he said. "How are you, my boy!"

"Little Buddha!" the Dodger gasped.

"Yes, my dear Dodger, Little Buddha himself at your service, what? You've lost your tongue. You're surprised to see me here. Still you knew that the dream of my life was to keep a wine shop. Well, here I am. What is a poor man to do? At my time of life one begins to have had enough of adventures. I've roamed about the world too long, and I want to settle down.

Now I am a respectable tradesman like any one else. And you, Dodger, are things as well with you as you hoped?"

The hapless Dodger did not know what to do with himself, and was cursing the moment which had brought him face to face with one of the witnesses of the sorry past, and he could only murmur:

"I thought you were dead."

"You had every reason to think so old man," returned Little Buddha, slipping a stool underneath him and seating himself beside the Marquis' secretary. "I must say that some of my best friends and I did our utmost to spread that belief generally. It was the wisest thing to do. Didn't you yourself change your name when you followed the fortunes of the Marquis du Touchais? And yet you had never, as far as I know, come into conflict with the police of your country, nor of any other. Still your friendship with the late Chéri-Bibi and the rather important part that you played in the mutiny of the 'Bayard.' . . . Eh? . . . What's that? . . . You want me to shut up. . . ."

"Hang it all," groaned the Dodger distractedly, "I should much prefer you to talk about something else. . . ."

"There's nobody here to overhear us," went on Little Buddha imperturbably. "So calm yourself. I have as much interest as you in not wishing to rake up the ashes of the past! The only person here is M. Bénevent—Jean Charles Bénevent—a respectable proprietor of a restaurant and café who is going to do himself the pleasure of offering a liqueur brandy to his old friend M. Hilaire, secretary to the Marquis du Touchais. You see I know all about you. And I'm telling you all about myself so as to prevent any possibility of error. . . .

"So make your mind easy, Monsieur Hilaire. Don't pull such a long and dismal face. We are bound to get on well together. I know that you would rather I had actually departed this life than have a drink with me. . . . But it can't be helped. Chance led me to buy this business, pure chance for which I am very thankful, since it brings me into touch with so true a friend. . . ."

Little Buddha, as we have already remarked, was at one time clerk to a sheriff's officer, and even after his trip to a convict settlement had not lost his habit of choosing his language. . . . "Well, here's to you. Dodger. . . . Just try this old brandy. Why, you're not going to be ill, are you, old man?"

"No, no. . . . I can't get over my surprise . . . astonishment. . . . You see . . . I never expected . . ."

"Of course you weren't prepared for it. . . . Well, is the governor keeping fit?"

"Quite fit . . ." sputtered the Dodger almost choking from a drop of brandy that had gone the wrong way.

"He's a decent fellow. Personally I like him very much. I owe everything to the Marquis. It's with my share of the proceeds that I've come to take up my quarters here, while the others fellows are squandering theirs down China way. As for myself, I've nothing but good wishes for the Marquis. . . . No need to tell him so, is there? . . . I'm not asking you to let him or any one else know of my arrival in these parts."

"Look here," said the Dodger with a perplexed look. "There's one thing that I don't understand. . . ."

"What's that, my boy? Perhaps I shall be able to enlighten you. . . ."

"Well, it's this: How is it that you've come to this part of the country where you were sure of meeting people who would recognize you?"

"Don't talk nonsense! Recognize me! Why, everyone thinks that I'm dead. First of all I hardly ever saw your Marquis. . . . And then there's every chance that he won't come to lunch here. . . ."

"All the same you've got a cheek, Little Buddha."

"Certainly I've always had plenty of cheek."

"Aren't you up to some mischief?"

"I'm settling down I tell you."

"You bought this place more than a year ago. Why haven't we seen you until to-day?"

"I'll tell you. . . . I thought that my death was a little too recent to set up as a respectable man. So I had one more year in the grave . . . and let my beard grow. . . ."

"That didn't prevent me from recognizing you at the first glance."

"Because you're fond of me, Dodger."

And Little Buddha clinked glasses with the Dodger and laughed ominously.

Just then Virginie came into 'the room with her trunk. She saw her intended husband in the act of drinking with the man who had behaved so grossly to her a little while before. She was taken aback and stood swinging her arms. At last she was able to say in an angry voice:

"Monsieur Hilaire, I wonder how you dare . . ."

"What. . . . What's the matter, my girl?" growled Little Buddha.

But Hilaire, who had turned pale, had already risen and he said in an agitated voice:

"Monsieur Bénevent, let me introduce you to Mlle. Virginie, my future wife."

"Oh really," returned Little Buddha. "I congratulate you. She's a superior woman, and I'm very sorry that she is already engaged or I should have offered her my hand!"

"I gave you my hand across your face, you old rascal."

"Don't you worry, I haven't forgotten it," replied Little Buddha, with a crafty and threatening look which made the Dodger shudder. "Come, my beauty, how much do I owe you?"

He settled the account, and asked her not to bear him any malice; and he forced the Dodger to have another drink with him while he sent for a conveyance to take the trunk, and stood in the doorway indulging in cynical and facetious remarks as Hilaire and Virginie disappeared in the direction of Le Pollet.

Virginie was incensed. Her future husband had not shone in the incident, and she threatened in the face of such cowardice to "go home to her mother."

To her great surprise Hilaire, who up to that moment had kept silent, recovered the use of his tongue, and told her that he entirely agreed with her, and that an immediate visit to her parents who lived in the neighborhood could not but do her good, and afford her a much needed rest before she entered upon her new duties. She left him in a state of intense annoyance, unable to understand what had happened.

The Dodger was no sooner alone than he ran like a madman until he reached the hill at Puys. Every now and then he stopped to take breath. He passed his fingers through his hair and quivering with emotion cried:

"It was too good to last, it was too good to last. Hang it all, what is the man doing here? What will Chéri-Bibi say?"

Then he started off again. When he reached the Villa on the Cliff he was told that the Marquis was out. His mother, the Dowager Marchioness, whose illness, it seemed, had taken a less favorable turn had sent for him.

CHAPTER VIII

CHÉRI-BIBI AT THE BEDSIDE OF HIS MOTHER, THE MARCHIONESS

It was not without certain trepidation that Chéri-Bibi proceeded to visit the old lady. It was to be his first interview with her. He had always dreaded to meet her.

The Marchioness, with the obstinacy of old people who are slow to forgive insults to their gray hairs, had hitherto refused to see her son, although after the departure of the "Belle of Dieppe," he had allowed her once more to take up her residence at the Château du Touchais in which she desired to end her days. Nor had she yielded to the entreaties of her daughter-in-law who represented to her that Maxime had completely changed in character, and that the change was all to the good.

Even when Jacques was born she refused to be moved by Cecily's appeal on his behalf.

"Later on," she said, "we will see if he is deserving of our compassion. Experience will teach us what value to attach to the fine sentiments of which you speak, but in which I cannot yet believe. It is impossible for me to forget, all at once, that he turned me out of my home."

"You are back again in it," Cecily reminded her.

"Only until it pleases him again to install here one

176

of those creatures," returned the Dowager with a harshness that struck a chill in her daughter-in-law's heart.

The truth was that the old lady was waiting for her son to take, by a spontaneous impulse, the step that was due to her after the affronts of the past, and to attempt, in person, a reconciliation in which she saw him at her feet, pleading forgiveness for the sins of his youth.

So long as he himself had not made up his mind to undergo this essential humiliation, she was inclined to think that Cecily had mistaken her husband's true feelings. And since Chéri-Bibi was in no hurry to fall at the Dowager's feet, but on the contrary shirked every opportunity of meeting her, the position had remained unchanged during the last year.

The Marchioness must have been really ill that day for Cecily to have sent word to her husband to come to the Château du Touchais. Chéri-Bibi sauntered very slowly to the stately home of his ancestors. He recollected reading stories in his youth in which mothers who were blind made no mistake about the identity of their children. Though he impersonated the Marquis du Touchais with great success he was, perhaps, not sufficiently the Marquis to deceive the perceptions of an old mother.

Nevertheless he could not avoid the test. He consoled himself with the reflection that if the Marchioness were the first to detect the incredible phenomenon, she would straightway be treated as out of her senses. Moreover he had confidence in his lucky star which, during the last year had shone in the firmament of his life with great and splendid brilliance. And it seemed

to him that his hopes were well founded, for he met
Sister St. Mary of the Angels who was on her way
to fetch a priest, and she cried:

"Be quick, Monsieur le Marquis. The Marchioness
is sinking. She is unable to recognize any one now."

"It's just as well," thought Chéri-Bibi.

He gave the nun a charming smile and she fled as if
she had seen an evil spirit.

He entered the drawing room without meeting a
servant, but almost immediately afterwards he was
joined by Rose, the Dowager's elderly companion, who
was as pale as her dying mistress must have been.

Whenever he saw Rose, Chéri-Bibi could not help
thinking of the story that his sister had told him on
the "Bayard." He said to himself: "Rose knows
everything. It is through her that we shall know one
day who murdered the old Marquis. It is through her
that I shall know one day who the man in the gray
hat is, the man who before he killed the Marquis with
Chéri-Bibi's knife, threw old Bourrelier over the cliff
after seizing the knife which poor Chéri-Bibi had un-
intentionally driven into his back!" Such were Chéri-
Bibi's thoughts whenever he encountered on the road
near Puys the enigmatic form of Rose who invariably
retreated when she caught sight of him.

It was through her that he hoped to be revenged one
day on the unknown individual who was the original
cause of his misfortunes. The reason why he had
not hitherto pursued that object with greater per-
sistence was that his perfect happiness as the new
Marquis du Touchais, had relegated to a second place
his scheme of revenge as Chéri-Bibi. He at once took

a step towards Rose who shrank back uttering an exclamation.

"What's the matter with you," he asked. "Are you afraid of me?"

Rose's pallor had increased, if that were possible, and trembling from head to foot she said without answering his question:

"Dr. Walter wishes you to go up at once to the Marchioness' bedroom. He hopes to save her life, but she must not undergo any excitement."

The few simple words were spoken in an almost inaudible voice, and she leant for support against the furniture as she crept from the room after casting a peculiar look upon Chéri-Bibi.

"There's another who will never forgive the Marquis' evil deeds," thought Chéri-Bibi. "Certainly I shall have to lead an exemplary life if I am to wipe out his sins. But I feel that in Cecily's love I have the strength of a saint, and I shall win Rose over like the others. I have nothing to ask from Providence to-day but that Dr. Walter should not restore my honorable mother to too great a clearness of mind."

Deep down within himself, he cursed the return of that confounded doctor whom he did not know, who had left the place at the moment when he himself had arrived, and appeared on the scene in time to perform the miracle of saving his mother's life when her departure to another world would have solved his difficulties.

But he would have been ashamed to acknowledge such a thought. It was unworthy of the husband of Cecily. He strode up and down the room resigning himself to the play of that good fortune which had been spoiling him for so long.

With his hands behind his back he sometimes stopped to take a long look at an old painting. The portraits of several of his ancestors hung on the walls. He was not sorry to make their acquaintance. He smiled or groaned at them as their faces pleased or displeased him. And thus he arrived before the portrait of his "father," the Marquis du Touchais who was supposed to have been murdered by Chéri-Bibi.

He could not repress an exclamation.

Under the portrait, fixed to the frame, was a velvet case in which, held in place by gold wire, was the knife, the butcher's knife, which had dealt the fatal blow. The Dowager Marchioness had obtained it, and brought it with her when she returned to the Château.

Chéri-Bibi recognized the knife. It was indeed his knife, the deadly weapon whose discovery had brought him to the Assize Court and secured his conviction for murder.

Stains of rust had not been removed from the steel, and these were the stains of the Marquis' blood. What memories were associated with the tragic object! How the past flashed before Chéri-Bibi!

His eyes were rivetted on the knife when the servant came to take him to the bedside of the sick woman.

He had the consolation of learning from the servant that the Marchioness was worse in spite of Dr. Walter's efforts.

When he entered the softly and dimly lighted room he saw Cecily on her knees by the bedside. Rose was standing near the doctor at the foot of the bed, and the

Marchioness seemed to be already sleeping her last sleep.

The lady's companion was weeping quietly with her handkerchief before her eyes. As to the doctor, he was watching the patient in silence, as if he expected some result which had not come to pass.

The doctor was a somewhat tall, thin, youngish man of English appearance, with clean shaven upper lip and sandy colored side whiskers. He paid no attention to the entrance of Chéri-Bibi.

Chéri-Bibi, thinking from the awful silence that the Marchioness was all but gone, and consequently that he had nothing to fear, threw himself on his knees beside Cecily, took the Marchioness' hand that lay on the bed, pressed a filial kiss upon it, and in a broken voice said:

"Mother!"

It was as though the inanimate figure was only waiting for that word to come to life again, for she heaved a deep sigh, opened her eyes, fixed them on her son, and recovering her forces which seemed to have ebbed away forever, she withdrew her hand, and pointing to the door said with a sigh:

"Go!"

Dr. Walter's voice was at once heard.

"Her life is saved," he said.

When the Marquis heard those words which ought to have filled him as a son with joy, he raised his head in dismay, and wild-eyed, stared at the man standing at the foot of the bed, while his lips murmured to himself in unspeakable horror.

"The Kanaka!"

And Chéri-Bibi fell in a dead faint like an ordinary mortal.

CHAPTER IX

A PASSING SHADOW

WHEN Chéri-Bibi came to himself in an adjoining room where he had been carried, he observed that he was being tended by Dr. Walter, and that Cecily was bending over him with a face of wild anxiety. But it was not Cecily's face that concerned him. It was the face of the ghost, of the man who knew his terrible secret, the man to whom he owed everything, and who might ruin everything, the man from whom he believed that death had relieved him.

It was the Kanaka right enough, it was the Kanaka right enough.

Neither the new color of his hair nor his sandy whiskers could deceive him. He recognized him beyond the shadow of a doubt. He recognized his nose, his ascetic profile. He recognized his lackluster, cold, blue eyes; and still more the voice which had encouraged him on the "Bayard" to undergo the frightful suffering which had transformed a Chéri-Bibi into a Marquis du Touchais.

What, by all the gods, was going to happen? What did he want? Why had he returned?

Alas, was it not quite obvious? It was only too easy to imagine his object. He was about to extort hush-money. What amount would he require? It might be one, two, three or four million francs. And afterwards

182

there would be other demands, still further demands, until Chéri-Bibi was ruined. What could he refuse a man of his caliber? Nothing. The Kanaka had only to open his mouth and Chéri-Bibi was done for. There would be no more Marquis, no more riches, no more Cecily. And his own son would be doomed to everlasting shame. His happiness would be a thing of the past.

His good fortune had not lasted long. Providence had not spoilt him for long. The counterstroke had soon fallen.

Fate was bearing down anew on the unfortunate Chéri-Bibi with a terrible weight that nothing, no human force, could resist. *Fatalitas! Fatalitas* in all its hideousness had reappeared.

The doctor had but to take off Chéri-Bibi's coat and turn back his shirt in order to disclose the chest and that part of the skin on which those indelible marks of his infamy and crimes were tattooed, those marks which the doctor had known how to preserve so that he might continue to hold him in his power, to make him his tool, his slave. Oh the misery of it! In truth there are people in this world who have more than their share of bad luck.

Chéri-Bibi instinctively turned his eyes to his chest and he perceived that his shirt still covered his "birth certificate." It was clear that the doctor had no interest in bringing about his immediate downfall.

The Kanaka had merely taken off his collar and partly opened the neck of his shirt. Chéri-Bibi let his gaze stray to the man with the sandy whiskers who was making him inhale smelling salts. The doctor's face still wore a smile, and the calm indifference with which he expressed himself, the quiet movements with which

he tended the poor being who in a moment had become
Chéri-Bibi again, far from rendering him easy in his
mind, caused him to shudder to the very marrow.

"There, that's over," said the doctor. "It's my fault,
Madame," he went on, turning to Cecily. "I ought not
to have told the Marquis so abruptly that his mother's
life was saved. It made him lose his balance. The
Marquis is very fond of his mother."

"Are you feeling better, dear?" asked Cecily.

Chéri-Bibi rose and quietly made himself presentable
again. He caught the reflection of his wife and Dr.
Walter in the glass. Both of them were so "natural,"
and the doctor seemed to trouble so little about him,
that the Marquis wondered if he were dreaming, or if he
were the sport of some optical illusion which in the
painful circumstances through which he had passed—
his mother's illness—might have been explicable.

The doctor gave Cecily injunctions as to the curative
treatment to be applied to the Dowager Marchioness,
whose condition was still serious.

"Have you a pen, Madame?" he asked.

After kissing her husband, without false shame,
Cecily left the room to fetch the necessary material to
enable the doctor to write out a prescription.

As soon as he was alone with his formidable enemy
Chéri-Bibi turned towards him. He was about to speak
when the doctor interposed and said in the calmest of
tones:

"Monsieur le Marquis, you must have been painfully
impressed by your mother's attitude towards you when
she came to herself after her attack. That attitude,
together with the sincere pleasure that you felt when
you learnt that she was out of danger, explains the

sudden weakness to which you succumbed. You must not be astonished at the strength with which old people, who are apparently in a comatose condition, revive and take up again ancient quarrels which ought to have been forgotten long ago. . . .

"Forgive me for alluding to family differences which I am the first to wish to see composed, for a doctor is almost like a father confessor. I had been attending the Dowager Marchioness for nearly a year when I found that I had to leave this place for a while; an event which coincided, I understand, with your arrival home. I had become almost a friend of the family, and I received certain confidences from my patient which assisted me, on more than one occasion, in diagnosing her illness. One's mental condition, in fact, often reacts upon one's physical condition. . . .

"Your mother, Monsieur le Marquis, has suffered more than I can say from the unfortunate relations which existed between you both. If you will allow me, I will take it upon myself, as opportunity offers, to bring about a reconciliation between you. I know that such is your dearest wish, and you must not read into my suggestion, which in other circumstances I should myself characterize as presumptuous, anything more than what it is in reality, namely, a desire to serve you and to bring back to health a patient for whom I have always felt not less respect than admiration. . . .

"Women, Monsieur le Marquis, are better than men are. They know how to forgive. I need look nó further as a proof of that than to your own wonderful wife. Nevertheless when they reach a certain age they are not free from some degree of small-mindedness which, like resentment, is the characteristic of all old

people. Leave her to me. Don't let us be in a hurry.
To-day she turned you out of doors; soon she will open
her arms to you."

"If you only knew, dear, how good Dr. Walter is,"
exclaimed Cecily, who had returned a moment before
and heard the doctor's last few words.

Chéri-Bibi himself seemed to have lost the power of
speech. The man who used such extraordinary language had shown so much unaffected sincerity, and
appeared so completely intent upon what he said, of
what he thought it right as a friend and a doctor to
say, that a strange and intolerable doubt began to
enter the Marquis' mind. Nevertheless it was the
Kanaka right enough. He could have sworn to it.

But what was the meaning of this farce? A few
minutes earlier, he was alone with him. How was it, if
he were the Kanaka, that he did not say bluntly: "You
have recognized me. Now to business," or something to
that effect?

For after all the Kanaka would not have taken the
trouble to come and practice his art on the du Touchais
family for the pleasure of doling out his medicines.
Yet there was nothing, nothing in his words, or in the
expression of his face, or in his general demeanor, nothing in his eyes which were fixed, calmly and frankly, on
the ex-convict; nothing in all this which could raise the
suspicion that a man was in that room who had something very particular to say to the Marquis du Touchais—or Chéri-Bibi.

Dr. Walter bent over the paper and his pen traveled
swiftly. When he finished writing out his prescription,
he handed it to Cecily and told her that he would call
again during the evening. Then he rose, bowed to the

Marchioness, and held out his hand to the Marquis. Chéri-Bibi took the proffered hand and gave him a penetrating glance.   The Kanaka did not move a muscle of his face, and withdrawing his hand without appearing to notice anything unusual in Chéri-Bibi's manner, took his leave.

"What is the matter, dear?" asked Cecily.   "The scene with your mother upset you, I suppose. . . . But tell me. . . . You don't say a word. . . . You alarm me."

"Let me be, my dear Cecily.   Do let me be quiet. . . . I was really very much affected by it. . . ."

He opened the window.

"I must have some air."

In reality he leant out of the window to catch another glimpse of that incredible specter.   Could he doubt his own intelligence?   Was he losing his reason? Was he in very truth ill?

He saw the doctor below meet the parish priest whom Sister St. Mary of the Angels had been sent to fetch, and he heard him say cheerfully:

"You won't be wanted this time, your Reverence. Luckily I was ahead of you.   There's no need to excite our dear patient, so allow me to see you home."

Thereupon he took the priest's arm and led him away.

"It's he, it's he!" Chéri-Bibi repeated to himself. "It's absolutely his walk.   There are no two men like that.   It's he."

"What do you think of Dr. Walter?" asked Cecily in her soft voice.

He turned round.

"Eh? . . . What's that?" he stammered. "Dr. Walter? . . . Oh, all right, all right."

And suddenly, violently, he caught her in his arms and strained her fiercely to him, against his throbbing heart, and covered her face with wild kisses, while Cecily, startled by this sudden outburst, tried in vain to release herself from his frenzied grasp.

"My wife, my wife," he cried in a choking voice. "You belong to me . . . me, I love you. I worship you. Oh, let them come here. Let any of them come and try to take you from me. I'll kill them. . . . I'll kill them like dogs. I'll cut them in pieces. . . . My Cecily . . . my darling Cecily. Don't be afraid . . . believe me. . . . Don't be afraid. I am with you. I love you. They can do nothing against such love . . . nothing, nothing. . . ."

And as Cecily grew more and more distraught as she saw him in a condition of mind which nothing seemed to justify, she tried to understand it all, and asked him in terrified accents to explain; and suddenly becoming calm once more, he said to her:

"Forgive me. . . . I don't know what I'm saying. . . . I don't know what I'm doing. . . . I love you so!"

And he lay back in a chair.

"My poor Maxime, what is the matter? It's dreadful to see you in this state," said Cecily, who could not keep back her tears. "It's your mother's unkindness which must have affected you like this."

"Yes, yes. . . . It's my mother. . . . That's it. . . . My mother. You understand, you understand everything. You divine everything. You are so good. To think that my mother should turn me away from her death bed. Have you ever heard of such a thing? It's awful."

"Awful," agreed Cecily. "She is really too bad. And yet I told her how good you were to me, how much you loved me, and how well you were behaving to both of us. It's incredible that she should continue to treat you in this way. And yet there were times when I really thought that she would give way to me, and ask me to bring you to her. I have often seen her cry when I spoke of you, and I fancied that the estrangement was all over and done with, when suddenly she would yield to her anger, become as cold as stone, and refuse to allow your name to be mentioned. . . . Listen, Maxime, I'll tell you something, something that I was keeping to myself, because in reality it's my own idea and I'm not certain of anything."

"What is it, dear? Tell me," said Chéri-Bibi, who wondered what was coming next, for during the last few minutes he had lost his nerve.

"You remember Rose?"

"Yes, her companion. What about her?"

"Well, I think she dislikes you."

"That's quite natural if she is devoted to her mistress. I haven't behaved well to my mother."

"Oh, there must be some other reason. I have often tried to get her on my side, to make her understand how pleased I should be if she'd join her endeavors to mine to obtain your mother's forgiveness for you. She always received my proposal with coldness and disfavor. I feel that she hates you. It is she who must destroy all my efforts with your mother. What have you done to her? Did you make an enemy of her in the old days?"

"Upon my soul I couldn't tell you," returned Chéri-Bibi. "Rose meant hardly anything to me, but it is quite possible. Try to tax your own recollection. There are so many blanks in my memory since my illness."

"But, dear, I don't know anything. After all I'm telling you what is in my mind and what I fancy that I've noticed."

But Chéri-Bibi had something more to do at that moment than to concern himself with Rose. He stood up and heaved a deep sigh.

"Rose is of no consequence. What she thinks of me or what she would like to do doesn't matter in the least. Only one thing is serious and important, and that is your love for me. Do you love me, Cecily?"

"I do, indeed."

Their lips met, and for the time Chéri-Bibi forgot all about the terrible Kanaka.

Nevertheless the doctor's form came back to him and obsessed him when, on leaving Cecily, who was obliged to remain with the Dowager Marchioness, he was once more on the road which Dr. Walter had traversed a little while before. The evening was soft and mild; a fragrant air swept the meadows; the music of the sea breaking on the beach was a caress. An atmosphere of happiness enshrouded him. How could he think that this glad hour was but the calm before the storm?

The Kanaka! But the Kanaka was dead; his death was vouched for by the authorities. The man whom he had met was not and could not be anything but a spurious likeness of him. Resemblances of that character had created a stir in the world before now, and were the cause of incredible miscarriages of justice.

Many voices, too, were alike, possessing the same reso-
nance and deceiving those who heard them. He had
been driveling like a child.

These thoughts reassured him to some extent. All
the same he felt very uneasy, and when he heard the
sound of hurried footsteps behind him he gave a start.
He recognized the Dodger, who came up to him in great
excitement. He had the foreboding that a new calamity
was about to fall on him. He was soon informed. The
Dodger did not wait to take breath but blurted out at
him:

"Monsieur le Marquis, I've just met Little Buddha."

They exchanged a glance as though they had seen a
ghost. They were back again, both of them, to their
worst days when they were engaged in sinister adventures against the law, when the police were on their
track, and when an irresistible fate drove them into a
position from which there was no escape. Little
Buddha! After what had come to pass with the enigmatic Dr. Walter, Chéri-Bibi felt indeed stricken. He
reeled.

He was no longer valiant as of old. He no longer
defied the Heavens. He no longer worked himself up
into a delirium with his misfortunes, to fling himself on
every obstacle reckless of the victims that he left in his
path. In those days he had nothing to lose. But
now! . . .

With weary limbs he sat down on a bank by the
roadside.

He held his head between his hands and listened as
the Dodger told his story. When it was finished he sat
for a while without speaking. He was taking time to
think, or at least he was endeavoring to concentrate his

thoughts on the two facts: Little Buddha had arrived in Dieppe, and the Kanaka had taken up his abode in Puys.

For he now felt that he had in fact met the Kanaka. The Kanaka and Little Buddha were obviously in league. What were they about to attempt against him? If he could not satisfy them both at one stroke and hear no more of them! He would not begrudge the price that he would have to pay.

But that was a hope with which it would be foolhardy to delude himself. Had not the Kanaka come to hunt him out at Dieppe a few months after he had received a million francs? So what did it all mean? . . . It meant that the whole business was to begin over again.

Well, there was one solution of the problem which he would not have hesitated to employ in the old days. Those two persons stood in his path, and he had but to make away with them. Obviously it would be easy work for Chéri-Bibi, but after a year in which he had lived a respectable life with Cecily the thought of murder was repugnant to the Marquis du Touchais. . . . Blood now terrified him. . . . Heavens! he had felt so safe, so secure. . . . Was it indeed possible that he would have to set to work again?

In a voice of infinite weariness which betrayed the confusion of his mind and his lack of spirit to take up again the everlasting struggle, he recounted to the Dodger the extraordinary apparition of the Kanaka in the guise of Dr. Walter.

"Oh," exclaimed the Dodger, "then it was the Kanaka who passed me in his buggy. Well, he let fly with his tongue and I said to myself: "Hullo, I know that voice.' "

"Yes, it was his voice, wasn't it?" said Chéri-Bibi with an air of hopelessness. "It was the Kanaka's voice."

"Yes, undoubtedly it was his voice. What did he say to you?"

"Nothing."

"What do you mean, nothing? Were other people present?"

"I was alone with him for a minute. He merely spoke of my mother's health."

"Didn't he make any sign?"

"None."

"But what did you do, what did you say, Monsieur le Marquis?"

"I did nothing and I said nothing."

"I can't understand it. Did you leave him without a word?"

"Without a word."

"That was not very clever of you."

"I'll explain, Dodger. I was so taken aback when I saw him that I doubted whether it was he, and even now there are moments when I wonder if it is he."

"That being so, you are sure of nothing. After all, it may not be he."

"Since you tell me that you've met Little Buddha, my opinion is that they came here together. It's the Kanaka who brought him, you see."

"Little Buddha came here, perhaps, to worm a little money out of the Marquis, or simply to fix up a business and settle down, as he declares. Little Buddha doesn't know our secret, and if the Kanaka is really dead nothing is lost. . . . You may perhaps have fancied that it was the Kanaka. Personally I should like to have a look at the fellow."

"He went off with the parish priest. They must have taken leave of each other on the hill and Dr. Walter probably went home.

"Where does he live?"

"Cecily pointed out his house to me one day when we were walking in the sunk road. It's a little house standing in its own ground and is called "The Fronds."

"I know where it is. I say, Monsieur le Marquis, I'll make a little tour of the place. We must know where we stand. Anything is better than this uncertainty. Don't you think so?"

"I do," agreed the other. "But if you ask me, it's the Kanaka right enough."

"Excuse me, Monsieur le Marquis, you know nothing. Sometimes you say one thing and sometimes you say another. You are a complete wreck. It hurts me to see you. Leave it to me. Where shall I join you again?"

"I won't leave this place," groaned Chéri-Bibi, like a little child.

The Dodger started off at a rapid pace and cut across country to reach the sunk road, and he soon disappeared from view.

Chéri-Bibi went through a terrible half-hour.

At length the Dodger came back.

"Well?" said the Marquis with visible anxiety.

"Well, it is not the Kanaka. Oh, I'm giving you my opinion. Something was wrong with our sight! Of course it was easy to be mistaken. He has a look about him of the Kanaka, but the Kanaka was never like that, and this man hasn't altered for a long time. I've seen a portrait of him in his youth. He looked then as he looks now. His voice? Well, yes, the voice is like the Kanaka's but he never had that slight English accent. And then, you know, I've had a chat with him. Besides you must remember that Dr. Walter took up his residence here some two years ago. At that time, if the Kanaka was not dead, devil take it, he was still in the East."

"You're right, Hilaire. I am still the Marquis," said Chéri-Bibi, making an effort to hold himself erect, for his body had been drooping just before.

"More than ever," declared the Dodger. "And Little Buddha is not the man to frighten us. He knows nothing. If the sight of him gets on our nerves, we can always make arrangements for him to go and hang himself elsewhere."

"I'll leave that to you."

"Rely on me, Monsieur le Marquis. He won't trouble you, but his presence will annoy me. I shall go back to the restaurant in the harbor and I'll soon find out what that fathead is driving at."

They returned to the Villa on the Cliff thinking to themselves that they had little cause for alarm, but nevertheless neither of them slept soundly.

CHAPTER X

LIFE during the following days appeared to have resumed its normal course. The Dowager Marchioness grew better day by day. Cecily was radiant, and Chéri-Bibi after his sudden outburst of passion increasingly revealed himself as the devoted lover. He was doing his utmost to drive out the thought that Dr. Walter might not be Dr. Walter, when one fine morning Cecily told him that the doctor was coming to lunch with them.

The Dodger was not present. For the last few days little had been seen of him. He was keeping watch on the restaurant in the harbor.

Chéri-Bibi did not display any great satisfaction when Cecily told him. The doctor might very well not be the Kanaka, but he sufficiently resembled him to bring back to the sham Marquis' mind a period of his life which he would fain have forgotten.

"You don't seem very pleased to hear of my invitation," said Cecily. "Have you anything against our friend?" She called the doctor "our friend."

"No, no, dearest, but I'm so glad to be alone with you and the children that when you tell me that a stranger will be present, it is never good news to me."

"Dr. Walter is not a stranger to us, and we must at least behave politely to him. I have invited his wife as well. You don't mind that, I hope."

196

"His wife? So the doctor is married?"

"Oh, yes, she had returned from the Indies. I don't know her. I didn't even know that she had arrived home. When I invited the doctor to lunch, he begged to be excused because it so happened that his wife was at 'The Fronds.' I couldn't do other than ask him to bring her with him, and say that I should be charmed to make her acquaintance."

"That's all right."

"What's the matter?"

"With me? . . . Nothing."

"You look quite upset."

"Upset? Why should I be? Not a bit of it. . . . I don't object to the doctor and his wife. After all we can't be unsociable."

"Of course we can't, dear." There was a ring at the garden gate. "Ah, here they are, I believe."

"Very well, I'll go and make myself presentable and have a look at Jacques, and be with you presently."

"Good-by for the present. Aren't you going to kiss me?"

"Dearest!"

"I say, Maxime, are you ill? You seem to have changed during the last few days—since your fainting fit. One moment you are all affection and the next you are abstracted, absent-minded. . . ."

"It's your fancy, Cecily, it's your fancy."

He heard the sound of footsteps on the gravel path and slipped away. He hastened to his room and sank into a seat. A mirror hung in front of him. He saw that he was ashen in the face.

"Why, but what's the matter with me?"

He might have looked out of his bedroom window into

the garden to see what was happening. Strange to say, he dared not. He was smarting under the blow of a great and inevitable misfortune. And, quivering all over, he thought only of putting off the evil moment when he would possess the dire certainty of the irretrievable catastrophe. At length he heaved a sigh, reasoned himself out of his fears, argued that he was foolish to become so excited because he was to meet at lunch a doctor who resembled the Kanaka, a doctor who was bringing his wife with him. Why should the doctor not be married? What business was it of his?

He rose to his feet, took a few paces, plunged his face into a basin of water, called himself a silly ass, brushed his hair, pulled down his cuffs, coughed and said aloud: "Come, Monsieur le Marquis, don't be childish," and went down stairs.

As he drew near the drawing room he could hear voices and his limbs trembled under him. Still he forced himself to open the door, and he saw before him the two guests who had risen to meet him. Luckily he still held the handle of the door. He could lean on it. Facing him was the Countess with dark red hair instead of her wonderful black hair, but unmistakably the Countess, and of necessity he no longer doubted the doctor's identity.

"Good gracious, how pale you are," exclaimed Cecily.

The three of them sprang forward to support him, but he had already recovered himself.

"It's nothing, nothing. . . . I felt dizzy. . . . You must forgive me, Madame."

He endeavored to fight against the shock, to act the strong man, and he knitted his brows. He would have liked to appear at that moment terrible. But the effect

was almost pitiable. Cecily was grieved beyond measure, and explained that her husband for some time had
been far from well, and she asked the doctor to call and
examine him carefully and prescribe some proper form
of treatment.

Chéri-Bibi interposed, cleared his throat, and looked
fondly at his wife, seeming to acquire renewed strength
and a firm determination to brave the danger.

"We'll say no more about it, at least for the present,"
he said. "The Marchioness didn't invite you to lunch to
consult you about my health. I may tell you that I had
no time to breakfast this morning, which is the cause,
perhaps, of a certain physical discomfort. I have a
wolfish appetite. I hope, Madame, that you are equally
ready for lunch. Let's begin. Doctor, give my wife
your arm."

He offered his arm to the Countess, who pressed it
with a mysterious smile.

They went to the veranda, where the luncheon table
was laid.

Chéri-Bibi had Madame Walter on his right. He
found courage to look at her, to talk to her. He ques-
tioned her about her travels, and while she readily
described the splendors of the Ganges and the wonders
of Benares he marveled that she should still retain her
youth and beauty.

He bore without flinching her piercing gaze.

He recalled to mind that she had loved him, and that
he had treated her with disdain. He thought to himself
that she, too, would wish to be revenged on him. But
now that the first stroke had fallen he knew that he had
the power to give them battle.

A fierce hatred began to possess him against the two

beings who were so deliberately attacking him when his cup of happiness was full. Yes, he would have to set to work again. They had willed it so. He would not shrink from the task. The wretched creatures had brought it on themselves. They only had themselves to blame. . . . He would show them what Chéri-Bibi was capable of doing even though he wore the skin of the Marquis du Touchais.

And so he had with him in his Villa on the Cliff, seated at his table opposite his wife, his adored idol, this wretched woman, this flower from the penal settlement, this companion of convicts and hardened criminals who struck terror in the hearts of the most callous by her ferocity at the time of the mutiny on the "Bayard," and amused the most cynical by her extraordinary command of slang.

Of course she had helped him when he escaped from his manacles, and he would never be able to forget it, but she had acted under the impulse of the worst of passions, the desire to hold in her arms Chéri-Bibi, the celebrated criminal, the famous man of blood as he then was. Faugh! it filled the Marquis with disgust.

The very thought that he had been in contact with that wanton and was forced to repel her reckless advances, brought a blush of shame to his cheeks. And now she played the lady, was full of affectations, gave herself airs, and astonished Cecily and the Marquis du Touchais himself by her assurance, her elegance, and her choice of language, which was pretentious and artificial almost to the point of absurdity.

Women know how to dissemble. However eager she was to be revenged against Chéri-Bibi, against Chéri-Bibi's happiness, against the love that he had for

another woman and refused to her, she smiled at him,
she made herself agreeable. "What an awful creature,"
the Marquis thought to himself.

Just then he felt a knee brush against his own. He
drew back slightly. But the knee pursued him, pressed
against him, and a little foot fixed itself upon his.

Chéri-Bibi did not budge this time nor did he speak.
It was as though he had been turned to stone.

Oh, the cool impudence of it in Cecily's presence!
She was but a couple of steps from his wife! He was
bound to permit this odious contact in order to avoid a
scene. It seemed to him that, as a respectable husband
and father, he was committing a sacrilege in allowing
that foot to rest upon his own. Nevertheless he did not
repulse her, not only because he wished to avoid any
action which might arouse suspicion in his wife's mind,
but also because it suddenly occurred to him that the
Countess still loved him and had not abandoned the
hope of making him love her.

If that were so, his defense against the Kanaka would
become less difficult. He might, perhaps, make an ally
of her even if he had to get rid of her as occasion offered
after he had disposed of her husband.

It behooved him to learn as soon as may be, what
precisely he had to fear from the Kanaka, what scheme
was being hatched against him; in a word, what the
Kanaka's plan of campaign was. If he played his cards
well the Countess might end, perhaps, by revealing the
whole plot.

He responded to the pressure of her foot by a sympathetic movement and he at once perceived from her
look, from the inflection of her voice, from her entire
bearing which was not sufficiently reserved, that she

was grateful. Fortunately Cecily was far from suspecting any such duplicity.

Nevertheless, Chéri-Bibi was not easy in his mind and he very gently withdrew his foot from under hers. But at that moment, in order doubtless that he might be fully conscious of the agitation that his presence produced in her, she placed her hand, her small hot hand on his, and said in the most animated manner:

"And you, Monsieur le Marquis, you also have traveled a great deal. People haven't yet forgotten that terrible affair of the 'Bayard.' You were made prisoner by convicts. Oh, how I should love to hear the story of your adventures. The very thought gives me a thrill."

Dr. Walter did not hesitate to add his entreaties to his wife's and Chéri-Bibi whether he liked it or not had to comply.

Dr. Walter went so far as to ask some particulars about the famous Chéri-Bibi and also the Kanaka.

"I understand there was a woman on board whom they called the Countess," said Mme. Walter, replacing her foot in a peremptory manner on Chéri-Bibi's.

"Yes, Madame," returned the Marquis, who would have liked to choke the life out of the pair of them on the spot. "She was, as it happens, the Kanaka's wife."

"Was she a beautiful woman?"

"Well, Madame, she was very handsome."

"I hear that at one time she was a woman of fashion."

"I have heard so."

"It was said, too, that she was in love with Chéri-Bibi. Is that true?"

"I can't say, Madame. I was not in her confidence. Still I believe that Chéri-Bibi had a certain liking for her."

Gratitude from Mme. Walter expressed by a movement of her foot under the table. Shame of Chéri-Bibi,
who dared not look at Cecily, and regarded himself as
the worst of men, the lowest of the low. . . . Oh, the
scoundrels. . . . They should pay dearly for it, the
pair of them!

"Is Chéri-Bibi really dead?" asked the doctor
abruptly, looking the Marquis straight in the face.

He did not lower his eyes; and his voice when he
answered assumed so grave an accent that Cecily was
surprised.

"Yes, doctor, yes. Chéri-Bibi is dead. I myself saw
his body, tied up in the usual sack, thrown into the sea,
and for some days before that he was little more than a
corpse. His sister, who lives in this neighborhood, was
present like myself at the funeral service. He is dead.
And you can take it from me that he won't come to life
again."

"Why do you say that, dear?" asked Cecily, who did
not grasp the importance or the expediency of the
declaration.

"Because Dr. Walter seems to doubt it."

"That's because Chéri-Bibi is an extraordinary
being, and it is difficult to imagine that he died a . . .
natural . . . death," replied the doctor with a composure which at least equaled the Marquis'. "Other
people have said the same thing before. Listen, two
years ago—perhaps he still comes to Dieppe—there
was a Detective Inspector. . . ."

"You mean of course a man called 'Costaud,'" said
Chéri-Bibi, with disarming frankness.

"Yes, that's the man. Well, Costaud does not believe
in Chéri-Bibi's death. It's no use telling him what you

have said to us, his invariable reply is: 'Chéri-Bibi is not dead. It was his interest to disappear. He deceived every one on the ship as he deceived every one at the penal settlement. And, mark my words, one day people will learn that he escaped death just as he escaped from Cayenne. He will pop up again under another name or under another disguise.' Costaud seemed convinced of it in his own mind when he said that."

"Everything is possible," said the Countess, "but nothing can be less certain. What you say is what we call a gratuitous assumption," she added, turning to Chéri-Bibi, and from the look in her eyes he realized that she was on his side, and left it to him to play the game with her against the Kanaka.

He thanked her quietly with his foot under the table. And he had a feeling of renewed hope, notwithstanding the diabolical audacity with which Dr. Walter proceeded to enlarge on the matter:

"I assure you that one never knows what may happen with such people. How do we know that we are not rubbing shoulders with him every day, that we don't come up against him in the Casino? Costaud said to me: 'I don't despair of seeing Chéri-Bibi again in Dieppe. He belongs to the place. It was the scene of his first exploits. He will come back again.' For my part, I who am very fond of serial stories and find a relaxation in them from my daily routine, I confess that it would amuse me greatly. . . . Suppose they should arrest him one evening in the Casino? People might have had dealings with a man, thinking that he was a marquis or a baron, and then find out all at once that he was Chéri-Bibi!"

"You have remarkable powers of imagination," said the Marquis, who turned slightly pale.

He stood up. Coffee was served in the garden. Cecily and the doctor were the first to leave the veranda. Certain that she could not be observed, the Countess motioned to Chéri-Bibi to remain behind.

"We know all about his imagination," she muttered between her teeth, but loud enough for the Marquis to hear.

She had taken his arm and Chéri-Bibi pressed her hand warmly.

"I still love you," she whispered.

"What are you here for?" asked Chéri-Bibi, keeping still further behind.

"To save you, Chéri-Bibi. . . . To save you if you will have a little pity on me. They are preparing a frightful blow against you."

"Who are 'they'?"

"The Kanaka and Little Buddha."

"I thought as much. . . . The blackguards."

"But nothing is lost if you'll listen to me."

"I'll kill the Kanaka."

"That won't help you. He has taken every precaution. I know. He told me so himself. He has written out your story and made his will, in which he discloses your real identity and furnishes the means of proving it. The whole thing is in a sealed envelope which is to be opened the day of his death."

"Then I can't go for him."

"That's why he thinks he's so clever. Look at him. I loathe him."

"I'm done for, Countess."

"We must see about that. . . . Do you love me?"

Before Chéri-Bibi had time to reply Cecily turned round and called them. While she was serving the coffee her husband watched her graceful movements without concealing his extreme dejection. The Countess' revelations had paralyzed him. He was foiled; he was powerless against the Kanaka. He would be a mere plaything in his hands. The Kanaka would be his master, his torturer, his executioner, and he would be debarred from any thought of getting rid of him. Such a crime would be the signal of his downfall, his ruin.

Oh, the Kanaka had prepared for every emergency. And Chéri-Bibi would have to submit to him to the uttermost, until he had stripped him of the last farthing —him and his. Poor Cecily! Poor little Jacques!

Chéri-Bibi slipped one of his hands underneath his waistcoat and under his shirt, and his nails tore the skin of his chest, causing red streaks in the infamous and indelible blue tatoo-marks which stamped him as Chéri-Bibi for life and even beyond the grave.

Cecily and the doctor walked away to admire the view from the top of the rising ground, whence they could have a sight of the sea.

"But look here," growled Chéri-Bibi when he was once more alone with the Countess, "how much money do they want?"

"The lot."

"But what will be left for me?"

"That's what I asked him. He replied that you would be left with your love for your wife. If you really love her, Chéri-Bibi, there's your consolation! . . . And at the finish it's I who will have nothing at all. Oh, I see that quite plainly. I noticed how you looked at her just now."

"Don't talk about it; that's no business of yours."

He flung the words at her savagely and she muttered in an extraordinary transport of delight:

"Oh, that's almost like your old self before he flayed your jaw, Chéri-Bibi! . . . Well, I assure you that the last word has not been said between the three of us. I hate him and I love you. The rest will come in due course. . . . You mustn't lose faith in Providence."

"Look here, what scheme have you concocted? You can very well tell me. How is it he came here two years ago? Did he leave the 'Bayard' at once?"

"Yes, directly after you did. We returned to France, where we thought we should meet you again. Of course he always intended to blackmail you on a big scale. The million francs were a mere nothing to him. His life's work was you. He had failed with so many others. You can imagine that he wasn't going to let you out of his sight after making a success with your face! No, the million francs were of no account. He proved that by losing them in a month on the gaming tables at Monte Carlo. It was then that he came and established himself here, thinking that you would arrive soon."

"What about you?"

"I left for the Indies with a rich Englishman. I preferred to get away. I had no wish to take part in what was to come. It hurt me too much. And then I was still thinking of you. You have always treated me like a dog, but you are a part of my life. . . . Oh, don't speak, I'm not asking you for anything, Chéri-Bibi. I know how to wait. My time will come. . . ."

"The villains," growled Chéri-Bibi to himself.

He longed to have a knife at the end of his fingers and to plunge it into his flesh and to lacerate and mortify himself for putting himself in the power of those two beings, who were about to crush him when he had attained the summit of happiness.

The Countess fixed her eyes on the Kanaka and the Marchioness, who were on the hill discussing the landscape and breaking into raptures over the view, and she went on with her story in quick sentences. It was the Kanaka who introduced her to the Englishman with a view of "clearing him out," because they needed money until the Marquis' great stroke was a definite success. She continued to send him money from abroad. The Kanaka held her by the link of the awful past that they had in common. The Englishman died, leaving the Countess a considerable sum, and the Kanaka—informed by his police, the international police of convicts, which is the most effective police of all—rejoined her at a time when she was hoping to be rid of him. During the last year they had been living on the money left to the Countess. Now that it was exhausted, they were preparing their blow against the Marquis. And this time the Kanaka was determined to make himself rich for life. That was the scheme. It was a simple one.

"You'll have to submit to whatever he pleases, my poor Chéri-Bibi. Oh, you thought of killing him. But you can't kill him."

"I can't kill him nor can I kill myself, for I know what he would do after my death."

"He would blackmail your wife by pointing to your body and by disclosing to her that her son was Chéri-Bibi's son."

"Oh, don't, don't," said Chéri-Bibi in a hoarse voice, and he uttered a hollow groan: "*Fatalitas!*"

"Be careful, here's your wife. . . . I was saying to your husband that you have a delightful place. . . . Oh, delightful. . . . The view from here is wonderful and the air delicious. It is very different from 'The Fronds,' where we live, and where the damp penetrates everything. I don't know why my husband took the tumble down old place. It's not a cottage, dear madame, it's a sponge! I assure you it's a sponge. The doctor, who suffers from gout, will soon find this out. . . . Beware of rheumatism, dear!"

"If I were rich enough," said the doctor, "I should buy the Villa on the Clic, assuming that the Marquis would be willing to sell it. In the meantime, dear, if you don't mind we'll take our leave and return to 'The Fronds.' I am expecting some letters."

"Madame," said Cecily, "we shall be very pleased to see you whenever you care to come to the Villa on the Clic."

At the moment of departure Cecily and the doctor exchanged a few words about the Dowager Marchioness' health, leaving the Countess and Chéri-Bibi alone for an instant. She bent forward and whispered quickly in his ear:

"I want to see if you are the Chéri-Bibi of old or an imitation Marquis. Little Buddha has the will. It's in an old mahogany writing table on the first floor in the restaurant in the harbor. Take the will first and kill the Kanaka afterwards . . . and then we'll have a talk."

Cecily came towards her with outstretched hand.

"We shall meet again soon, I hope, dear Madame."

"We shall meet again soon, Marchioness."

CHAPTER XI

CHÉRI-BIBI SETS TO WORK AGAIN

IT was a stormy night, a night on which, as the saying goes, no one would turn a dog out of the house. The wind and rain were tempestuous; the sea broke upon the rocky coast with resounding violence. On the storm-swept cliff darkness had fallen like a pall. Not even the outlines of the houses were visible ten paces away in the dense obscurity. No lights shone.

The church clock in the little valley struck two. The wind blowing from the sea seemed to gather increasing fury from moment to moment, and its sinister voice howled like the messenger of an inexorable catastrophe. Alas for the seafarers who had not returned to harbor, and the luckless landsmen driven from their homes by their occupations or their misery, and flung into the heart of the storm.

But was there a being so abandoned of God and man that he must needs remain in the open on such a night? Nature, less rigorous than man, offers a refuge against the fury of the elements to the most wretched. There are cavities, crevices, curves in the rock in which men can find shelter even as there are lairs and dens to which animals may retreat.

So what were those two shadows doing in the torrential rain and the icy blast, those two shadows bending under the weight of the storm, and creeping forward amidst the impenetrable darkness? What object—darker perhaps than the night itself—was before them? What was their destination? What force was urging them forward?

Fatalitas.

It was fate which was guiding those two suspicious shadows, the inevitable fate by which crime breeds crime, and never lets go of the man whom it has once marked down with its blood-red hand; and it was fate, perhaps, which had determined to envelop in the storm the two beings whom it had doomed to tragic deeds.

"*Fatalitas!*" muttered Chéri-Bibi, clutching the Dodger as he nearly slipped on the wet ground. "What a night, my dear old Dodger."

"Why complain, Monsieur le Marquis? It's much better to have this sort of weather for the job we've got to do than a moonlight night."

"I'm wet to the skin, and it's a certainty that I shall catch a fine cold."

"The Marchioness will look after you."

"Dear Cecily! She thinks I'm asleep in a nice warm bed."

"That's as it should be," returned the Dodger in a tone of philosophy. "We couldn't have asked her to come with us."

"Oh, I say, if it goes on like this we shall have to creep along on all fours."

"All the better. We shan't risk running up against Costaud."

"I'm surprised to see you in such good spirits, Dodger."

"That's because I said to myself that we've got to go

through a rough time, but afterwards we shall feel safe
again."

"Let's stop a moment under cover of tne semaphore."

"It'll be a mistake if we do."

"I'm out of breath."

"We've got over worse nights than this."

"Exactly, but I've lost the knack of it. . . . Wait a
bit. . . . Besides you're not going to tell me that it
isn't a good thing to get one's breath back again.   In
truth you are wonderful.   Doesn't it worry you to have
to set to work again?"

"Perhaps more than it does you, Monsieur le Marquis,
because I haven't so much to lose.   But my devotion to
you impels me to endeavor to keep you from losing
courage.   I am still only a poor devil, but I realize the
effort that a man like you must make to put on an old
cast-off coat, to dress up in patched-up rags and to
wear that dirty cap."

"You're right, Dodger.   When I looked at myself in
the glass before I slipped out of the window, I admit
that a shudder passed through me.   I frightened even
myself.   And then when I recognized myself under it all,
I couldn't help shedding tears.   The fact is, Dodger,
that I've got out of the way of doing it.   And then I
really thought that all that sort of work was a thing of
the past."

"Oh, please, Monsieur le Marquis, this is not the
moment to give way to weakness.   You must show the
stuff you're made of."

"I will show it.   But let me tell you that I'm ashamed
to be out of doors in such weather as this and dressed
like a dock laborer.   If Cecily were to see me now."

"Of course we don't look ladies' men!   I admit

myself that if Virginie saw me, her affianced husband, in this rig-out it's very likely we shouldn't go to the altar. . . ."

"Have you got all the tools?"

"Yes, in the bag."

"The keys? The picklocks? The jimmy and the dark lantern? Where did you get the jimmy?"

"I stole it . . . of course. It's I who was the first, as you see, to begin work again. Well, I would never have believed that it was so hard to appropriate other people's property when once, as you say yourself, we've got out of the way of doing it. I trembled all over and felt like nothing on earth . . . I ran away like a child."

"That shows your naturally good disposition."

"Yes, but listen to me. We mustn't be too childish either. If you are weaker than I am we shan't do good business. That's why I carried it high and tried to buck you up just now."

"That's true. We've got to get it over and done with. Come, let's be off."

They sallied forth once more in the rain and storm and murky darkness.

"The best of it now is," gasped the Dodger, attempting to be consolatory, "that the wind is in our favor, for it's behind us and is blowing us towards the restaurant in the harbor."

They soon caught sight of the first street lamps on the hill and rapidly made their way down to Dieppe. They crossed the bridge and the wharves without encountering a living soul. The Customhouse officers were buried inside their wooden huts.

They halted for a moment a couple of steps from the

fish market and took a long look at Little Buddha's windows.

It was a house of two stories and stood at the corner of the quay. No light penetrated through the shutters on the ground floor; nor was there the faintest glimmer from the first and second floors. The place seemed to sleep like the houses in the vicinity. They went down a narrow street and quickly reached the Square in which loomed the somber mass of Duquesne's statue.

They leant against the pedestal and their forms became merged in the shadow of the great sailor; and they stood scanning for a few minutes the surroundings before entering upon their adventure, availing themselves of the respite to put the finishing touches to their plan of operations.

One entrance to the restaurant was in the small courtyard of an old building, the front part of which overlooked the Square. The entrance to this courtyard was through a large oak door embossed with iron bars and nails, and in this door was fitted a smaller one of which the Dodger held the key.

Virginie had given him the key at the time when that comely daughter of the Caux country was a waitress at the restaurant and lived under its roof. Consequently the Dodger knew the way. He could not refrain from observing:

"Monsieur le Marquis, you have on more than one occasion reproached me for my love affairs, which you considered unworthy of the position that I held under you, but don't you think to-night that we were, in some way, being assisted by Providence, which made me fall in love with a girl whom I could only visit in a particu-

lar way, the knowledge of which is of great use to us
now?"

"Not so many words, Dodger, let's be up and doing.
And be careful to drop calling me marquis in this business. My name must not be mentioned. I told you so
before. Don't let me have to repeat it."

"Very good, Monsieur le Marquis."

"There you are again!"

"Would you rather I called you Chéri-Bibi?"

"Don't call me anything at all, unless you want to
feel the weight of my boot. . . . Tell me, are you sure
that there's only one room on the first floor?"

"Yes, and the article of furniture in question stands
in that room. The room was used as an office by the
governor, and sometimes as a private room by sundry
customers who didn't want to mix with the crowd
below."

"You say it is impossible to get in by the servants'
door which opens on to the courtyard?"

"Impossible, because it is fastened by an iron bar
which is padlocked, and the woman cook who keeps the
key is in the habit of sleeping quite near it. We must
get direct to the first floor through the window in the
courtyard, by using the ladder."

"Is the ladder there?"

"Yes, Monsieur le Mar . . . It has always been there.
It won't take long, I repeat. Little Buddha sleeps on
the second floor, just as the old proprietor used to do.
I made sure of that only yesterday by carefully getting
the cook to chatter when I met her doing her shop-
ping."

"So there's no danger?"

"I believe I can secure you there's none at all, Monsieur le Mar. . . ."

The sentence did not end without a slight exclamation from Hilaire, who received a sudden kick from the Marquis. He had already been warned, and it would teach him to be less polite.

"Can the people living in the house in the courtyard hear us?" asked Chéri-Bibi roughly.

"Well, we must go to work as discreetly as if we were keeping an appointment in a love affair. They have never disturbed me," returned the secretary, rubbing the spot where the Marquis' kick had been planted.

"Now I must tell you, Dodger, that nothing would induce me to let myself be discovered. Not for the world would I place a certain individual whom you know in a false position. If any one turns up here it will be a bad look out for him."

"I see, Mons . . . I see. Oh, we're up against a stiff proposition. . . . Yes, it'll be rather hard lines on that particular person."

"We shall have to settle him in a trice, and you'll exert yourself as much as I do, won't you?"

"In a trice, Monsieur le . . . in a trice! If it must be so we won't hesitate. But I hope we shan't be driven to such terrible extremities."

"I hope so, at least as much as you do," returned Chéri-Bibi with a sigh. "What's the time?"

"About a quarter to three."

"We must finish the entire job in half an hour because we've got to be at 'The Fronds,' as arranged with the Countess, before the Kanaka has the time to make a fresh will. But in that quarter the affair will soon be finished. We have a friend at court."

"It's a great pity, monsieur, that we couldn't begin work an hour earlier."

"You told me yourself that Little Buddha didn't go to bed until very late."

"That's true, but I dread getting back to the Villa on the Cliff in the early morning. Dressed as we are we can't avoid attracting the attention of chance wayfarers if we meet any."

"I know a little path through the hedges which will get us out of that difficulty," returned Chéri-Bibi, who seemed to have thought of everything. "Come, are you ready? Hand me the diamond. Look after your dark lantern and let's get on with it."

"Heaven be with us!" sighed the Dodger.

He all but made the sign of the cross, he had become like his master so orthodox.

A couple of minutes later the two shadows had opened the door and were in the rear. The Dodger found the ladder in the cellar, and placed it with the greatest care against the wall so that the top rung rested on the window-sill of the room on the first floor.

Chéri-Bibi mounted first.

The Dodger followed, carrying the bag of tools.

Chéri-Bibi began his work in silence. With his glazier's diamond he neatly cut out the glass, caught it smartly and passed it to the Dodger. Then he slipped his hand in, and turned the latch of the window and opened it.

The two men lost no time in entering the room. They were wearing bathing sandals for the occasion.

"Oh!" exclaimed Chéri-Bibi in a low voice, seating himself in an easy chair, for his heart was throbbing more wildly than he would have dared to confess to his assistant, and he wanted to pull himself together. "Oh, here we are! All the same I'm not so rusty as I thought I should be."

The Dodger had switched on his dark lantern and he threw its beam on one corner of the room. Their eyes fell on the mahogany writing table.

It was an old piece of furniture and did not look very formidable. Chéri-Bibi rose and with a certain distaste searched the bag in which the Dodger had collected the necessary housebreaking tools, and advanced to the table with a somewhat varied assortment of keys, master keys, picklocks and levers.

They managed to pick one of the two locks, but the other withstood every attempt to force it.

Moreover, truth to tell, they were all of a-tremble. The least noise caused by their implements compelled them to stop for several minutes while they listened, the perspiration breaking out on their foreheads, to discover whether they had been heard or had given the alarm.

The position became still worse when they had to use the jimmy. The table creaked, and they came to a stand in their work, holding their breath, their limbs shaking under them.

At one moment they thought that they heard in the distance a deep, painful gasp. They stood stock still, dismayed.

"It's some one yawning on the next floor," suggested the Dodger.

"Then some one is awake," said Chéri-Bibi.

"Well, let's get on with it, we've no time to lose."

Nevertheless they did lose time, for a violent effort

was needed to break the catch of the lock, and they were afraid to make it because of the inevitable noise.

"Oh, I'm not so expert as I used to be," groaned Chéri-Bibi, wiping the perspiration which rolled down his cheeks. "In the old days I'd have done it in no time."

"And then we haven't got the pluck either," confessed the Dodger.

"No, we haven't got the pluck either. A mere miserable piece of furniture like that. I would never have believed that I was such a muff," muttered Chéri-Bibi.

"Come, monsieur, show a little more courage. Remember that we're working for your wife and son."

The Dodger's dignified reminder of the duty which the Marquis du Touchais owed to his family was not lost upon him. Chéri-Bibi drew himself up as if he had received an electric shock; and he set to work again filled with a deceptive and momentary energy. He pressed with all his might on the jimmy and this time the lock gave way.

The top part of the desk fell back upon Chéri-Bibi, and the Dodger was barely in time to catch it in his outstretched hands. Nevertheless there was a considerable crash, and the wood groaned loudly, and almost at once there came an answering human groan from above.

"Good Lord, what's happening," said the Dodger.

"We snap our fingers at it. Come, hurry up with the lantern."

To search the desk for the will, seize it, and to get clear off would now be a question only of seconds. Chéri-Bibi already longed to be outside. The Dodger with the light from his lantern ransacked every nook and corner of the table, opened the drawers, began to lose patience, but could find nothing, absolutely nothing; the desk was completely empty. There was no paper of any sort in it.

Stay, there was one paper, a paper which he at length discovered, fastened by drawing pins to the back of the desk like a show-card. On this card was some writing, a sentence which a flash of light revealed word for word, and which made Chéri-Bibi and the Dodger start back uttering fearful oaths.

The sentence which they saw and which was written in large characters, emphasized by ironical notes of exclamation, was:

LITTLE BUDDHA PRESENTS HIS COMPLIMENTS
TO MONSIEUR LE MARQUIS DU TOUCHAIS ! ! !

CHAPTER XII

The two friends clasped hands in a gesture in which was concentrated their utter despair.

"We're in for it," growled Chéri-Bibi.

He dragged himself to the window, followed by the Dodger, who had extinguished the lantern. The ladder was no longer there. And in the courtyard into which they might have jumped at the risk of breaking their necks, they distinguished two forms, muffled up in great coats, keeping watch.

They drew back into the room and felt their way along the walls to the window that gave on to the harbor. It was an iron barred window like the windows in most of those ancient buildings. They were caught like rats in a trap.

"The baggage!" exclaimed Chéri-Bibi, cast down.

The expression was certainly applied to the Countess, who had succeeded in leading him into a snare from which there was no escape. She had humbugged and played with him as if he were a greenhorn. At least, he thought so.

Nevertheless Chéri-Bibi's fury was not so great as his fear. How was he to get out of the place? It behooved him above all to avoid a scandal. He would have to fight the scoundrels whose prey he feared to become, without giving the alarm to respectable people.

He moved carefully in the small room and in a choking voice said:

"We're in a nice mess, we're in a nice mess."

"Yes, Monsieur le Marquis, we're in a nice mess," groaned Hilaire, who agreed with his master more than ever now, and undoubtedly owed the fact that he was not called to order as severely as before to the gravity of the position.

Yes, Chéri-Bibi was overcome with fear. Nevertheless if in the midst of such dread events he was able to retain the power of deliberate judgment which, since he had been lifted to a new career, had transformed him into one of the justest men of his day, he would not have failed to realize that if his turn had come it served him right. For, after all, he had often, in his time, terrified honest people at night, and it was right that he should himself experience, at least once in his life, that feeling of intolerable anguish which renders the bravest man powerless, and makes him quiver like a child surrounded by the mysteries of the night.

The Dodger had lost his courage. Groping in the dark his hands encountered a door which he shook in vain. It was a door that led to the upper floor, and it was locked. He made for the other door. He felt the lock; there was no key. But he lifted the latch and the door gave way. He had but to push it open.

"This door opens on to the staircase leading down to the restaurant," he whispered to Chéri-Bibi, who was bending over him. "We have only to go downstairs. We can then open a window and jump out on the quay."

Chéri-Bibi seized him by the wrist.

"Don't open it."

He feared some trap.

It was hardly likely that this way out should have been reserved for them out of friendliness. And as they stood there in absolute bewilderment, Chéri-Bibi pressed his forehead with feverish fingers, not knowing whether to advance or to retire.

He thought of his wife and child, all that he loved in this world of misery. And he beheld the swift and harrowing vision of the sweetness of his home, of the calm restfulness of the soft nest at the Villa on the Cliff in which he ought to have been then, instead of wandering in the secret channels of darkness and crime, dressed and armed like a malefactor.

"You see," he said to the Dodger, who was holding on to him like a child to the skirts of its mother, "there are some trades in which it is best to be without a family."

As he uttered those words of wisdom he felt something fall lightly on his hand. It was as though drops were trickling one by one from the ceiling. And at that very moment the terrible gasping which they had heard before broke out anew. It still came from the floor above.

He caught a slight sound as of some one dragging himself along the floor. They had not moved a muscle and Chéri-Bibi's hand was still clasped to his forehead; and he again felt the warm drops fall on his burning skin.

What was happening in the room above?

What was about to happen in that room? What was being planned against them? Into what snare would they be hurling themselves if they made the least movement. And what was the meaning of that gasping?

Chéri-Bibi leant towards the Dodger, who was suffering unutterable anguish, and took his lantern from him. He uncovered the light with extreme care and looked at his hand. It was red with blood.

Blood was dripping from the floor above.

Chéri-Bibi started back in affright. It was long since he had been accustomed to that particular kind of dew.

And drops of blood continued to fall from the ceiling on to the floor with the monotonous cadence of drops of rain trickling through a badly soldered gutter spout. The rain of blood added immensely to their feeling of terror.

Brought to bay, they both stood in the gloom, their backs leaning against the door through which they dared not pass. The Dodger was armed with a knife, and Chéri-Bibi waved on high his jimmy as if it were a club, for they had forbidden themselves the use of fire-arms. Thus they waited for some event to take place which would enlighten them as to the extent of the calamity which was prepared for them. They would have preferred an open attack to this state of pitiable suspense in the darkness, while above their heads some one seemed to be lingering in his death agony.

A small part of the floor was lit up by the rays of the lantern which they had placed at their feet. And within this compass of light the rain of blood continued to fall. . . .

Suddenly a white scrap of paper fluttered on to the same spot. . . .

There must have been sufficient room for the letter to slip between the rotten planks of the ceiling. Perhaps it contained a warning. Perhaps it would be the saving

of them. Perhaps it set a new trap for them. . . . The
thing was to be certain. Chéri-Bibi crept up to the
bloodstained note, picked it up and held it to the lantern. The few words on it had been written in blood:

*Tried to save you . . . I am dying . . . Beware . . .
Chéri-Bibi I love you . . . torture you until you sign away
everything . . . the will I believe . . . gime.*

A few words were written between "I believe" and the
last syllable "gime," but they were so intermixed with
the blood with which the note was smeared that they
had become illegible.

Chéri-Bibi lifted his eyes to the ceiling, but the gasping had ceased; nor could he hear any movement along
the floor.

"The Countess," he muttered, tearing up the note
and placing the pieces in his pocket.

In order to read it, he lay stretched on the floor
nearly level with the lantern. He was greatly surprised
when listening for the sounds from above which had
suddenly stopped, to hear distinctly the murmur of
voices from below.

He glued his ear to the floor.

And now he caught sundry phrases exchanged
quickly in an undertone, such as: "Let's wait"; "He
must be at the job still"; "The safe is very strong";
and then a sentence which revealed to him his adver-
saries' plan: "They'll have to come downstairs."

The enemy was lying in wait for them below, as he
had feared. It was there that they had made ready
their trap. He congratulated himself on having pulled
up the Dodger at the moment when he was about to go

downstairs. If he had not done so both of them would now be held prisoners by these miscreants, while, after all no such thing had happened.

In spite of the appalling rain of blood which continued to drip from the upper floor, Chéri-Bibi gradually recovered his self-command. He knew that they were looking out for him. He had time to think things over, to consider what risks he could take. He no longer had anything to fear from the upper story so long as he did not go upstairs, while he had everything to fear from the ground floor if he went downstairs.

He had no intention of venturing upstairs to the assistance of the hapless woman who was in her death throes. The part which the Countess had played seemed to him too suspicious for him to spare any pity for her, or to cease to be on his guard against her interference. That blood and that death agony were perhaps only play-acting. No, the thing that he would like to know there and then was: How many men were below?

At the moment when, to his surprise, he clearly heard the conversation between the accomplices below, he noticed that he had flattened his ear against a small trap door the ring of which fitted almost exactly into the wooden floor.

It was a tiny trap door, not more than the width of two hands. It must have been used by the proprietor either to supervise the work of his staff when he happened to be upstairs, or to shout his orders to them, or to observe for himself the character of his customers.

Chéri-Bibi motioned to the Dodger to switch off the lantern once more, and he managed quite easily to put his finger in the ring and lift up the small board. He stooped over the hole thus exposed in the flooring. His face seemed as if it were lit up by a distant and mysterious glimmer, and almost immediately he drew back stifling an exclamation. Notwithstanding the quickness of the movement his companion had caught a momentary glimpse of Chéri-Bibi's startled face.

The Dodger taking a look in his turn, cast a glance above the small space so strangely luminous, and he, too, instinctively fell back in the same way. And both of them, holding their breath, returned and crept to their peep-hole, and head to head, stared in dismay at the sight below them. Their hands, meantime, met again in a nervous grip which conveyed from one to the other the extent of their excitement.

The spectacle that met their gaze was hardly calculated to reassure them. Lit up in ghostlike fashion by the niggard light of a small lamp, which was almost entirely turned down, and shrouded by way of greater precaution with a band of paper which prevented its rays from penetrating throughout the dining room, parts of which were in complete darkness, certain faces, terrifying because they were the faces of men, who, as it were, had come back from the dead, loomed up silent and motionless.

Four men were seated round the table.

The unspeakable dismay which filled Chéri-Bibi and the Dodger was comprehensible inasmuch as the four ghostly figures whom they recognized were the Toper, the Top, Carrots and another hardened criminal from the financier's cage, called Barefoot, who was notorious for his cowardice and brutality.

Thus the flower of the "Bayard" was there. They had accompanied the Kanaka in his travels and were reckoning on a stroke of fortune which, doubtless, he had promised them if they would assist him in his project against the Marquis. The Marquis had been far too easy a prey in the first instance, and they would attempt to repeat the experiment on a large scale, and after subjecting him to a new imprisonment, fleece him, this time, to the skin.

From all appearance the Kanaka, who was physically weak and devoid of courage, had not dared to risk a struggle with Chéri-Bibi alone. And hence he had brought the gang with him so as to have Chéri-Bibi at his mercy.

Suppose they knew everything? Suppose the Kanaka had told them the whole story? Chéri-Bibi put the questions to himself torn with anguish. Suppose they knew whom they were pursuing in the guise of the Marquis du Touchais?

He called to mind Little Buddha's satirical greeting to him on the card in the writing table.

"The scoundrels know everything," said Chéri-Bibi hoarsely, dragging the Dodger into a corner of the room. "Did you recognize them? They all come from my cage. Oh, the misery of it? The entire past comes back to me."

"Monsieur le Marquis, listen to me," said the Dodger, shivering all over and conscious that since he had seen those terrifying faces his courage had ebbed away. "We had better give in."

Chéri-Bibi made no reply. He was deep in thought. He thought with the full force of his mind. In the interval between the crime that had been committed on the upper floor from which blood continued to drip, and that which was being prepared down below, he still found time to think. Little Buddha, the Toper and the others knew everything. They were fully aware of the secret which the sham Marquis du Touchais came to wrest from the mahogany writing table that stormy night. And since they were in possession of that secret, they would by degrees squeeze him until they drove him to death, after robbing him of every sou.

Could he enter into negotiations with those men? Would it be possible to live with that menace perpetually hanging over him? Seven persons now were in the secret. Heaven only knew what they would do with it. Seven persons who would scatter over the four corners of the world, and who from time to time would return and show him their hang-dog faces and hold out their hands anew; seven persons who were brought together that night; for he did not doubt that the Kanaka was somewhere near, superintending the plot as well as the agony of the Countess if it were true that she was suffering death for trying to save him, of which he was not certain. Yes, they were all there, all the men who knew or, at least, who were likely to know. Providentially they were all there! It was thus that the affair presented itself to him in the frightful blaze of conflicting thoughts with which his mind was consumed.

And so after his waverings and fears he was himself again, the Chéri-Bibi of the old days, when he rushed headlong against his fate in order to triumph over it once more. But this time he was grateful to *Fatalitas* for bringing together for a single and definite task the last survivors of the men who could have encompassed his undoing.

He would kill them all. He felt that he was a match for them all. The mania for murder was already throbbing in his hot veins. He turned to the Dodger, whose trembling ceased when he saw, or rather felt, that he had become suddenly strong, and said:

"Kill the lot without a sound."

From that moment his plan was formed.

Knowing what they wanted to know about the gang in the restaurant below, they had a marked advantage over them because the gang knew nothing of what was happening on the floor above, a fact which would end by unnerving and wearying them, and by forcing them to mount the stairs and see.

Well, then, they should see. After all the thing was to dispose of two or three of them without creating a disturbance.

Chéri-Bibi took up a position a little at the back, near the door, armed with his heavy jimmy.

The Dodger returned to his post of observation. The ominous figures below had not stirred. Vaguely he caught on the table the pale glint of glasses which were being drained in silence.

The Dodger had looked in vain for any sign of the Kanaka and Little Buddha, when suddenly the latter emerged from the darkness and, bending his yellow face over the Toper, whispered in his ear.

The Toper's eyes were raised to the ceiling; and it seemed as though they were talking of those whom they could already regard as their prisoners, and were expressing surprise that no further sound came from them. The Dodger almost at once discovered Little Buddha making signs, and the lamp which shed a feeble light was still further turned down and then taken away and placed on the mantelpiece. The Dodger went over to Chéri-Bibi and told him what he had seen.

Chéri-Bibi pushed him aside so as to retain full liberty of movement, and standing him against the wall
opposite, gave him instructions not to budge.

The rain had now ceased and, as often happens after
a violent storm, the moon shone out between two great
clouds.

Chéri-Bibi seemed to hear in the absolute silence the
creaking of one of the stairs. He imagined that Little
Buddha was tired of waiting, and had made up his
mind to see for himself what was occurring on the first
floor, and he held his breath. He was not mistaken.
The sound was repeated, and soon after the handle of
the door was turned and the door quietly opened.

The moonlight streaming into the room revealed
clearly the look of amazement on Little Buddha's face,
for he expected to find the two men engaged in opening
the writing table. At first glance he could perceive no
one.

His second look, perhaps, would have discovered
Chéri-Bibi and his lieutenant standing against the wall,
but he was not given the time for a second look.

Like a beast in a slaughter-house which receives a
blow from the ax which it does not expect, and which
falls to the ground without a groan, Little Buddha
collapsed without a sigh into the arms of the Dodger,
who laid him with the utmost care on the floor, drawing
him slightly back from the door so that his body might
not be in the way of other inquisitive persons who would
not fail, doubtless, to make their appearance.

Chéri-Bibi's jimmy, which a little while before had
smashed the mahogany writing table somewhat clumsily, had cut open Little Buddha's head quite neatly.
In short Chéri-Bibi set to work with not a little

promptitude and was "getting his hand in" to such purpose that without presumption he need not despair of completing his task.

A good five minutes elapsed when they heard, through the little peep-hole which remained open, the noise of moving feet and some amount of whispering followed by the echo of a footstep on the stairs which there was no attempt to conceal.

The door had been softly pushed back by the Dodger.

The footsteps came to a stand half-way up and after a pause of a few seconds the Top's hoarse voice was heard shouting aloud:

"Well, what's happening, Little Buddha?"

Little Buddha was unable to reply, and for a very good reason.

"Damn it all," screeched the Toper, "I bet they've cleared off." And he shouted "Little Buddha! Little Buddha!"

When he reached the door he made the error of thrusting forward the tip of his nose to "see what was going on."

The terrible jimmy swooped down like a hammer on an anvil, only the anvil offered no resistance.

"That's two of them accounted for!" said the Dodger in a tone of philosophy, placing the second body beside the first.

The unfortunate part was that this fine performance could not be kept up with the same regularity. The Toper had fallen with a crash; and the three other men rushed pell-mell to the stairs.

Chéri-Bibi and the Dodger recognized distinctly the voices of the Top, Barefoot and Carrots. They were all jabbering at once. There was no need to worry any more about the Kanaka. They had not seen him, nor had they heard them.

"Oh, the swine they've done 'em in, they've done 'em in, they've done 'em in," they shouted.

"Hold your jaw," growled Carrots. "One cannot hear one's self speak. If they don't behave themselves upstairs we shall know how to cook their goose."

"Please let me speak," begged the Top, of financial fame.

Barefoot shouted:

"Dodger, be sensible up there! Look here, Dodger, we don't want to do you any harm."

In other circumstances the three miscreants would have rushed headlong into the fray, and put their hearts in it without asking by your leave, but they seemed to have received some definite order which hampered them, notwithstanding that the fate which had befallen their two confederates was by no means calculated to reassure them. Some one must have said to them:

"Whatever you do, don't make a noise to disturb the neighbors, and don't fire your revolvers."

It was not, of course, their business to kill their hostages, but to deprive them of all power of resistance, to have them at their mercy, and their numbers were five against two, not forgetting the Kanaka and the Countess and the fact that the Dodger, in their eyes, might be left out of account. It should have been easy for them to complete the business. Therefore they were taken aback, distraught, by the brutal fact that what had happened above had deprived them of two of their best men.

They thought it well in view of the persistent silence on the first floor to bring out their knives.

If they could have made a bold attack they would have got the better of the fight, but they had before them a narrow wooden staircase which only permitted one person to pass up at a time, and they ran the risk of being bled one after the other like so many rabbits.

And that was why Barefoot held back the impetuous Carrots and why the Top tried to make his two men keep silent, in order to enter into negotiations with the enemy.

"Dodger, please tell Monsieur le Marquis that we don't want to do him any harm. He's our prisoner. He can't get away from us whatever he does. Well, it's not worth while to hurt any one. We've only got to come to terms."

Meantime Chéri-Bibi reflected that he had but three men against him, two of whom, Carrots and Barefoot, were possessed of no ordinary strength. He began, however, to think that the match was becoming an equal one, unless the Kanaka had prepared some plot against him in his own particular manner the nature of which he could not guess. He quickly made up his mind.

"I'll leave the Top to you. You must tackle him," he told the Dodger.

"I'll do my best, Monsieur le Marquis," returned the Dodger with a shudder, for he had no liking for a fight. His courage rose only when it was absolutely necessary, and his part in the adventures of the old days consisted, in most cases, of playing the spy.

"Listen to me. I'm going to make a rush on them.

You'll have the advantage of being on your feet. But don't waste any time."

Voices below were taking up the refrain again.

"Monsieur le Marquis, surrender," shouted the Top, "otherwise we shall be compelled to get at you by the door and the window at the same time. You will be caught between two fires, and if you show fight we'll have to take strong measures."

"Thank you for the warning," sneered Chéri-Bibi.

In a flash something tremendous fell upon the group of men, a huge massive body which knocked them backwards with its full force, scattering them in the darkness. The ruffians scrambled up, groped about and grabbed hold of each other.

The first man on his feet was Barefoot, but Chéri-Bibi at once seized him by the throat in an iron grip, and was choking the life out of him while with his free hand, which held the jimmy, the hero of the "Bayard," the king of convicts, whirled it so violently that Carrots, who was trying to run him through with his knife, was kept at a distance.

Realizing that he could not reach the terrible fighter with his blade, Carrots leapt back and with lowered head, taking his chance, charged from the darkness at Chéri-Bibi.

The men were once more sprawling on the floor.

Chéri-Bibi and Carrots came to grips.

Meanwhile the Dodger had made an end of the Top by ripping him open before he had the time to pick himself up. He did the work so thoroughly that the wretched man died almost instantaneously. The Dodger afterwards finished off Barefoot, who was already half dead.

When he had completed his work he stood up, holding his knife free in readiness to go to his master's assistance.

But in spite of his good intentions the Dodger was not called upon to intervene in the giant combat which was being fought out on the floor of the dimly lit restaurant.

In truth as he watched in terror the shapeless mass of the two bodies rolling on the floor as if they were but one, the Dodger could not tell to whom the arm which was suddenly raised in the air, or the leg which was kicking out, or the shoulders which were weighing down upon the other man really belonged.

The gleam from the lamp on the mantelpiece threw a feeble and fantastic light on the last movements of the struggle.

The two men as they spun round overturned chairs, tables, glasses, bottles, everything, as if they were so many skittles.

The Dodger had no wish to be caught and perhaps struck down by the tumultuous and rebounding forces which were struggling backwards and forwards in the obscurity, and he climbed several stairs and, leaning over the balusters, encouraged Chéri-Bibi in a low voice, advising him to show no mercy to his vicious enemy.

"Kill him, Chéri-Bibi. Kill him, kill him, I tell you," he cried.

It is probable that Chéri-Bibi was nothing loth and if he had not already done so, it was not his fault.

Carrots was still defending himself.

Suddenly out of the darkness in which the fight was reaching its climax, an awful moan of pain and death went up. And then nothing more. . . . Silence fell.

. . . Who had uttered that moan? The Dodger, trembling with anxiety, could not tell, for at the moment of death nearly every voice and nearly every death-rattle is alike. Who was dead? Who was waiting until the other was motionless to leave go his hold and to come either to reassure the Dodger or to "do him in" in his turn?

In spite of the prolonged silence we must do the Dodger the justice to say that he entertained little doubt of his master's victory.

"Is it over, Chéri-Bibi?" he asked.

"I'm waiting to see if he's shamming," replied Chéri-Bibi.

But Carrots was not up to any tricks. Chéri-Bibi chanced while disporting himself on the floor to touch the jimmy which slipped from his hand in his fall, and with rare good fortune he had driven it into Carrot's brain by the ready-made road of the eye.

Carrots was dead. Chéri-Bibi was not even wounded, protected as he was from the knife by a splendid chain of mail belonging to his ancestor, Marshal du Touchais, who wore it at the Battle of Argues, fighting on the side of the Duc de Mayenne against Henry IV, the Huguenot king.

This strong and delicate masterpiece of the olden-time armorer's art had attracted his attention at the time of his first visit to the Château du Touchais when he had arranged for his mother to return to it with all the honors due to her rank after the departure of the "Belle of Dieppe." He put the chain of mail in his pocket, saying to himself: "Here we have something which will be of great use in fights with cold steel."

The event showed that he was right, but all the same

he did not explain to the Dodger the secret of his invulnerability, preferring to witness his amazement at such luck and desirous not to lose prestige in the eyes of his "staff."

CHAPTER XIII

CHÉRI-BIBI having risen, requested the Dodger with a sight to go and see if there was "anything else remaining to be done."

The Dodger took the lamp from the mantelpiece and made for the battlefield, ready to give the finishing stroke to the vanquished if necessary. But he realized from the open mouths, the glazed eyes, and the absence of breathing that the three convicts were dead. The Dodger vouched for it and Chéri-Bibi turned his head.

"My dear Dodger, you were very plucky. . . . Have a look at the two men upstairs," said Chéri-Bibi, who was a man of system but to whom subordinate tasks were always repugnant.

The Dodger's voice was soon heard:

"Both are dead."

"The world is well rid of them," returned Chéri-Bibi. Thus he conferred on himself a diploma of good citizenship which was intended if needs be to pacify a possible feeling of remorse.

"At all events dead men tell no tales," said the Dodger, who certainly was possessed with a hatred of gossipers. "It's all the better even if they knew nothing of your secret, for they knew mine. We must regret, Monsieur le Marquis, that the infamous Kanaka is not included in the picture."

239

Chéri-Bibi, who had rejoined his lieutenant on the first floor, did not deign to smile at the bold cynicism of the phrase.

"Let's be off, Dodger. We may have a chat to-morrow morning. There's nothing more to be done."

"I've known the time when you would have shown much more curiosity," said the Dodger.

"What do you mean?"

"I mean that nothing presses since the Countess is no longer waiting for us at 'The Fronds,' and we've got plenty of time to have a look upstairs where that red blood comes from, and also to see if by any chance the Kanaka is hiding in the roof."

"Perhaps you're right, but I'm very tired," sighed Chéri-Bibi.

"Oh, you can stand a lot yet," objected the Dodger in a tone of the basest flattery, "and I feel certain that one good blow from your shoulders is all that is needed to break in this door which leads upstairs."

"I'm afraid of some trap."

"Monsieur le Marquis, after seeing you just now on the job, I'm only afraid of one thing, which is that we may be leaving the place without going to the assistance of a poor woman upstairs who is perhaps dying on your account."

"What you say shows that you've got a good heart, Dodger, but I can't forget that it was that woman who lured me here by her clever lying."

"I don't agree with you. She was in love with you. It was she who was deceived. The Kanaka must have known that she was in sympathy with you. He said to himself: 'If I tell her the story that the will is in the writing-table in the restaurant she will repeat it to the

Marquis, who will go there and hunt for it.' If you ask me, that's the whole story."

"Upon my word, what you say is quite likely."

"And what is even more likely is that the poor woman, learning at the last moment that the will was somewhere else, realized that she had been fooled and feared they were setting a trap for you. She must have hastened here determined to thwart their schemes. And the Kanaka killed her. . . . Listen, Monsieur le Marquis, listen. . . . She is gasping again upstairs. The blood has stopped dripping, but she is still moaning. Perhaps she is conscious. . . . So let's make up our minds what to do," said the Dodger, amazed at his master's inaction.

"Of course it's not very cheerful work to carry on a conversation with dead bodies around us, so whatever we do let's do it quickly, and get away from this place as soon as we can," said Chéri-Bibi.

"Come on, give a good blow with your shoulder. We may get up to the poor thing in time for her to tell us, if she really knows, where the will is."

"Well, go ahead, but bear in mind, Dodger, that up to now I've never had any luck when murder has been done and when I've been found by the police near the dead bodies."

"Oh, Monsieur, listen . . . listen."

The Dodger pointed to the ceiling. The sound of painful gasping could still be heard, and the blood again began to drip.

"God help us!" exclaimed the Marquis, using the favorite expression of sailors when they venture upon some desperate maneuver in a storm, and he threw himself against the door.

The door gave way and the two men reached the upper floor in a bound. The Dodger opened a door in which the key had been left outside, and in the moonlight they beheld a body lying on the floor. A low wail went up from it.

"Bring your lantern," ordered Chéri-Bibi.

The Dodger had to go downstairs to fetch it. When he returned he found his master bending over a woman whose head he was supporting. It was the Countess in her death agony. Her throat and breast had been stabbed with a knife.

"Oh, the poor thing, the poor thing," groaned Chéri-Bibi. "Who could have had the cruelty to treat her like this? If it's the Kanaka, I'll avenge her . . . I'll avenge her."

The Dodger threw the beams of the lantern over the awful spectacle. The room was in disorder. The Countess had obviously endeavored to defend herself, and later, when her enemies left her for dead, had managed to drag herself to the desk, and with a hand covered with blood leaving traces everywhere, to find a sheet of paper, and write in letters of blood those last words to Chéri-Bibi; the final memory of herself that she left him, longing with the last strength of her dying soul for her words to reach him and show that she had not betrayed him.

The Dodger found a basin and water, moistened a towel, and wrapped it round the poor woman's head, and she opened her eyes. Death had already imparted a glassy stare to them. Nevertheless she must have recognized Chéri-Bibi, for her wan lips were touched by the flicker of a sad smile.

He remembered that she had saved his life once

before, had loved him, and that he had never shown her the slightest affection, and, bending over her, he pressed a kiss upon her forehead.

Her face seemed to light up, her eyes opened wider and recovered a last gleam, her lips moved and she breathed a name. . . . And then after a pause and a supreme effort another name.

Chéri-Bibi thought of "gime," the last syllable on the bloodstained letter.

"Maître Régime," he cried, "The will is with Maître Régime. . . . Countess, I swear that I will avenge you."

But she could no longer hear him. She was dead.

After climbing to the roof, inspecting all the rooms, and making sure that they were leaving nothing behind them but dead bodies, Chéri-Bibi and the Dodger carefully opened the front door, which was locked on the inside, and looked out on to the quay through the arcades. Not a soul was outside. The rain had started to fall again, offering them the protection of its kindly screen.

Less than an hour later they reached the Villa on the Cliff without meeting any untoward adventure. They cast off their old rags and hid them where they knew they could find them in a hole which they covered with stones, for they anticipated that they would need them again. They had worked hard enough for one night and deserved a rest.

The Marquis himself slept until eleven o'clock, when he rang for his valet. He learnt that some one had come that morning from the Dowager Marchioness to fetch Cecily since the former had suffered a relapse. Dr. Walter was in attendance on her.

"Are you certain?" inquired Chéri-Bibi, amazed at the man's effrontery. "Are you certain that Dr. Walter is at the Château?"

"Quite certain, Monsieur le Marquis. I myself went to fetch him."

"Very well. Let me dress."

"Do you wish me to assist you, Monsieur le Marquis?"

"No, you clear out."

Chéri-Bibi for reasons known to himself invariably dressed alone, and had no need of his valet to help him with his shirt.

Ten minutes later he descended to the hall and was on the point of leaving the house when two unshaven gentlemen appeared, hat in hand.

"Are you the Marquis du Touchais?"

"Yes, what do you want with me?"

"We are detective officers, Monsieur le Marquis, and our orders are not to allow you to leave your house."

Chéri-Bibi grew white and retreated to the far end of the hall.

"Who gave those orders?" he had the strength to articulate, mastering by an immense effort of will the terrible agitation which was suffocating him.

"Detective Inspector Costaud himself, Monsieur le Marquis. Besides he will be here almost at once and will give you the necessary information."

"Very well, gentlemen. I'll return to the drawing room."

And he disappeared, shutting the door in their faces.

As soon as he reached the room he collapsed, and said in a smothered voice:

"It's all up with me."

Meanwhile Costaud was on his way. He hadn't a moment to lose. The window was open. He thought he might scurry away and escape across country. He leapt forward and was getting ready to bestride the window when a form rose up before him coming from the garden.

"Good morning, Monsieur le Marquis."

It was Costaud.

CHAPTER XIV

CHÉRI-BIBI was still in a state of great excitement when
Detective Inspector Costaud, who came to him in the
drawing room, apologized for the liberty that he had
taken in keeping him under observation.

"Monsieur le Marquis," explained this honest detective, "I did not wish you to leave your house this morning without being warned of the danger that hangs over
you. A murder or rather a series of murders have been
brought to light in Dieppe. Chéri-Bibi has returned!"

The Marquis raised to the worthy Costaud a face
whose pallor was pitiful to see, and the detective did not
fail to attribute to the ominous news of which he was
the bearer the agitation of which he was very far from
suspecting the real cause.

The Marquis, however, after uttering a deep sigh
seemed to recover from his sudden alarm. Costaud
helped him to feel better by promising him, for his protection, the devoted assistance of his men. Costaud was
literally beaming. An extraordinary delight shone
upon his features, usually rather frigid. But since the
event had proved only too clearly that he was right, no
one could bear him malice for showing somewhat im-
properly his joy in his triumph. He had always said
that the notorious Chéri-Bibi was not dead and would
be heard of again. And now the murderer of M. Bour-

246

relier and the old Marquis du Touchais had appeared
once more on the scene of his early exploits!

"How reckless," the Marquis could not refrain from
observing. "Doesn't he know Monsieur Costaud, that
you are here?"

"That's a detail," returned the elated Costaud in no
way disconcerted. "That's a detail which did not deter
him since he knew that he would have the pleasure of
meeting you here."

The Marquis cast a sidelong glance at Costaud fearing lest he was jesting, but the Detective Inspector was
never more serious. Moreover, he at once explained
himself.

"It's you, Monsieur le Marquis, who are most threatened in this business. There's no doubt that the
wretches have returned to these parts with the object,
in the main, of extorting another little million out of
you. The gang with whom you had to do on the
'Bayard' were not exterminated as people were pleased
to say."

"Are you sure that Chéri-Bibi is with them?"

"Yes, Monsieur le Marquis. He brought back a certain Little Buddha with him and those other flowers
among convicts the Toper, Barefoot, Carrots and the
Top. You need have no concern about them. They
were murdered last night."

"Murdered . . . Who committed the deed, Monsieur Costaud?"

"In my opinion, Chéri-Bibi himself. Their bodies
were found in the restaurant in the harbor which Little
Buddha had rented—under a false name of course. It
was there, no doubt, that they were going to carry out
their scheme which would have placed you in their

power, because we found on them certain papers in which mention is made of a trap laid for you, and we saw a card in a writing table bearing an odd inscription in Little Buddha's handwriting in which he presents his compliments to you, and this, everything considered, must be regarded as a threat."

"What cheek!"

"It's precisely as I tell you, Monsieur le Marquis. Only at the last moment they could not come to terms among themselves, and they determined to get rid of Chéri-Bibi who, no doubt, was considered too tyrannical and, of course, had marked out for himself the lion's share. They joined together to kill him; but it was an unlucky thought for them. Chéri-Bibi reduced the lot of them to a bleeding pulp. You ought to see it, Monsieur le Marquis, it's a remarkable piece of work. . . . Oh his hand has lost nothing of its cunning."

"But there's nothing in all this to prove Chéri-Bibi's intervention."

"Yes there is, Monsieur le Marquis. To begin with, there is this butchery which bears his imprint as I will undertake to prove to the public prosecutor; and then, in order that every one should know it, there is a little piece of bloodstained paper, unfortunately torn, on which is written in letters of blood: 'Beware Chéri-Bibi! . . .' That warning must have been written by one of the confederates who was on the upper floor, and whom the others half-killed, for he has disappeared leaving on the first and second floors frightful traces of blood. Perhaps Chéri-Bibi himself, after his victory, carried him off since he was dying, not wishing to leave such a good friend in the hands of the police."

"The whole story is terrible," said the Marquis du
Touchais.

"If I may give you my opinion, Monsieur le Marquis,
the whole thing should put you on your guard. . . .
Be careful! Take no risks until we have captured
Chéri-Bibi, who must be thinking only of one thing; how
to seize a man of your importance as a hostage. My
men will not lose sight of you."

Chéri-Bibi made a wry face and since he was above
all a good husband and father, said:

"Upon my word, Monsieur Costaud, I can only thank
you for showing such praiseworthy zeal. Nevertheless
I should like this watch to be kept with discretion and
not too near me as I don't want to alarm my family. I
am particularly anxious that the Marchioness should
have no suspicion that the infernal Chéri-Bibi's return
may expose me to danger. I know her, the dear lady,
and it would make her ill."

"You can rely on my tact, Monsieur le Marquis."

"I do rely on it, Monsieur Costaud."

Costaud took his leave, for the ghastly business would
impose on him a considerable amount of work; and
Chéri-Bibi turned his steps to the Lodge where the
worthy Dodger was still sleeping like a top.

The news of the murders in the restaurant spread
with great rapidity, and by the afternoon the entire
population was on the quays. One name flew from
mouth to mouth: Chéri-Bibi. Chéri-Bibi had come
back. . . . And to make himself welcome his first action was to commit four murders. What a man he was!
And he was supposed to be dead!

The story went that he had escaped by the roofs,
that he was disguised as a policeman; indeed a thou-

sand silly tales were current. People suddenly stopped talking and let their gaze stray stealthily to the faces around them. He was thought to be far away and he was, perhaps, quite near, listening with both ears, and quite capable of revenging himself, there and then, on such persons as were indiscreet enough to let their tongues run away with them.

A great crowd assembled in the arcades and the fish market, and in spite of the policemen on duty, an indescribable confusion reigned outside the restaurant itself.

Suddenly the morbid interest and curiosity of the multitude seemed to be transferred to that part of the quay beyond the bridge at which the suburb of Le Pollet begins. There was a general movement to this place resulting in a great crush at the bottom of the hill leading to Dieppe. It was due to an extremely gruesome discovery made at low tide in this quarter of the harbor. Some sailors had fished up, from the mud, the body and leg of a woman.

The horrible remains were removed to the Morgue to the accompaniment of a concert of maledictions, and it was soon known that these were the dismembered parts of some woman who had been murdered only a few hours before. Chéri-Bibi again! The monster's image seemed to grow in horror, and many persons who were present went home and barricaded themselves in with a shudder of fear. Gunsmiths coined money, for every one wanted to be armed. A rush was made for the local newspapers which told the outrageous story almost as it had been imagined by M. Costaud. In an interview he requested the people to retain their self-control, and to furnish him with any information which

might assist the police. M. Costaud hinted vaguely
that he was already on the track of the criminal, and
that it would not be long before he laid hands on him
for the third time.

The Paris evening papers contained huge head-
lines in which the four resounding syllables Chéri-Bibi
stood out conspicuously as was only natural. The shop-
keepers in the Grand Rue closed their shutters early.
In the neighboring seaside places similar precautions
were adopted. At Puys and Pourville no person loi-
tered in the streets or highways.

Among the most apprehensive, mention must be made
of Maître and Madame Régime who were staying at
Pourville. They heard the frightful news at Dieppe
through which they were passing, intending to pay a
courtesy visit to the Marquis and Marchioness du Touchais whom they had not seen for some time. As soon
as they heard of Chéri-Bibi's fearsome presence they
interrupted their little trip. The Marquis more than
any other person, it was said, was menaced by his old
jailor of the "Bayard," and it would certainly be un-
wise to "rush into the lion's den," as Mme. Régime
suggested in a tremulous voice.

"You are right, Nathalie," agreed Maître Régime.
"Let's go back home. It's no business of ours. Besides
I shouldn't be of any assistance to the Marquis, and
they say that he's well guarded."

They went back to their villa "Sea-Mew," at Pourville, which they had rented quite cheaply because it
was the end of the season and also because it was somewhat lonely, standing in a wood not far from the cliff.
The former tenant was no other than M. de Pont-Marie

who never lived there, and suddenly disappeared from the country after pretty well ruining himself.

When evening came and they found themselves and their old servant alone in the house, which was much too large for them, they regretted their isolation at a moment when Chéri-Bibi's notoriety had been given a new birth.

With a revolver in his hand, an old family revolver, all rusty, which was never loaded lest it should burst, Maître Régime accompanied by his trembling spouse made the tour of the premises, and personally assured himself that the doors were properly fastened. Then they "supped," as they say in those parts to denote the meal at eight o'clock. They were full of Chéri-Bibi's crimes, old and new, but they spoke in an undertone as though the ruffian were in hiding near and could overhear them.

At the finish their conversation had reduced them to a condition of painful trepidation, and they determined to leave Pourville and Dieppe the following day.

They retired upstairs to bed and blew out the candle but were unable to sleep. Every moment they seemed to hear unnatural sounds. Yet the noises were but the wind whistling through the trees, the crackle of a branch outside, the groaning of a worm-eaten piece of furniture inside.

"Let's have a light," begged Nathalie.

They lighted the candle and blew it out again several times. At length towards midnight they dosed off into a sleep under the bedclothes in the darkness.

Suddenly both awoke at the same time. It seemed to them as if the candle had flared up of its own accord. There was a light in the bedroom, but a queer

light, a spindle-like gleam which wandered over the
walls and furniture and abruptly flashed full in their
faces, blinding them while they gave a despairing groan
in mortal terror.

Two men were in the room. . . . Maître Régime put
up a head under his cotton night-cap and, dismayed,
cried in a stifled voice:

"Mercy! Who's there?"

His distracted better half drew back under the bedclothes without waiting for the reply. To Maître Régime's question a voice made answer:

"It's me, Chéri-Bibi!"

From the depths of the bed a prodigious groan came
forth. Maître Régime's head fell back on to the wooden
bed with a hollow sound, and the top of a night-cap
arose in a flutter as if even inanimate things were conscious of the horror of the situation.

Nevertheless Chéri-Bibi attempted to tranquillize the
affrighted couple:

"Pull yourself together, Maître Régime," he said,
"And you too madame. We shan't kill you unless it's
absolutely necessary!" Fresh start of the night-cap;
fresh groan under the bedclothes. "We're not here to
do you any harm, but to ask you to do us a little service. We know that your friend Dr. Walter placed in
your hands a sealed document which is, in fact, his
will. Is that correct?" The night-cap moved in a way
that might be taken to signify an affirmative. "That
being so, give us the will and we will be satisfied."

Chéri-Bibi had no sooner finished speaking than
Madame Régime's scared features appeared above the
coverlet.

"Give him the will, Polydore," she exclaimed.

Maître Régime never opposed his wife's wishes when she called him by his Christian name, and this was not the occasion to make an exception to the rule. He stretched out a trembling hand above the bedside table, and not without difficulty managed to slip it into the drawer which contained his bunch of keys; but the old family revolver lay in this very drawer and Chéri-Bibi leapt on to the poor fellow seizing him by the throat.

Mme. Régime uttered a shriek of terror while Polydore gasped for breath.

"Ah, you wanted to get hold of your revolver. You shall die," said Chéri-Bibi.

"Have pity, my good sir . . . it's not loaded . . . not loaded," cried Mme. Régime in a frenzy, clasping her hands.

Chéri-Bibi dropped Polydore, and the night-cap fell back limp on to the side of the bed. He was incapable of uttering a single word after this attack, and it was Nathalie who took charge of the proceedings.

"My good sir, the bunch of keys is in the table by the bedside . . ." and she pointed it out to the two masked shadows standing erect before her . . . "there . . . there and that's the key which opens the desk . . . there in front of you. You'll find the will on the first shelf. It bears the words 'Will of Dr. Walter.' You'll also find some money there, about fifteen hundred francs and a little change . . . take it all. We give it all to you."

"Yes all," said the night-cap, which had come to life again.

"Do you take us for thieves?" demanded Chéri-Bibi.

"No, no," cried Polydore and Nathalie in unison.

"Well, keep your money. We make you a present of it."

Chéri-Bibi with the bunch of keys in his hand stole to the desk which he opened and in which, in fact, he easily found the will. By the light of his dark lantern he examined the seals, and then stowed the document away in his pocket.

"Now we've only one thing more to say to you, dear sir and madame, which is, that if ever you breathe a word about our visit, your numbers will be up. . . . A word and you'll die. . . . Take it from Chéri-Bibi. You quite understand, don't you? No one has taken the will away from you."

"No, no, we'll say we lost it," promised Nathalie.

"If you say you've lost it, you'll be dead within a couple of hours."

"Heavens above! . . . Then we'll say nothing at all about it."

"That'll be the best thing for all of us," returned Chéri-Bibi. "Good-night, monsieur; good night, madame. We shan't see you again unless you want to lose your tongue or have your throat cut, at your option!"

"Messieurs we give you our word of honor," said the night-cap.

The two shadows bowed and disappeared in the most imperturbable and normal manner, namely, through the doors of which they possessed the keys.

Standing at the window, behind the Venetian blinds, and holding each other in a final grip of distress, Polydore and Nathalie watched them as they plunged into the darkness and made for the road to the beach.

"Well, he is not so black as he is painted," considered Mme. Régime.

"Why does Chéri-Bibi want Dr. Walter's will?" asked Maître Régime, thinking aloud.

"If you want to please me, Polydore, you won't ask any one that question."

"No one," swore M. Régime, and at Nathalie's suggestion they fell on their knees, as they were wont to do in the days of their childhood, and thanked Heaven for saving them from the clutches of the terrible Chéri-Bibi at no greater cost to themselves than a breach of professional duty.

Out of doors the night was now dark and anon bright for masses of clouds floated across the sky and concealed or discovered the moon. Chéri-Bibi and the Dodger crept forward with caution. They reached the beach unimpeded. It was low tide.

They went back to Dieppe and Puys over the shingle, thus avoiding the roads in which they might have encountered the numerous detectives whom Costaud had brought down from Paris.

The Dodger was delighted with their expedition which had succeeded to perfection. Nevertheless Chéri-Bibi betrayed some dejection as he reflected that his task was not yet finished, and that though he had seized the will, it still remained for him to kill the testator.

"Oh the villain," cried the Dodger, "he little suspects what's in store for him. He'll have a nice awakening soon in his bye-bye; for he must be sleeping calmly, the wretch, feeling sure that he's absolutely safe and that we are bound hand and foot."

"Yes," growled Chéri-Bibi, "and the insolence of the man! If you had seen and heard him as I did in my

house a few hours after the murder of the poor Countess, and in spite of the slaughter of his men! . . . Yes
in my own house. He dared to show himself and talk
as if nothing out of the way had happened."

"What cheek!"

"Oh nothing shames and nothing frightens him. He
came from the Château du Touchais to the Villa on the
Cliff with the Marchioness, my wife, and was reassuring
her as if he were an honest man as to the result of
the Dowager's new attack. . . . He advised me, in
Cecily's presence, to keep calm. I had a longing to
fly at his throat, and he realized it quite plainly. He
smiled satirically, knowing that since he told me,
through the Countess, that he had made his will, he
held the whip hand. And when Cecily, as he was leaving
us, asked him to remember her to Madame Walter, he
answered in the calmest of tones, fixing his eyes on me,
'Madame Walter had left home for a short journey.' "

"I think you'll have the pleasure of making him taste
death," said the Dodger.

"Yes, although I'm feeling the strain," returned
Chéri-Bibi. . . . "It was absolutely horrible to cut her
into pieces like that."

"He must have returned to the restaurant to do that
particular little job, because, if you ask me, he slipped
away from the place when he saw that matters were
going against him. The Kanaka never had any physical courage, and then he reflected that her body would
be found and recognized as that of Dr. Walter's wife.
So he went back to the place and cut the poor thing into
pieces because in that way it was easier to dispose of
her and less easy to identify her."

"Poor thing, she was very much in love with me," sighed Chéri-Bibi.

"Tut, tut, don't lose your nerve, Monsieur le Marquis. Things couldn't have turned out better. The Kanaka's death will be put down to the abominable Chéri-Bibi, while M. Costaud's men will continue to guard the Marquis at the very door of the Villa on the Cliff, and provide him with an alibi which will remove all suspicion, if any such should arise, which I refuse to believe."

"Dodger, I am very weary . . . weary."

"Sit down then."

"That's not what I mean, old man. I mean that I'm weary of bloodshed."

"But, Monsieur le Marquis, seeing there's nothing else to be done." . . . And the Dodger gave a grievous sigh. . . . "And to think that all this is owing to that infernal tatooing business. Oh the man who tatooed you didn't waste his ink!"

"That's what I always said when you asked me to get the marks removed. Oh how hard I tried! Before I escaped I went to all the tatooers and asked them to get rid of the marks. They could do nothing. It was no use working with the needle. And since they did not succeed in effacing the confounded marks, they tried to modify them, to transform them by adding other letters, by extending them, and by decorating them, but it was all to no purpose. The words 'Chéri-Bibi' still stood out above the others. . . . My tatooer was very proud of the fact. He told me that the work was done with an indelible ink which was unlike any other ink, and he alone possessed the secret of it. It was ink distilled from plants gathered in the primeval forest."

"But couldn't he himself get rid of the marks?"

"No, he couldn't. I offered him anything he liked, liberty, a share in our store of gold in the forest . . . anything. He couldn't do it. The good Lord himself couldn't do it he told me. . . . And, look here, I'll tell you something so that you needn't bring up the subject again. Last winter I went to Paris alone for a fortnight. Well, the object was—that and nothing else— to try and get the marks obliterated. I had heard of an electric treatment of high frequency currents which remove marks from your skin as easily as if your skin were a water color painting. I tried it. Yes, I was treated several times by the d'Arsonval method. . . ."

"But you must have had to take your things off to do that. The doctor who gave you the d'Arsonval treatment must have seen you."

"No, you need not strip entirely. You keep certain things on. So you can imagine my excitement when I got back to the hotel and took off my shirt. Well, upon my word, all the other tatoo marks, and all the decorations disappeared by degrees. But the words 'Chéri-Bibi' stood out more boldly than ever. It was like a decree of fate. *Fatalitas.*"

They continued their way in silence after uttering this last word which had emphasized for so long their misfortunes. They swam across the Dieppe canal without any great difficulty, and stood once more, soaking wet, on the beach which led to Puys, and they soon entered the village. They were creeping along the sunk road to "The Fronds" with the utmost caution, when the sound of voices made them draw back quickly into a footpath near a church.

They stopped concealing themselves behind a hedge, in order to allow two shadows to pass which were coming towards them at a rapid pace. They recognized the voices. One was the Kanaka's and the other was Rose's. The lady companion had come to fetch Dr. Walter in the middle of the night, for the Dowager Marchioness' illness had taken a turn for the worse.

When they passed out of hearing Chéri-Bibi, losing patience with this interruption of his plan, could not repress an oath.

"That's another who would do well to die now once for all," he said, referring to the old Marchioness.

"Monsieur le Marquis!" protested the Dodger. "How can you say such a thing. It's sacrilege to wish for the death of one's mother. It will bring us bad luck."

"You're quite right, Dodger. Touch wood."

The Dodger was to remember for the rest of his life his master's impious wish, and, alas, to regret it with sincere tears for he was devoted to him.

"And now what are we going to do?" asked the latter. "Suppose we go to bed."

"Oh no, certainly not," returned the Dodger. "We must finish the business to-night come what may. We will go back again to the beach, and stay at the foot of the cliff not far from the flight of steps which leads up to the Château, and by which the Kanaka is bound to descend. He will be alone this time. You'll only have to stretch out your arm to strike him down."

"Well, go ahead old man," agreed Chéri-Bibi, "and let's hope that the villain won't make us wait too long, for I'm quite frozen in these abominable wet rags, and I'm at the end of my tether."

They were dressed for their night's work in the old rags which they wore the night before. They looked like real tramps and were shivering from head to foot.

They sat on the beach behind a hut and waited for the Kanaka to return. Lights gleamed from the Château windows above them.

"Oh the villain keeps us waiting," sighed Chéri-Bibi. "How irritating it is for me, the Marquis du Touchais, to be here on this deserted beach, at this hour, and on a dull night like this, in this horrible get-up, prepared to use the knife again as in the worst days of my life. Dodger, I will confess to you that I am really out of heart. . . .

"I can't go on like this. I feel as if I had been degraded and that I've got to begin all my work and life over again in order to win back the position which I gained with so much difficulty. Here I am again like a poor soldier of crime, like a ragamuffin who has neither house nor home nor God. The whole thing, you see, doesn't become me at my time of life. It's pitiable and it's not right."

As Chéri-Bibi gave utterance to his thoughts his voice grew so dejected that the Dodger was moved to pity, and it was with tears in his eyes that he replied:

"One more little effort, Monsieur le Marquis, and we shall be at the end of our troubles. . . . A tiny little little effort, a mere trifle."

"Yes, another murder. You call it a little effort, a mere trifle. I've done nothing else all my life, and now I'm tired of it. Certainly fate never spares its victims. I am still wading in a sea of blood. There isn't a more miserable man on earth than I am when I think of it. If Cecily were not so much in love with me, and if I hadn't got a son, I should blow my brains out without a doubt."

"Come, Monsieur le Marquis, come. . . ."

"Look here, Dodger, be fair. Have you ever heard of such a career as mine? Men in the world have been driven to slaughter before now, and poets have sung their miseries in tragedies and dramas. Their lives were as nothing compared with mine. . . .

"I have seen those plays performed. Fate again led me to see them when I went to Paris last time to undergo the d'Arsonval treatment. I saw *Hamlet*. Well, *Hamlet* is bad enough. All the characters in the play die—drowned, strangled, stabbed or put to the sword. But this is nothing compared with what has happened, with what is happening in my family. And then last year I went with Cecily to see Mounet-Sully in *Œdipus the King*. Well Œdipus is more miserable than Hamlet. Fate in his case did not do things by halves. Œdipus killed his father without knowing it. He married his mother without knowing it. He was the brother of his own children. He put out his own eyes and thus became blind. And he was not to blame, it was *fatalitas;* he suffered the decrees of fate. I too am the victim of fate. . . .

"I am a kind of Œdipus. When I saw the play it made me ill. I longed to interrupt the performance, to rush upon the stage, to call a halt to Mounet-Sully and to cry: 'It's not Œdipus who is acting a farce, it's I . . . I. . . . I. . . . I who killed my father-in-law, who caused my wife's husband to be killed, I who am the murderer of my children's father, I who have killed myself in order to live with a face that is not my own.' I left the theater foaming, without troubling about Cecily who ran behind me. People took me for a madman. *Fatalitas!* Œdipus was more wretched than Hamlet but less wretched than I."

And Chéri-Bibi lifted his hand to the Heavens and cursed as of old as he contrasted his woes with the woes of the son of Laius. The Dodger hardly dared to speak another word when he saw him so utterly cast down. Nevertheless he would be wanting in his duty if he allowed him to remain in a state of prostration at a moment when he needed the full possession of his energies to kill Dr. Walter.

"Monsieur le Marquis, when I consider the nature and character of the persons who died by your hand, I see no grounds why you should unduly distress yourself; and you do wrong to find fault with Heaven which has so justly distributed your blows. Let us begin at the beginning as the Kanaka hasn't appeared yet, and is giving you the time to read yourself clearly before you inflict the punishment on him which he deserves more than any one. First there is old Bourrelier who took advantage of your sister. Abandoning every thought of revenge, in the true Christian spirit, you were on the point of saving his life when he was about to be hurled over the cliff by some wretched man in a gray hat. But instead of hitting the man in the gray hat you inadvertently planted your knife up to the hilt in old Bourrelier's back. Do you pity him? No, because he deserved his fate, and Heaven took care that he should submit to it. . . .

"Personally, I see the hand of Providence in everything that has happened to you as a result. Providence assuredly desired to punish a certain number of other persons in the world who were quite as contemptible as old Bourrelier, and that is why it caused you to be unjustly prosecuted and condemned for crimes which you did not commit, so that in your irritation and in the exceptional difficulties of your life, you should become the blind instrument of which it stood in need. . . .

"Don't forget that you have never killed any one for the pleasure of killing, but only when driven into a corner by the necessity of defending yourself. Doubtless it was written that those whom you struck down should go under as a punishment for their sins. But for you, Madame Cecily's first husband would have continued to torture that divine creature. So you cannot regret the death of her tormentor seeing that she would never have been rewarded for her virtue in this world if you hadn't taken the place of a man unworthy of her. . . .

"Then again had it not been written that Little Buddha, Barefoot, Carrots and the Top should meet the end of their detestable lives in this country, do you suppose that fatality, as you call it, would have taken the trouble to bring them here so that all four of them should die by your hand? Moreover, fatality knows what it is about in seeking to throw the defenseless Kanaka into your arms. It will not be long before he expiates the crime of killing a poor woman whose mutilated body is being found all over the place."

"What you say does me good, my dear Dodger," confessed Chéri-Bibi. "Nevertheless I cannot find myself again on the beach without going back in imagination to that fatal night two days after Bourrelier's death, when in this very spot where I now am, I saw the man in the gray hat mount the cliff steps leading to the Château du Touchais. That man more than any one else deserved to be brought to book by me, and yet he has always escaped me. . . .

"After attacking old Bourrelier two days before, and

stealing his pocket book, he determined to murder the
Marquis du Touchais, a worthy man who never harmed
a soul. Oh I can see myself now following the scoundrel's footsteps and arriving too late, unfortunately,
to save the Marquis' life, but early enough to be arrested as the murderer! And do you think it just that
after so many years he should still remain unpunished,
and people should still be ignorant of his crime, while
the name of Chéri-Bibi should still serve as a bogy with
which to frighten little children?"

"And grown up people as well," the Dodger thought
it well to interpose; "but don't lose patience, everything comes to him who waits, and I am convinced that
that villain's turn will come like the rest. Didn't you
tell me that Rose knows much more about him than we
do?"

"Yes, she took Sister St. Mary of the Angels into her
confidence to some extent and then refused to say another word. There's no reason why she should speak
now after keeping silent so long. Why did she spare
the man in the gray hat? I have an idea that he may
belong to our world. She is certainly afraid of creating
a scandal. . . . She knew him. She must have seen
his face while I caught sight only of his back, first of
all on the cliff, and afterwards on the steps, at that
spot revealed by the moon."

So saying, Chéri-Bibi pointed to the cliff, and suddenly he sprang up quivering with such excitement that
the Dodger followed his gesture and anxiously asked
him what was the matter.

"Don't you see, don't you see? . . . There. . . .
there on the cliff."

The Dodger at length observed the cause of his agitation. Skirting the rock and going along an almost perpendicular path which appeared impracticable for a human being, a shadow glided and reached one of the stair-heads of the narrow flight of steps leading to the Château du Touchais. Suddenly the shadow appeared in the full light of the moon and Chéri-Bibi cried:

"That's the man in the gray hat. . . . Yes, it's he, it's his movements, his bearing, his form and figure. Besides he was exactly the same; he was ill at ease like this man."

Chéri-Bibi was ready to dart forward and the Dodger had great difficulty in holding him back.

"Let me go. I tell you it's he. He took the same path."

Chéri-Bibi roughly hustled the Dodger, and at that moment the man above them turned round apparently to see if there was any one on the beach and as if he feared to be discovered from below. The two men, hidden from view behind the hut, uttered the same exclamation:

"De Pont-Marie!"

Chéri-Bibi threw himself on his hands and knees and crept along, his jaw thrust forward, like a wolf. The Dodger stole behind him to the foot of the cliff.

"Leave him to me," said Chéri-Bibi, "I ought to have suspected it. Never mind. That man's time has come!"

"But what takes him to the Château?"

"Cecily is staying there to-night with the Marchioness. The villain must be up to some mischief. Stay here and, whatever you do, don't budge unless I call you."

As de Pont-Marie seemed to make up his mind to

ascend the last steps, Chéri-Bibi took advantage of a cloud which floated across the moon to go forward.

When the moon appeared once more he was on the top steps, but de Pont-Marie had disappeared as if by magic. Had he heard footsteps behind him, and drawn back to the cliff, or had he slipped into the Château through the little door leading into the garden which was still slightly ajar, as it was on the night of the tragedy? Dr. Walter and Rose must have passed through, and in their hurry omitted to close it.

Chéri-Bibi pushed the door and went in. He looked round him. No one was there. And this nocturnal expedition which was no part of his program stirred up within him all the old memories. Nevertheless he did not delay, but pursued his investigations. He hunted throughout the garden with the utmost caution. De Pont-Marie was not there. Chéri-Bibi assumed that he himself was to blame, for making a noise, and revealing himself prematurely. The argument was quite plausible.

He sat down on a settle in the shadow of a thicket and continued in silence to keep a lookout round him. De Pont-Marie certainly had had no time to enter the Château as the doors were locked.

Lights gleamed from the windows of the first floor, in the wing occupied by the Marchioness. Chéri-Bibi discerned through the windows the silhouettes of Cecily and Rose moving about as if busily engaged. A third person came to them and a brief discussion ensued. The third person was Dr. Walter who was doubtless giving his last injunctions.

Chéri-Bibi was so greatly perturbed by the discovery which he had just made, and his heart was so full of

wrath against de Pont-Marie in whom he saw the sorry
being whom he had, in the old days, vainly endeavored
to trace, that he forgot his mission to kill the Kanaka
that night. It was left to events to remind him of it
by showing him that the death of the Kanaka was
within reach.

A light shone through the turret window of the staircase which ran down to the ground floor. Chéri-Bibi
clearly saw Rose descending the stairs, going before Dr.
Walter and lighting the way. Ere long both were in
the great drawing room in which the old Marquis du
Touchais had been murdered. Rose and the doctor
stopped for a moment at the glazed door to have a talk.
Then Rose unlocked the front door and opened it.

"Do you wish me to go with you, doctor?" she
asked. "The little garden gate is open."

"No, no, go upstairs at once to your mistress and
carry out my instructions. Oh, have you any paper
and ink? I'll give you a prescription now which you
can have made up in the morning. . . ."

"Here you are, doctor."

Their voices sounded clear and distinct in the silence
of the night. She took him to a table on which he
found writing material. He sat down while Rose, in
answer to a call from Cecily, left her candle in the room
and went quickly upstairs, telling him that she would
come down again presently and lock the front door; and
asking him to leave his prescription on the table before
taking his departure.

The Kanaka sat at the table and bending over it, for
he was slightly shortsighted, began to write. His back
was turned to the door which Rose had left ajar. Chéri-
Bibi had but to go in. He would never have a finer

opportunity. He could kill the Kanaka as he sat writing out his prescription. He drew his knife and went in.

Treading stealthily he moved, with weapon upraised, towards the back which was presented to him, and he was about to spring forward when an unfortunate creaking of the floor caused the Kanaka to turn round with a celerity which showed that this queer doctor must always have been on his guard. He was so thoroughly on his guard that Chéri-Bibi, in his impetus, found himself up against a revolver, with the result that the hour of the murder which, in his mind, was already done, was postponed. It was a false move which forced a painful sigh from Chéri-Bibi and a ghastly grin from the doctor.

"Do you know that I could shoot you like a dog?" said the Kanaka.

"You have nothing to gain by shooting me," returned the sham Marquis du Touchais in a voice of utter weariness, "so I'm not afraid of you."

"Nor am I afraid of you," said the Kanaka in mocking tones. "You know that I have taken my precautions and that my death would be the signal for your downfall; the end of the Marquis du Touchais and, without a doubt, the end of Chéri-Bibi as well. Why do you come here with a knife and in that get-up? You wouldn't be such a fool as to kill me, would you? You wanted to frighten me."

"Yes, because I absolutely insist on having a talk with you. Don't be too clever. I won the first rubber only yesterday, and now you are left alone against me."

"With your secret."

"How much do you want?"

"First I want you to drop your knife and I'll put away my revolver. As weapons are useless, and we can't kill each other, let us do without these stage properties and talk frankly and openly."

"As you please," agreed Chéri-Bibi, who put his knife in his pocket.

Now that they had laid down their arms, they steadily gazed at each other in silence for a few moments. They took stock of each other, each endeavoring to gauge from a look the mettle of the other. Chéri-Bibi suddenly staggered back for he heard footsteps above him.

"Don't be alarmed," said the Kanaka, going towards him. "Rose won't come downstairs yet. I have given her work to do. Yes, she and your wife cannot leave the Marchioness, your mother, just now. We can talk business."

And he repeated with a sneer:

"Your mother! . . . Your wife!"

"Leave my wife out of it you villain."

"As you please. What shall we talk about then? Ah, yes, you want to know 'my price.' Are you aware that you're a pretty fellow?"

"Why?" asked Chéri-Bibi innocently, still falling back as if the Kanaka's masterful air and flashing look seriously intimidated him.

"Why? Because, my dear fellow, one oughtn't to be such an ass as you are. What! Do you suppose that I made you the Marquis du Touchais for a million francs? And now you ask 'my price.' You think, apparently, that you'll be able to get rid of me for another million."

"No," returned Chéri-Bibi. "How much do you want?"

"I'll tell you something: I thought of taking everything from you, or pretty well everything. That was my object in bringing my staff here with me."

"Your staff no longer exists. How much do you want?"

As Chéri-Bibi spoke he continued imperceptibly to retreat, and the Kanaka followed him, without hesitation, for Chéri-Bibi was brought to a standstill in a corner, and could not move a step, while his enemy was able to keep a sharp eye on his every movement. Moreover, the Kanaka was obviously easy in his mind as to Chéri-Bibi's purpose, for he had quietly crossed his hands behind his back.

It had resolved itself into a diplomatic bout between the two men on the question of money.

"Yes," went on the Kanaka in a jesting tone, "yes, I dreamed of plundering you, of taking from you by force, and if necessary by torture, all your property. That plan would have succeeded if the Countess hadn't put you on your guard."

"Poor woman!" said Chéri-Bibi.

"God rest her soul," said the Kanaka. "I really think that she did me a service without suspecting it. First of all, thanks to her, you have relieved me of a quartette who began to embarrass me, and afterwards the event gave me pause. What could I do with all your millions? I leave you your millions, Monsieur le Marquis."

"Indeed."

"Yes, so that they might multiply in your hands.

You shall be, as one might say, my agent. Does that
suit you?"

"Go on."

"You're pulling a face. Don't you understand then
that you are my thing, my property, my world? That
I brought about a new life of you in order that you
might work for me? Be sensible and I will be sensible.
. . . I will leave you enough to live on. The remainder,
the amount of which I will fix for myself, you will pay
over to me at regular intervals in the usual way. And
if I am satisfied with you, I'll make you a little extra
present on Michaelmas day. Does that suit you?"

"It's very nice of you," returned Chéri-Bibi in icy
tones, "but I prefer to tell you at once that it does not
suit me."

"I'm very sorry, my boy, because I've no other proposal to make to you."

"You think you're very clever, Kanaka."

"Clever enough to feel positive that you'll think it
over, and we shall be the best friends in the world."

"No. . . . You see, Kanaka, there's one too many
of us in this world."

"I don't agree with you. Each of us complements
the other."

"Don't you know that I've sworn to avenge the
Countess?"

"Childish babble! If you lay a hand upon me I
know some one who will take my will to the public
prosecutor."

"No he won't."

"Oh nonsense."

"Maître Régime won't take your will to the public
prosecutor."

The Kanaka, when he heard the name, could not help betraying his excitement.

"To begin with, you don't know whether Maître Régime has my will or not."

"Yes, he told me so.   And he won't use it because he hasn't got it now."

"What's that?" cried the other, turning pale.

"I tell you that I've got your will."

Chéri-Bibi had no sooner uttered these words than the Kanaka gave a muffled exclamation, fearing the worst for his own life, and though Chéri-Bibi still kept his hands behind his back, and he knew that he was unarmed, he felt in his pocket for his revolver.   But he was too late, for with a startling gesture Chéri-Bibi wrested from behind his back the deadly knife, held in place by gold wire under the portrait of the murdered Marquis du Touchais, and plunged it into the Kanaka's breast, and he fell in his death agony.

"That's one for me," snarled Chéri-Bibi.

The Kanaka's death rattle was soon over for the second blow cut his throat.

"And that's one for the Countess. . . ."

Chéri-Bibi stared for a second at the Kanaka's lifeless body.   Then he fled like a man bereft of his senses, for the thought of the dead now terrified him.

CHAPTER XV

AFTER his last crime Chéri-Bibi was conscious of a great feeling of tranquillity. Not only was the Kanaka's death unlikely to cause remorse to any honest man, but with his disappearance Chéri-Bibi's fear lest his secret should be known was gone forever. A period of perfect happiness followed in the Villa on the Cliff. To the two friends it was like paradise regained.

M. Costaud was the only person in the whole drama whom it was painful to see. He was still endeavoring to discover Chéri-Bibi, to whom he attributed every crime committed in the country. To begin with, there was no doubt, in his mind, that the notorious convict had murdered, with his own hand and knife, Dr. Walter, whose dead body was discovered in the drawing room of the Château du Touchais. Moreover, every trace of Chéri-Bibi gleaned by the worthy M. Costaud led either to the Château or to the Villa on the Cliff, which was ample proof that Chéri-Bibi had not relinquished his plan of capturing the Marquis. Accordingly M. Costaud kept guard over the Marquis with greater zeal than ever, but with the gloomy despair of a detective who is weary of pursuing a shadow which always eludes him.

At length the Countess' head was picked up and the identification of this fresh victim placed another murder to Chéri-Bibi's account.

Such a series of horrors sent a shudder through the Caux country, but did not disturb the digestion either of the Marquis or of Hilaire, his devoted secretary. As a matter of fact, Chéri-Bibi and the Dodger had only to allow life to take its course, and to enjoy thenceforward a well earned peace. Chéri-Bibi's love for Cecily increased, while the Dodger married Virginie and both men allowed themselves to be molly-coddled and made much of, conscious that they had omitted nothing to achieve that summit of happiness from which they had nearly slipped at a moment when they believed that it was within their reach.

They lived, it may said, in clover. Chéri-Bibi was putting on girth. Cecily in whose eyes the Marquis had always been a handsome man threatened him smilingly not to love him any more unless he kept an eye on himself. So he bound himself down to certain exercises which delighted the youthful Jacques. He went on all fours and with the boy on his back pranced about the garden paths. He was indulging in what he called Swedish drill. And as though to put the finishing touch to his happiness the Dowager Marchioness died.

Chéri-Bibi betrayed unspeakable delight when he was alone with the Dodger, notwithstanding that his secretary did not fail to reproach him with the impropriety of such sacrilegious demonstrations of satisfaction. But Chéri-Bibi had no love for his "mother."

And yet she had scarcely troubled him during her life and it may be said without anticipating the course of events, that her death in no way added to his good fortune.

On the day of the funeral all Dieppe walked behind the hearse, and came to offer their condolences to the

Marquis who on the Dodger's suggestion assumed an air
of great grief. But what was his amazement suddenly
to perceive de Pont-Marie approaching him with a suitable expression on his face and outstretched hand.

"My dear Maxime," said de Pont-Marie shamelessly,
"there are times when old friends meet again, and it is
their duty to forget everything that has come between
them and remember only what brings them together."

The Marquis stood as though petrified by such amazing assurance while de Pont-Marie grasped him by the
hand and shook it with every sign of boundless devotion; and observing that Chéri-Bibi was more than ever
dumbfounded, and made no effort to withstand him, de
Pont-Marie bent over his ear as if he were about to
kiss him—as is the custom in moments of great sorrow
—and sinking his voice said:

"Hand me over a hundred thousand francs and you
shall never see me again."

So saying he did not wait for an answer but plunged
into the crowd loudly lamenting the blow which had
befallen the house of du Touchais.

Chéri-Bibi, leaning on the Dodger for support, followed him with his eyes.

So he had come back again! He had dared to come
back. He was no longer prowling in the dark round
Cecily; but had come forth in the light of day to brave
and insult him and to endeavor to extort hush-money
from him. Such was de Pont-Marie, the man in the
gray hat, the man whom he had recognized on the
cliff . . . the murderer of the Marquis, his father.

Suddenly Chéri-Bibi clutched the Dodger's arm.

"Look!" he cried. "Look, I tell you!"

The Dodger followed the direction of his master's

exasperated gaze, and he saw the Vicomte de Pont-Marie go towards Rose who, all in tears, and supported by Sister St. Mary of the Angels, presented a sorrowful figure in her heavy mourning. De Pont-Marie stopped and held out his hand to Rose, who uttered a shrill cry and threw herself back into the nun's arms. The Vicomte, amazed at such an unexpected attack of nerves, said in a loud voice:

"Poor thing! She's going out of her mind."

And he left her. A number of persons bustled about her.

When the funeral ceremony was over Chéri-Bibi motioned the Dodger to step into his car and they drove away.

"Well, you saw that for yourself," he said. "You saw him go up to Rose, and you saw what happened. You heard Rose cry out. Rose knows everything. And de Pont-Marie is the murderer."

"Well, monsieur, it's no business of ours."

"What's that! No business of ours! Do you want me to quarrel with you for saying such a thing? Have you forgotten all that the wretch made the Marchioness suffer? Do you suppose that I'm going to forget it and be magnanimous enough to forgive him for all the misery of my past life and the punishment which I suffered in his place?"

"You ought to remember, for that matter, that if you hadn't undergone that misery you wouldn't have attained your present happiness."

"Perhaps you think I ought to be thankful to him for it?"

"Why not, monsieur?"

"Shut up! You talk like a rotter. What! Here's a

man who tried to take my wife away from me and murdered my father, and you want me to leave him alone. Hang it all, if I listened to you I should say thank you to him and give him what he wants into the bargain."

"What does he want, monsieur?"

"A hundred thousand francs so that I shall hear no more of him."

"Well, give him the money. Give him the money right away."

"Are you dreaming?"

"No, monsieur, I'm wide awake and in full possession of my senses, and I say to you: Give this man the hundred thousand francs that he's asking for, and don't let us trouble about anything but our own happiness. We have escaped from so many shady transactions with honor that I should be infinitely sorry to see you drawn into this new business. No one dreams any more of revenging the death of the old Marquis du Touchais. And it is anything but certain, after all, that de Pont-Marie is his murderer. To whitewash Chéri-Bibi is beyond human power. Let us, I entreat you, be happy in our home life."

"You've no pluck, Dodger. No, my boy, you've no pluck. You prefer the fleshpots of Egypt. Very well, I shall set to work on my own. You can get out of the car."

"No, monsieur."

"You won't get out?"

"No, monsieur. I am convinced that you are wrong," said the Dodger, changing his mind under his master's threatening gesture, "but I'm willing to do anything you wish."

"Ah, and not a moment too soon! Well, my boy,

Rose must be made to speak out, I feel certain that she has only to say one word, and we shall get rid of de Pont-Marie much easier than by giving him a hundred thousand francs. He will be always wanting a hundred thousand francs. Listen to me. You must go and see Sister St. Mary of the Angels."

"On your behalf?"

"No. I don't want to appear in the thing at all."

"That'll be safer," said the Dodger.

"I don't want to appear in it because I have no wish for any one to think that the blow which falls on de Pont-Marie is the result of any vindictive act on my part. People know that trouble has arisen between him and me and my wife, and I don't want Cecily, any more than myself, to be mixed up in it. He will be accused of the murder because Rose will declare that he is guilty of it. It's very simple."

"What must I say to Sister St. Mary of the Angels?"

"You will tell her that there are certain people—no need to mention names—who are sorry for her, and not less grieved to see the stir which is made about these last crimes as though they were the work of Chéri-Bibi; that they, like herself, are convinced that her brother is really dead and had no hand in those atrocities, but is as innocent of them as he was of the murder of the old Marquis. You can tell Sister St. Mary that they know of Rose's confession to her about Chéri-Bibi's innocence, and they consider that the time is come for Rose to reveal the truth. They understand clearly that she has delayed for so long naming the guilty man because he was a close friend of the family and in particular of Maxime's. But now things have changed and she has nothing to fear from a living soul; she will be

backed up in her work of justice; and she must not
delay if she wishes to prevent the wretch from committing other crimes. In short, you will give her to
understand that the persons who are interested in Rose
saw her faint at the Dowager Marchioness' funeral
when de Pont-Marie went up to her, and they understood the cause of her agitation."

"Is that all?" asked the Dodger, with a look of great
uneasiness.

"That's all. You see there is nothing complicated
about it. Only you must find out what Rose intends
to do, and what reply she makes to Sister St. Mary of
the Angels."

"Very good, monsieur. When shall I see Sister St.
Mary?"

"At once. Go and seek her out now. You must strike
while the iron is hot. Cadol will put me down at the
Villa and drive you back to Dieppe. You can then call
at the hospital and ask to see the nun."

Chéri-Bibi rejoined Cecily who was feeling the strain
of the long nights passed at the bedside of the old
Marchioness, and had been ordered by the doctor not
to attend the funeral. She threw her arms round the
Marquis' neck as soon as he came in. Whenever he
was away from her, she was on tenter hooks for, according to Detective Inspector Costaud, Chéri-Bibi was
continuing his crimes and was the murderer of the
worthy Dr. Walter.

"Do you know who came and shook hands with me
at the cemetery? The intolerable de Pont-Marie."

"What cheek!" she exclaimed.

"Yes, what cheek; and do you know what he wants

from me so that we shan't hear of him again? One hundred thousand francs."

"Give him the money," she returned without hesitation.

"Hullo," thought Chéri-Bibi, "she says the same thing as the Dodger."

"Give him the money twice over. Don't let's see him again. He'll bring us bad luck."

"I'll consider the matter," said Chéri-Bibi wrapped in thought.

An hour later the Dodger came in with the best of news.

"You were right, Monsieur le Marquis," he said, when they were alone in the study. "You did well to refuse to give de Pont-Marie the hundred thousand francs. It's all up with him. Rose has decided to speak."

"Is that a fact," cried Chéri-Bibi, whose eyes gleamed with malicious satisfaction so great was his detestation of de Pont-Marie.

"Oh there was no need to make a long speech about it. Sister St. Mary of the Angels was at first very uncomfortable when I opened up the subject, and then seeing that I was so well informed she said: 'Tell the people who sent you to me that they can rejoice as much as I do. Rose will speak within the next fortnight.' She confided to me that poor Rose was very excited as a result of what she saw at the cemetery; and de Pont-Marie's audacity in coming to shake hands with her had greatly unnerved her. 'The villain,' she said when she came to herself, 'will be punished for his crime.'"

"Did she say that?"

"Sister St. Mary repeated her words to me. The brave little sister was beside herself with joy. It was a pleasure to see her. She looked quite young again. 'At last we shall see the justice of God. Poor Chéri-Bibi,' " she said.

"Did she say 'Poor Chéri-Bibi'?"

"Yes, and as she said it she cried."

"She's a good girl."

"I slipped away because I myself felt moved to tears."

"Didn't you ask if Rose had any proofs?"

"Oh, yes, monsieur. We must take it that there are proofs. She spoke to me in ambiguous terms of a pocket book."

"You don't say so! De Pont-Marie is nicely done."

"I think so."

"Well, let's dance a jig."

Chéri-Bibi caught hold of the Dodger and they danced together, so true it is that man, in his ignorance of all things, and in particular of the fate that lurks ahead of him, will weep over events which pave the way to his happiness and blindly rejoice over those which lead to his destruction.

During the following days, while they were waiting for Rose to speak, Chéri-Bibi made preparations for a short journey. They intended to pass the winter in the South, far from the scene of old troubles which would be forgotten by the Spring. While the family were away great alterations would be made at the Château du Touchais which was to be rebuilt in a manner worthy of the famous mansion's new fortune. In fact next season they would leave the Villa on the Cliff for the Château. The work of alteration was already in progress in the roofs and roofing which greatly needed repair. Workmen were busy scraping off the old paint from the rooms on the second floor which were to be entirely redecorated. The Marquis du Touchais in his eagerness to put the rebuilding in hand remained at the Château with the builder.

Truth to tell he deliberately sought in this activity an artificial channel for his thoughts, a distraction from his restlessness. Would Rose at last make up her mind? What was she waiting for?

De Pont-Marie still remained at Dieppe in full expectation of receiving the hundred thousand francs, and Chéri-Bibi who had to enter into correspondence with him, let matters drag on so that he could not go away. Nevertheless he feared lest de Pont-Marie would lose patience. Accordingly he sent the Dodger from time to time to Sister St. Mary of the Angels who made answer:

"The day is at hand, the day is at hand."

Meanwhile Detective Inspector Costaud had become convinced that Chéri-Bibi had once more left the district, and he gave notice of his impending departure, with his men, for Paris.

Costaud had displayed so much devotion to the Marquis' interests that he did not wish to let him go away without giving him some special mark of his favor. In spite of his recent mourning he invited him to dinner. Cecily who was not less grateful to Costaud seconded her husband, and as their old friend Maître Régime had returned to Dieppe on the Marquis' business, she invited him as well. It was to be a farewell dinner without any sort of formality about it.

For once in his life Chéri-Bibi could not regard the

departure of his friend Costaud without regret. He wanted this model officer to be present when Rose made her revelations, and to see him lay hands on de Pont-Marie as he was wont, in the old days to lay hands on Chéri-Bibi. So he said to the Dodger:

"My boy we must make that old crack-brained Rose come to the point. Go and see Sister St. Mary of the Angels and tell her that M. Costaud is leaving the place but before he goes is to dine with the Marquis du Touchais. The dinner is fixed for to-morrow evening. Convey to her that no one seems more suitable to arrest the old Marquis' murderer than M. Costaud, the man who arrested Chéri-Bibi."

The Marquis' delight knew no bounds when Hilaire returned from his mission with a decisive answer.

"The evidence which Rose placed in safekeeping and for which she was waiting, has now reached her. Rose will speak out to-morrow evening at the Marquis du Touchais' house, in the presence of Detective Inspector Costaud."

"I am delighted," exclaimed Chéri-Bibi. "Well, we'll have some fun. Rely on me, my dear Dodger. It'll be splendid."

"May I ask what you mean?" ventured the Dodger diffidently.

"It's no business of yours. Oh, I say, while I think of it. Nothing will be easier than to invite Rose to the dinner."

"Don't do that. Her intention, so the nun tells me, is to appear unexpectedly at dessert time, and she wants every one to be kept in ignorance of her coming, even yourself, Sister St. Mary says."

"She's afraid, apparently, that at the last moment

I may warn de Pont-Marie whose friend I used to be. Well, yes, Dodger, I shall warn him. There's no mistake about that!"

In point of fact on that very evening the Marquis du Touchais sent de Pont-Marie a note which was couched in the following language:

"I agree with you. We must get the business over and done with. Be at the small gate which leads from the Château du Touchais to the cliff steps at six o'clock to-morrow evening. I will admit you myself. Bring with you the photographs of the letters in question. If you give me your word of honor that you are not keeping back a single one, I will give you mine that you shall receive one hundred thousand francs."

It was the month of October; and when de Pont-Marie arrived at the appointed spot at six o'clock the next evening it was pitch dark. Chéri-Bibi himself opened the door, and led the way through the deserted garden into the Château from which the workmen had departed more than an hour before. He took him up to the first floor, and when he pointed to the staircase leading to the second floor de Pont-Marie made a gesture of impatience. The Marquis turned round, put his finger to his lips as a call for silence, and pointing to the door said:

"The Marchioness is there. Let us settle our business without disturbing her if you don't mind."

He was lying; but de Pont-Marie followed without suspicion. When they reached the passage on the second floor, Chéri-Bibi said:

"We shall be quite at home here."

And savagely, before de Pont-Marie had time to say a word or to make a sign, he sent him sprawling into a small dark room, flung himself upon him, bound him hand and foot as he alone knew how, gagged him, emptied his pockets of a packet of photographs and a revolver, and rising to his feet said:

"See you presently."

He double-locked the door and then imperturbably left the Château, proceeding to the Villa on the Cliff. On arrival he informed Cecily that the dinner was not to take place at the Villa, but in the large dining room at the Château. Cecily was astonished and asked for an explanation.

"My dearest," he returned, "be glad of the change, and don't ask me now the reason of it for you will soon know. I have a pleasant surprise in store for you. Only you must do as I say without asking questions. We shall dine to-night at the Château du Touchais. Please have three extra covers laid."

"But have you reflected, dear? We have already invited M. Costaud and Maître Régime. Three extra covers will make a big dinner party of it. . . . A fortnight after the Dowager Marchioness' funeral!"

"Please do as I say without asking questions."

"Very well, dear, it shall be as you wish."

"That's only what I expected from you, my dear Cecily."

"May I ask who the three other guests are?"

"Why, certainly. They are the Commissary of Police who saved us a great deal of worry at the time of the inquiry into the murder of Dr. Walter; the Examining Magistrate who was himself very considerate; and the President of the Court who was a great friend of my mother's."

So saying he went out, calling for his car, and Cecily

stood for some minutes wondering why her beloved husband was anxious to have so many magistrates round the family table that evening. She could not imagine the reason, but the main point was that the Marquis had given the order for dinner to be served at the Château and she set about it without further ado.

Chéri-Bibi was driven to Dieppe where he paid several visits. He returned to Puys with five men armed to the teeth. They were Costaud and his detectives. The Marquis had informed the Inspector of the Criminal Investigation Department, with an air of mystery, that he was reserving a surprise for him "at dessert time"; a surprise of such a nature that he persuaded him to bring with him some of his most reliable men.

"Are we, after all, going to arrest Chéri-Bibi?" asked M. Costaud who thought of nothing but his pet criminal.

"Who knows?" returned the Marquis with an increasingly mysterious air.

The guests came at eight o'clock and were greatly astonished to meet together at so imposing a dinner party, for as the du Touchais' were in mourning it was incomprehensible to them. But Costaud winked at them like a man who is in the know, giving them to understand that it was not for nothing that their host had disturbed such distinguished representatives of justice.

They were equally astonished when the dinner was served, not at the Villa but in the Château, which was already disorganized by workmen, and filled with the odor of plaster and turpentine. But Costaud with another wink replied that the Marquis "must have his reasons."

Detective Inspector Costaud ordered his men, on Chéri-Bibi's suggestion, to walk about the park and to hold themselves in readiness to come up at the first signal. As to the Dodger, he was left behind at the Villa on the Cliff to wait for Rose and Sister St. Mary of the Angels and to bring them to the Château.

The dinner passed in comparative silence, for the guests had no inkling of what was coming, and each man searched with a look the Marquis' face, who however kept his secret.

Chéri-Bibi continued to watch the park as if he were expecting some one who was late in coming. At last he descried—and he was the only one to notice them in the light that filtered through the windows—the Dodger accompanied by Rose and Sister St. Mary of the Angels.

The two women seemed to be very pale. The Dodger took them, according to his instructions, to the drawing room next to the dining room. Then Chéri-Bibi rose, made his apologies, and asked the company for permission to leave them for a few minutes, begging them to be patient should his return be slightly delayed, and went up to the second story where his prisoner lay bound on the floor in the small dark room. He carried him to the next room and placed him in an easy chair. He lighted a lamp, removed the gag, waited until his man had breathed freely to his heart's content, and stopped, from the outset, de Pont-Marie's indignant protests:

"Monsieur, I have looked at the photographs and find that they are all there. You promised me that you would not keep back a single one for your own purposes. I believed your word and I did well to do so. But you won't receive the hundred thousand francs. I shall pay you for your audacity and your crimes, as is proper, by having you arrested at the very place where you murdered the Marquis du Touchais, my father."

CHAPTER XVI

"What's that!" roared de Pont-Marie leaping from his chair and striving in vain to set himself free from his bonds. "What do you say?"

"I say that you murdered my father."

"Well and you?"

"What do you mean 'you'?" demanded Chéri-Bibi taken aback.

"Look here," growled de Pont-Marie, trembling with rage in the bonds that held him, a threatening look in his eyes, his whole figure expressing revolt as he came up against the face of the sham Marquis. "Look here, you can't play that game with me for long, my boy, and if you think you're going to get rid of your friend de Pont-Marie like this, you must have completely lost your head . . . Ah . . . you're not serious."

"I am so serious," he returned in a voice in which there was less assurance, for there was something in de Pont-Marie's furious language which he could not understand. "I am so serious that Detective Inspector Costaud is down below with his men waiting to arrest you, and nothing can prevent you from receiving the punishment which you deserve . . . you murderer and blackmailer!"

De Pont-Marie opened his eyes in amazement endeavoring to understand the Marquis' attitude towards him, and looking upon him as clean off his head.

"No, no, you won't do that," he snapped out. "You take me for some one else. You won't rake up that story. You'll do better to hand over the hundred thousand francs, I assure you, and let me clear out. You can't frighten me. Though I am your prisoner I hold the whip hand."

"And why may I ask?"

"Why? Because you know that I shan't let you have your own way. What's the use of pretending to have a short memory my boy? You can't have forgotten that when I stabbed him you were a consenting party."

It was now Chéri-Bibi's turn to give a start for he was beginning to understand, and the horror of the position which he had brought on himself without suspecting it, made his hair stand on end. He lent over de Pont-Marie and gasped, foaming at the mouth.

"You lie . . . You lie."

"That won't do," returned the other. "No, no, that won't do. You hold your jaw, or I'll give you away."

"You lie," repeated Chéri-Bibi in a smothered voice, "You know that you're lying."

"If you are absolutely bent on it, all the world shall be told that the real murderer of the Marquis du Touchais was his son," de Pont-Marie threw at him furiously and with harsh contempt.

Chéri-Bibi let go de Pont-Marie and drew back uttering a hoarse groan. Breathing heavily, wild-eyed, he stared at his prisoner who in sullen and sneering accents, sure of himself, went on:

"I was never anything but your accomplice, you see.

You know that quite well. It was only to save you that
I stabbed him. Some things are never forgotten my
dear man. Come release me, and have the kindness to
show me the door with as little fuss as possible. We'll
resume this conversation some other day. This evening, my poor Maxime, you have a screw loose."

And as Chéri-Bibi seemed now to be turned to stone
and did not move a muscle, he went on:

"Come on, hurry up. What's the meaning of this
farce? You intended to terrorize me. You don't want
to hand over any more dibs. Since you came back
you've been deuced miserly. Possibly you think that I
have already cost you a pretty penny. You ass!
Think of the time when you were head over ears in
debt, when we were hard up for a thousand francs . . .
Think of the night when you said to me: 'Old Bourrelier has gone to Dieppe this afternoon to collect a
large amount of cash. His pocket book will be well
lined.' Think of when, still acting on your information,
I went for him on the cliff. Think of our rage when
we found that his famous pocket book contained only
an insignificant sum compared with the amount that
we stood in need of, so that I regretted the deed for
which the police were already trying to find poor young
Chéri-Bibi . . . Think of the night—the following
night—when you said to me: 'Nothing is left to us
but to rob my father,' and when you sent me a note
making an appointment for that night in the park and
requesting me to bring with me the needful . . .

"Good Lord, how you trembled that night when you
met me. Oh, I'll refresh your memory for you! . . .
Well, I brought the needful with me. I even brought
the knife with which I stabbed your father when he

came upon us and caught us starting on the job, and
you came to grips with him, and I thought you would
have choked the life out of each other. Think how I
made him let go his hold—and not a moment too soon
—and how your teeth chattered when you hid me in
your bedroom, under the bed, while we listened to the
commotion in the house, and the police arrested the
heaven-sent Chéri-Bibi which saved us . . . Well,
what's the matter? What's up? Are you ill?"

"*Fatalitas!*" groaned Chéri-Bibi, sinking in a huddled heap on the sofa and tearing his hair. "*Fatalitas!*
I took the skin of an honest man and even he was a
murderer!"

He uttered this fantastic sentence, the meaning of
which de Pont-Marie of course was unable to compre-
hend, in an accent of such utter and infinite sorrow
and hopelessness that de Pont-Marie really believed
this time that his mind had given way. He saw him
draw himself up once more, heave a frightful sigh,
raise his clenched and trembling fists to the ceiling as
to an unseen victim and cry in a frenzied voice: "I
have shed the blood of my father . . . my father!"

"Well, don't shout so loud about it if it affects you
so much as all that—as you say it does. Let me go."

"My son's father is a murderer."

"Oh, he's absolutely mad . . . Let me go. Do you
hear?"

"Yes, yes," said Chéri-Bibi, passing his hands over
his face as if he sought to drive out the hideous shadows
which beset him. "Yes, yes. Go! . . . You must go.
You must keep silent. You must keep silent for ever
. . . for ever."

The last two words "for ever" set his brain on fire

and seemed to point to the only gesture which, in very
sooth, could set him free. He stared fiercely at de
Pont-Marie. "If I kill you, you will never speak again
. . . never."

De Pont-Marie saw him approach, a determined look
on his face, and he grew white giving himself up for
lost.

"Be careful," he shouted, "my dead body might be
awkward for you. Have I said a word during all this
long time? Haven't I as much reason as you to keep
my mouth shut? No one knows anything about it."

"That's where you make a mistake. Some one does
know. Some one who is here, some one who came to
denounce you, some one who is, perhaps speaking at
this moment to the magistrates whom I myself invited
here, some one who will give a description of you to
the police, who at my request, are surrounding the
Château. Some one to whom you will cry: 'I murdered the father but the son was my accomplice.' You
see yourself that you must die."

"What you say is unbelievable," growled de Pont-
Marie huskily, "impossible. Who is this some one?
What new things are you imagining now? What proof
has he? He would have made use of it long ago."

"It's Rose."

"Rose, your mother's companion?"

"Yes. Remember how she fainted when you went
up to her at the funeral?"

"But, you infernal lunatic, if she knows that I killed
the Marquis she knows that you helped me."

"Do you think so?" said Chéri-Bibi digging his nails
into his face which was bleeding.

"I do think so. Don't you realize that if she really

knows, she has only waited for your mother's death before speaking?"

"Wretch that I am! . . . Yes it was on the day of the funeral that she said she would speak."

"You see! If it were only a question of me she would have denounced me long ago. Well, we must get away . . . the both of us."

"Wait a bit . . . What proof has she?"

"How can I tell. Before bringing her here and tying me up like a sausage, you ought to have asked her."

"That'll do, no jokes. We haven't a moment to lose. God, let me think things out! Rose . . . Rose must not speak. If she has any proof she mustn't produce it."

"But look here, you who know so much know nothing. Perhaps she saw us on the night of the crime. But that's not enough, that in itself is no proof."

"I know there's a pocket-book."

"A pocket-book!" exclaimed de Pont-Marie. "Old Bourrelier's pocket-book."

"Do you know what it contained?"

"Wait . . . Oh damn it all! . . . I have it. It must be that letter which we looked for everywhere, and which I put in Old Bourrelier's pocket-book. It was the letter in which you made an appointment for that night at the Château du Touchais, and which you asked me to return to you. Yes, she has that letter. We searched high and low for it. In the end we came to the conclusion that I dropped it in the sea, seeing that I took a boat at Dieppe in order to come to you. Well, she has that letter. I must have dropped it in your room, under the bed, and that's where she found it."

"*Fatalitas*," growled Chéri-Bibi.

"Well, old man, we are badly done. Oh, curse it all, cut these ropes. She must hold her tongue or it's all up with both of us. You must not kill me, old man, you must kill Rose."

While de Pont-Marie was speaking Chéri-Bibi's haggard eyes roamed in all directions. He felt that he was choking, weighed down, doomed. He tore off his tie and uttered a cry and it was impossible to say whether he were dying or pulling himself together. The entire room seemed to be swimming round him. "You must not kill me, you must kill Rose" danced in letters of blood on the white wall.

A knock came at the door. He gave a start. Nevertheless he recognized the Dodger's way of knocking. He opened the door. It was indeed the Dodger holding a letter in his hand.

"A letter from Rose," he said.

Chéri-Bibi took the letter and while the Dodger stared wide-eyed and open-mouthed at the sight of de Pont-Marie bound in a chair, like a sausage, he said in a muffled voice:

"Ask Rose to come up here."

"Yes, Monsieur le Marquis."

"Do you understand? She must come up here."

"Yes, Monsieur le Marquis."

Chéri-Bibi closed the door, leant against the wall, and with a hand shaking like that of a confirmed drunkard tore open the envelope. He recognized his own notepaper; the notepaper that lay on his desk in the drawing room. Rose had written the letter that very evening. Had she changed her mind? Had she decided after all not to speak? With a mist before his eyes he with difficulty deciphered her writing.

"I am aware of the crime of which you and de Pont-Marie are guilty. It is unnecessary, is it not, for me to state more plainly to which crime I refer? I kept silent during your mother's lifetime, because I was devoted to her and loved her, and I verily believe that in watching over the peace and honor of her last days I have sacrificed the repose of my soul. Wittingly I allowed an innocent man to suffer. But the hour of expiation has struck. Knowing that magistrates would be here, I came to your house this evening with the full intention of delivering you up to the justice of man. Nevertheless as I crossed the threshold of this old Château in which I have lived so many years with an honorable family, my heart was touched with compassion, and I thought it would suffice, perhaps, if I assisted the justice of God . . . I have evidence of your crime. I swear on the grave of my dear mistress, your mother, that I will destroy this evidence if you have the courage to inflict punishment upon yourself. You must kill yourself, Monsieur le Marquis."

"Well," asked de Pont-Marie, "what does she say?"

"Nothing that concerns you," he returned, very pale. "She does not even mention you."

"What did I tell you? There's no doubt she was only waiting for the Marchioness' death . . . Oh the baggage! . . . Come, Maxime, release me . . . Release me, damn it. You see for yourself that we must make a bolt for it."

"Wait, I tell you," said Chéri-Bibi in an unspeakably mournful voice. "Perhaps she's coming up here."

"Is that our last hope?"

"Yes."

Again there was a knock at the door, and the Dodger appeared with Rose's answer.

The old lady was still in the drawing room with Sister St. Mary of the Angels, and sent word refusing to come up, for she had nothing further to discuss with the Marquis. Nevertheless she had written a few words which she enclosed in an envelope. Chéri-Bibi flung himself upon it. "I give you half an hour," said the fresh message. It was short but full of meaning.

Chéri-Bibi tore out a leaf from his notebook and wrote:

"You had compassion at one time on my mother, have compassion to-day on my wife and child. Do not deprive them of a husband and father who is devoted to them and bitterly repents his past sins. It is not so much myself whom you would strike as an innocent and hapless family. Think of it, and do not be more relentless than the justice of man to which there is a limitation."

He folded the note in four and gave it to the Dodger who stared in bewilderment at his distraught expression and trembling hands.

"Good Heavens, what's up?" asked the secretary piteously.

"I will explain things presently," said Chéri-Bibi in a hoarse voice. "Go. Ask Rose to read this, then tear it up, or rather bring it back to me for I don't want it to go astray."

The Dodger made off.

"Good Lord," exclaimed de Pont-Marie, "she refuses to come up. Well, we must go down and fetch her, and compel her to shut her mouth at all costs."

"Impossible," returned Chéri-Bibi in a voice of peculiar calmness. "She won't leave Sister St. Mary of the Angels."

"Well?"

"Well," returned the other in increasingly icy tones, "I can't kill Sister St. Mary."

"Why not?"

"That's no business of yours."

"Because she's a nun?"

"Yes, that's it."

Then de Pont-Marie began to bellow again.

"Good God, release me!"

"You call upon God which will bring you bad luck," said Chéri-Bibi, plunged in thought.

He sat down holding his head in his hands, and waited for Rose's answer, giving no heed to de Pont-Marie's protests and groans and oaths. The Dodger was not away five minutes.

"Oh, Monsieur le Marquis, Rose and Sister St. Mary certainly look as white as you do. I told you that you would do wrong to mix yourself up in this affair."

"Her answer?"

"Here it is with your own returned." He handed him an envelope which contained the two sheets of paper.

"Is there a limitation also for your last crime? And do you think that I shall have pity on a man who after murdering his father, killed almost before my eyes the unfortunate Dr. Walter? I came into the room in time to see you strike the blow. There is too much blood on your hands, Monsieur le Marquis, and I decline any longer to be an accomplice, by my silence, in your misdeeds. If at the time which I have fixed I am not certain of your death, I shall tell M. Costaud who it is that he must arrest instead of vainly searching in the shadow of poor Chéri-Bibi, your first victim."

Chéri-Bibi shot the letter in his mouth as he had done with the others. He munched it like an animal with an entire lack of intelligence. He seemed to be in a state of stupor. And silent tears trickled down his cheeks.

"But what's the matter, Monsieur le Marquis?" asked the Dodger in supplicating tones.

"The matter is that I must die, my dear Dodger. Yes, we thought that we were so happy and then crash! here I am about to die. Oh I have no luck." And he wept like a child wiping his eyes with the sleeve of his coat.

The Dodger unnerved, fell on his knees.

"Get up," said Chéri-Bibi, with a piteous smile, "get up and help me to carry this gentleman into the dark room. He is making too much noise. He worries my last moments."

De Pont-Marie was becoming in fact unendurable with his movements like those of a refractory frog. They carried him into the room, and as he started once more to shout aloud, they gagged him and then returned to their room.

Chéri-Bibi drew a revolver from his pocket and loaded it in great dejection.

The Dodger clutched him by the arm.

"God in Heaven," he groaned, "if it is a fact that you must die, kill me first. But I ask you, on the life of your son, to tell me what it is that forces you to kill yourself. Tell me the reason. I may, perhaps, find a way of saving your life."

"It's good of you, Dodger, dear friend, brave com-

panion of my sufferings; it shows your heart of gold
. . . There's nothing to be done, believe me, but to
fulfil the last decree of fate. I wanted to avenge Chéri-
Bibi, who was innocent of the murder of the old Marquis. And do you know who did murder him? Do
you know the man whom Rose came here to-day to denounce, bringing proofs with her? It's I . . . I the
son of the Marquis du Touchais . . . The man who
killed him was his own son. Oh Dodger as I have always said to you, I have never had any luck. But,
even so, think of the bad luck of it . . . God knew
what he was about when he struck me down . . . It's
enough to make a man weep, isn't it? True, I am
weeping like a poor brat, but it is not because I am
afraid to die—you know I am not afraid of death—
but because I am leaving Cecily and my dear little kid
of whom I am so fond . . .

"That's what makes me squeal. To think that I
shall never see them again . . . never. There, come,
give me your hand, Dodger . . . You must kiss them
afterwards for me; and watch over them. You will
understand the situation in two words: If I die Rose
will not speak. She has promised it; she has sworn
it. She is one of the best of women. She allows me
by my death to save my son's honor. At least he won't
have a murderer for a father. I am to kill myself for
their sakes, my dear Dodger. That in itself is enough
to restore my character in my eyes and give me courage." He looked at his watch. "I still have a good
quarter of an hour. All the same, I am very grieved
about it . . . My dear Cecily . . . My dear little
Jacques."

The Dodger fell on his knees again and mingled his tears with Chéri-Bibi's.

"My poor wife . . . She was worthy of my love. Yes, in spite of the wickedness of my life, my heart was as pure as the heart of a child. I kept it for her. I took it to her in my two terrible hands, and she knew that it was so. She accepted it and she loved me. So you see, my dear Dodger, it would be wrong to complain, for I must pay for having tasted such happiness, and as she loved me the doors of hell may open before me now."

The two men gave a sob. The memory of the past . . . Cecily's love . . . These were a softening and assuaging influence in that dying hour.

"Good-by Cecily, good-by little Jacques, good-by Dodger. Good-by Sister St. Mary who prayed so often for me and never knew anything of my happiness. Good-by all whom I have so greatly loved."

Chéri-Bibi raised his revolver, but the Dodger seized him by the arm once more with a great cry.

"Monsieur, you cannot kill yourself."

"Why not, my dear Dodger?"

"Because your death, instead of saving your wife and child, would dishonor them forever."

Chéri-Bibi was impressed with the Dodger's triumphant exaltation but he failed to grasp his meaning.

"I don't understand."

"You have forgotten the marks on your chest."

"My tatoo marks?"

"Yes, Chéri-Bibi's tatoo marks."

"Curse the thing!" said Chéri-Bibi.

"They would tell the world that your son was the son of a convict. They would reveal your secret."

"Wretch, wretch, thrice accursed that I am!" he cried breaking into a crowning lamentation. "Only my death can save my wife and child, and I cannot die. *Fatalitas!*"

Chéri-Bibi in his turn fell on his knees. He wrung his hands and tore his hair.

"Rose will speak. Rose will speak if I do not kill myself, and my son, poor little fellow, will have a curse upon him like myself. May God in Heaven crush me still further but have pity on my son! What's to be done? What are we to do?"

"Monsieur," returned the Dodger who was still a prey to a strange elation, "you must kill me."

"What do you say? Your devotion to me has turned your head."

"As Rose wants a dead body she shall have one. Kill me, monsieur . . . Give me your jewelry, rings, watch, and when you have killed me set fire to me and the house . . . Set fire to me and the Château of your forefathers. But burn me so that I shall be beyond recognition. Disfigure me and you and your child will be saved. In my case there will be no risk of Costaud finding some morsel of skin with which he might piece together a Chéri-Bibi. Kill me and save your own life . . . Disappear from the place. You can keep an eye on Virginie from afar as I would have kept watch over those whom you love had I lived."

Chéri-Bibi gave ear to the Dodger and as he listened his eyes shone with a divine gleam of hope.

"What splendid friendship!" he muttered, "what splendid inspiration!"

He rose from his stooping posture and pointing to

the door of the little room in which de Pont-Marie was imprisoned said:

"We have the dead body."

As a matter of fact Chéri-Bibi was slightly anticipating events for de Pont-Marie was still alive, but doubtless in his mind's eye he already saw him dead. The Dodger seized the idea.

"You see for yourself that there is a Providence," he exclaimed in delighted tones.

"Be quick," said Chéri-Bibi looking at his watch. "We haven't a moment to lose." And he slipped his watch into de Pont-Marie's waistcoat pocket after taking his prisoner's watch and placing it in his own pocket.

De Pont-Marie had been carried back into the room by the two men. Unable to understand the meaning of this exchange of watches, his eyes instead of his mouth, which was still furnished with its gag, asked for an explanation, which Chéri-Bibi and the Dodger did not deem it necessary to afford him. Then there was an exchange of rings between Chéri-Bibi and de Pont-Marie which was effected with a certain roughness owing to the need for hurry. Finally Chéri-Bibi began to undress himself and was about to pass over his clothes to de Pont-Marie when the Dodger stopped him.

"It's not worth while. He will be so thoroughly burnt that very little of him will remain. Wait a moment, please."

He was away for a few seconds, returning with buckets, pots, and bottles.

"It occurred to me to set the place on fire because it can be easily done. The workmen have left behind everything that is necessary for it. The passage and the little lumber room are full of pots of paint and turpentine. The house and poor M. de Pont-Marie will burn like matchwood."

So saying he put down his burden, rushed off again, and came back with a bundle of soiled rags and two liters.

"What's that?" asked Chéri-Bibi who was putting his own boots on de Pont-Marie's feet so as to be on the safe side.

"That," returned the Dodger throwing down the bundle, "is a house painter's smock and some overalls which I shall be glad if you will put on at once, for here you have, right at hand, a disguise which will enable you to escape by the servants' staircase when the place begins to burn. I'll go downstairs and get Madame Cecily and your guests away."

"I leave her in your charge, Dodger."

"Don't worry about that, Monsieur le Marquis."

"What are you going to do with that bottle?"

"You see, monsieur, I am pouring the contents over M. de Pont-Marie's clothes."

"But what does it contain?"

"Petrol, Monsieur le Marquis?"

The prisoner shuddered and rolled his eyes which seemed about to start from their sockets.

"He thinks we're going to burn him alive," said Chéri-Bibi, "he takes us for savages!"

Having said which, Chéri-Bibi went up to de Pont-Marie from behind and passed his handkerchief, which he had twisted into a cord, round his neck, and set about strangling him, endeavoring to hurt him as little as possible. Though de Pont-Marie continued, under the pressure, to open his terrified eyes still wider, Chéri-Bibi closed his own, because the business of executioner filled him with indescribable repugnance, and at that moment of desperation so little heart was left to him that he would have preferred to die himself rather than to send to another world, by his own hand, a man who was entitled to demand the services of the public hangman. But at any rate as Chéri-Bibi could not die himself and he wanted a corpse, he took the work in hand.

"Another one!" he groaned lifting his eyes to Heaven when de Pont-Marie ceased to give any sign of life.

Meantime the Dodger continued to sprinkle the passages and hangings on the second floor with the rest of the petrol. He came back with a second bottle.

"Is it all over?" he asked.

"Yes," said Chéri-Bibi with a sigh.

"Nothing remains now but to alter his appearance on the off chance, Monsieur le Marquis."

And as he knelt in front of the dead man and carefully passed over his distorted features a brush which he had previously dipped in the bottle, Chéri-Bibi moved by curiosity cast a glance on the label. His secretary was "painting" the face of the man in the gray hat with sulphuric acid. The vitriol effected the work of transformation with terrible rapidity.

"There! Now there'll be no danger of any one saying that it isn't the Marque du Touchais' face," said the Dodger rising and turning to his master. Then holding out his hand.

"Now shake hands, Monsieur le Marquis, we must say good-by." They shook hands.

"My dear old Dodger."

"My dear Monsieur le Marquis," said the Dodger, still polite in spite of his great emotion.

They parted after speaking once more of Cecily and the boy. Chéri-Bibi darted towards the servants' staircase while the Dodger made ready to "light the fire." But suddenly Chéri-Bibi appeared once more, gasping for breath, more haggard-eyed than ever.

"Damn it all, the staircase is guarded. I gave the order myself. I had forgotten it."

"By Costaud's men!" exclaimed the Dodger. "Well, what about it? Make a rush through them."

"They'll recognize me. They'll know that it's the Marquis who is running away. Rose will know that I am not dead and will speak."

He seemed to be in a state of frenzy.

"No," he cried, "No, the Marquis du Touchais is not dead . . . He is not dead."

He was a pitiable sight as his wild gaze wandered round the room and fell on de Pont-Marie's face eaten up by the vitriol, and the bottle which was but half empty. At the height of his delirium he repeated:

"The Marquis du Touchais is not dead as long as his face remains."

He went up to the Dodger with so tragic a gesture that the latter grasped his meaning, for he pointed to the bottle.

"No, no, not that, not that," protested the Dodger.

"If you refuse to help me, you understand, Dodger," said Chéri-Bibi in a smothered voice . . . "If you refuse to paint my face as you painted the face of that villain, you're no friend of mine."

"Not that, not that."

"No, you're no friend of mine, because everything

that we've done is of no avail so long as that face exists
. . . I can't get away as long as that face exists."

"Not that, not that."

"Look at those men who are guarding the Château.
Do you want them to see the Marquis du Touchais running away when the house blazes up? Do you want
Rose to see him? Come, be a man Dodger . . . Show
your pluck."

"Not that, not that Chéri-Bibi . . . Never . . .
never."

It was the first time for many a long day that the
Dodger called his master by the name which was his in
their adventures of old. He spoke the words in an
accent of such pitiable desperation and of such intense
and splendid friendship that Chéri-Bibi drew him to
his breast.

"Let us say good-by my dear old Dodger. No, no,
I won't ask you to do it . . . No, I won't ask you . . .
There, pull yourself together, I'll manage the thing
myself. Listen, I have suffered so much in the making
of this face that I may as well suffer a little more in
getting rid of it."

"Suffer a little more! Don't do it, Chéri-Bibi. Don't
do it. They say it's hell itself."

"I belong to hell, Dodger . . . I escaped from it and
I am going back to it. What do I care? I have not
loved the less on that account . . . My son will not
curse my memory. Good-by, my dear fellow. You
must clear out. This is a moment when I shall need all
my courage."

He said good-by once more and carried him, as if
he were a child, on to the landing while the Dodger
broke down as he lay in Chéri-Bibi's powerful arms.

"Come, think of what I said to you. Go and save them. In five minutes I shall have set the place on fire." He locked the door on the landing.

The Dodger clasped his hands and made his way downstairs like a drunken man. He crept along the walls, passed the dining room like a shadow and caught the sound of conversation. The President of the Court was telling a story . . . He entered the drawing room. He went up to Rose who was leaning for support on the arm of Sister St. Mary of the Angels, and the ghostly pallor of her face could be discerned underneath her mourning veil.

"Monsieur le Marquis says that he quite understands and that you will be satisfied," he said. And he left her lest he should kill her.

He plunged into the garden, walked round the Château, reached some rising ground, and looked to see if he could distinguish anything on the second floor in which there was at that moment but a feeble glimmer. Then he saw clearly, almost flattened against the window, the face of the Marquis du Touchais over whose mouth Chéri-Bibi was placing a gag.

"Poor fellow! He is doing that to prevent any one from hearing him shriek. Not another man in the world would show courage like that . . . My poor Chéri-Bibi, my poor Chéri-Bibi! And you are doing this for your wife and kid . . . Oh you are in very truth an honest man!"

He recalled to mind his promise to take care of those two dear creatures, and he returned to the Château still under the influence of grief. He must save Cecily's life. As to the two boys, they had remained at the Villa.

Cecily in the dining room was beginning to feel extremely anxious about her husband's prolonged absence. It was in vain that she remembered his warning, she could not conceal the agitation that beset her. The mystery in which the dinner was enveloped, became more and more incomprehensible to her; and the attitude of the guests and even the grimaces of M. Costaud added greatly to her anguish. Costaud, in particular, who seemed to be much better informed than the others, alarmed her instead of reassuring her by his assumption of special knowledge. Feeling that the hour was at hand he ventured to say:

"I think, madame, that we shall do a fine piece of work this evening, thanks to the Marquis. But don't upset yourself. We've taken every precaution and my men are here."

"What piece of work?" asked Cecily in great agitation.

"Ah, that's just it . . . It's a secret."

"Are you going to arrest Chéri-Bibi?" asked the President of the Court in a jesting tone.

"Very likely," replied Costaud gravely. "But you must ask the Marquis that question."

"You terrify me," exclaimed Cecily rising from her chair.

But she did not say another word, nor did she stir again, and the faces round her became, like hers, extraordinarily vigilant for they began to hear a sort of long drawn out wail, dull, faint, and funereal, which came from the upper floors and sent a shiver of fear through them.

"What's that?" stammered Cecily.

"Yes, what a peculiar wail," murmured the Examining Magistrate.

"It's like some one being smothered," said the President.

"Oh, but it's awful," said Cecily, who seemed about to faint.

Costaud not less startled than the others was instantly on his feet.

"We must see about this."

The wail penetrating the floors and walls grew louder and more painful, and the entire house rang with it as from a deep-toned drum.

They made a rush for the door with Cecily at their head, but at that moment it was violently opened and the Dodger appeared with the gestures of a man who was beside himself, shouting:

"Fire! . . . Fire! . . . Run for your lives! . . . Run for your lives!"

The party was thrown into an immense confusion. Fortunately the Dodger took Cecily under his protection or she might have been trampled under foot.

"Maxime . . . Maxime . . . Where's the Marquis? . . . Maxime where are you?" she cried.

She endeavored to release herself from the Dodger's grasp, for he had taken her out of the Château by force.

"It's Chéri-Bibi . . . Chéri-Bibi who has fired the place," Costaud shouted.

He summoned his men who came hurrying up from all parts of the park attracted by the first gleams of the conflagration. The fire had broken out on the second floor, and the roofing was already in a blaze. The rapidity of its progress was startling, and a tremendous flame licked up the darkness of the night. The men, too, shouted:

"Chéri-Bibi! . . . Chéri-Bibi! . . . Chéri-Bibi has set the place on fire. We saw him running about the top floor. He's still in the house. Can't you hear him? Can't you hear him shouting? . . . He must be burning.

"Ah we've got him this time. He'll be caught or roasted to death," bellowed Costaud.

Above the general uproar, the cries of the servants as they left the basements, the shouts of the detectives and magistrates who were searching for the Marquis; above even the despairing sobs of Cecily as she continued to call for Maxime and implore the men to rescue him; above all these things, the long drawn out, terrible, muffled lamentation could be heard; and the sound did not cease until the floor of the second story collapsed.

"If only he's had time to clear off!" muttered the Dodger who still supported Cecily, dreading every moment lest she should give way to some act of despair.

It was useless to tell the Marchioness that her husband must have left the Château, and that this was the explanation of his absence, she tried to go back to the burning house, and make sure that he was not there, or if he were there, to save him or to die with him.

"Maxime! . . . Maxime!"

It suddenly occurred to her that she might reach the first floor by the servants' staircase which was as yet untouched by the flames, and violently pushing the Dodger aside she ran towards it. The men darted after her.

"Take care. . . . Take care" the detectives shouted

"Chéri-Bibi. . . . Chéri-Bibi. . . . We saw him again just now . . . there . . . there at the turret window."

Costaud rushed up behind Cecily and this time a cry went up, a terrible cry from Cecily as she pointed out to Costaud and his men Chéri-Bibi himself.

The kitchen door was opened and emerging from a cloud of smoke, diabolically illuminated by the crackling sparks, a sort of half-nude monster loomed up, a hideous being whose face was one large wound, whose mouth emitted but one long hoarse cry and whose chest bore as though it were a flag the infamous sign *Chéri-Bibi*. There *could be no mistake*. It was he right enough.

He was mustering all his strength to charge through Costaud's men, in the darkness, when he perceived Cecily in front of him pointing him out to them and barring his way, shouting, "Chéri-Bibi! Chéri-Bibi!" like a woman who had gone mad. Then they saw the monster strike himself on the heart, and with a savage cry draw back into the furnace.

His flaming outline appeared here and there like an evil spirit in this inferno, and for the last time Chéri-Bibi hurled forth into the night his terrible battle cry *"Fatalitas!"*

And then confusion reigned. . . . And the fire at the Château burnt itself out undisturbed and in silence . . . for they carried Cecily away unconscious.

．　　．　　．　　．　　．

Next morning were discovered the mortal remains of the Marquis whom everyone pitied as Chéri-Bibi's last victim. But no trace was ever found of the remains of

Chéri-Bibi which impelled the obstinate Costaud to observe:

"Do you think he is dead? We shall probably hear of him again one of these days."

THE END

www.ingramcontent.com/pod-product-compliance
Lightning Source LLC
Chambersburg PA
CBHW030246030726
47493CB00023B/610

* 9 7 8 1 4 3 4 4 1 7 1 2 1 *